SPEAKING
OF
MURDER

TACE BAKER

Tace Baker

BARKING RAIN PRESS

Speaking of Murder

Copyright © 2012 Tace Baker (www.tacebaker.com)

Edited by Betty Dobson (www.inkspotter.com)

Barking Rain Press
PO Box 822674
Vancouver, WA 98682 USA

www.barkingrainpress.org

ISBN Trade Paperback: 1-935460-47-1
ISBN eBook: 1-935460-51-X
Library of Congress Control Number: 2012947341

First Edition: September 2012

Printed in the United States of America

9 7 8 1 9 3 5 4 6 0 4 7 3

DEDICATION

This book is for my late parents,
Allan Maxwell Jr. and Marilyn Muller.
They always told me I could be anything I wanted to be.
And now I'm an author, exactly what I want to be.

※

ALSO FROM TACE BAKER

"An Idea for Murder" (*Burning Bridges* anthology)

※

COMING SOON FROM TACE BAKER

Murder on the Bluffs

※

COMING SOON FROM EDITH MAXWELL

A Tine to Live, a Tine to Die

WWW.TACEBAKER.COM

WWW.EDITHMAXWELL.COM

※

ACKNOWLEDGEMENTS

I am indebted to many people for helping me make this book so much better than it might have otherwise been. Chief Louis Pacheco of the Raynham, Massachusetts, Police Department generously shared his time and that of his video forensics specialist to explain how they use the dTective video-clarification software that helps find the killer in this book. Kelli Hutchings of the Bristol County District Attorney's office also spent an afternoon with me explaining how she uses the application to find the guilty.

I read every word of this story to the fabulous Salem Writer's Group—Margaret Press, Rae Francouer, Kit Irwin, Bill Joyner, Libby Mussman, Joy Seymour, Sam Sherman, and John Urban—and am grateful for their keen ears and insightful critiques. Several readers of the entire book—Rae Francouer, Julie Hennrikus, and Ruth McCarty—gave me invaluable feedback on issues large and small. Sherry Harris delivered an eagle-eyed edit of the entire manuscript before it was accepted for publication by Barking Rain Press, where Betty Dobson gave it an expert final edit.

My writing mentors along the way include Susan Oleksiw, Jan Brogan, Hallie Ephron, Kate Flora, Roberta Islieb, and Hank Phillippi Ryan. Thank you, Sisters in Crime! The members of the Guppies (the Great UnPublished) subgroup of Sisters in Crime are an infinite source of cheers at success, commiseration at rejection, excellent information, and hope. May you all be published! I also thank Barbara Bergendorf, Janet Maxwell, David Maxwell, and Jennifer Yanco, as well as my fellow Quakers at Amesbury Friends Meeting, for their love and support. I plucked my pen name from Quaker archives; I also write as Edith Maxwell.

A lovely photograph of the Choate Bridge in Ipswich, Massachusetts, was used with permission from Elizabeth Thomsen in much of my prepublication publicity. Any similarity to the town of Ipswich, Massachusetts, is not accidental, but the characters and events are a work of fiction.

Finally, my sons, Allan and John David, provided endless encouragement, and my partner in life, Hugh, supported me in this crazy endeavor even when he didn't quite get what I was doing. I thank these three dear men in my life.

EDITH MAXWELL

CHAPTER ONE

I watched Jamal Carter stretch his dark, silken body like a tiger in my bed and wondered just exactly how I was going to get myself out of this mess. He turned to me. "Time to rise and shine, Professor." The early Saturday light shone into green eyes flecked with brown. He reached over and lightly smacked my naked hip. With a sly pull to his mouth, he winked one of those deep-set eyes.

I closed my own eyes and groaned. "You know you can't say anything about this. To anybody. Ever." I opened my eyes and trained them on my student. It was hard to be serious with a gorgeous man in the nude, but I tried.

"Hey, honey, I'm a big boy." Jamal's casual tone belied his sudden departure from the bed. "I'm not going to get my esteemed advisor in trouble for sleeping with me." The sarcasm on 'esteemed' was unmistakable. "That would be counterproductive."

I watched as he pulled on his slacks and buttoned up his long-sleeved shirt. I pulled up the covers then reached out my hand. "You're not mad, right? I had a wonderful night." I tried to smile. "It's just—"

"Not mad. This fling of yours is late for work, though. See you around campus." He pressed his palms together at his chest and lowered his head toward them for a moment. "*Namaste*."

I heard the door of my condo close behind him. "Nice, Rousseau. You got what you wanted. A casual Friday-night fling to take your mind off Zac. With your star student. How could you be so stupid?"

I stopped short after rounding a corner several yards down the hall and pressed myself against the wall.

"With all *due* respect, ma'am," Jamal said to Alexa Kensington, my department chair at Agawam College. He sliced a hand through the air for emphasis. "It's a perfectly good thesis topic, and Professor Rousseau agrees. Just because you don't value it doesn't mean you should cancel my fellowship."

It was Monday morning, and I had no intention of tangling with Alexa's fury if I didn't have to. Jamal could hold his own. I didn't really want to tangle with him right now, either. Luckily, neither faced me directly.

"Mr. Carter." Alexa's voice rang out in the empty hallway. She was almost as tall as my student and usually as pale as he was dark, but her neck and cheeks now flared dark pink. "We have had this discussion before. As you know, your thesis-topic appeal is being considered by the fellowship committee." She shook her perfectly coiffed silver cap of hair and looked around like she wanted to escape—until her eyes found me.

Uh-oh.

"Ah, Lauren." Alexa beckoned. "Won't you join us?"

Pretty much the last thing I wanted to do. But, the boss being the boss, I walked toward them then started when a door clicked closed on my right. The shadow of a figure appeared behind the glass. Probably someone smart enough to hide when they saw Alexa.

"Mr. Carter is apparently unhappy with the department, Lauren. Perhaps the two of you can settle the matter? I have a meeting to get to," Alexa said, avoiding Jamal's eyes. "You can take care of this, can't you? As someone in line for full professor?"

I sighed as the elegant figure strode away. Alexa's arm swung with purpose as she walked, and her boot heels planted firm resonant steps on the floor.

"What's going on?" I faced Jamal.

A couple of undergrads in uniforms of flannel pajama pants, flip-flops, ear buds, and book bags slapped by.

"Same old issue. Can we talk in your office, Dr. Rousseau?" Jamal asked, still looking down the hall.

"You know the way."

We walked in silence. I felt him fuming.

Helmut, another Linguistics undergrad, emerged from a classroom right in front of us. He stared at Jamal, at me, and back at Jamal. I nodded at him. Why was he staring? Were we walking too close to each other? Jamal ignored him as we passed. I hoped Helmut didn't see the blush that raced up my neck.

Jamal and I continued to my office. A moment later, we sat in two deep armchairs covered in indigo cloth. The chair behind my wooden desk might be more appropriate for me to sit in, but it housed stacks of stapled papers and several piles of books and journals. My bonsai Chinese elm sat on the window sill.

Jamal extracted a stapled sheaf of papers from his bag and handed it to me. "First draft." He seemed all business. Good.

"'The Impact of Black Children's Speech on Their Socio-Economic Success.' Thanks. I look forward to reading this. You know, not that many undergrads even write honors theses." I rose and pushed up the window sash then sat again. The air held a refreshing cold bite of mid-March in Massachusetts. The old building was always too hot.

"Anyway, Jamal, what's going on with you and Dr. Kensington?"

"She's a racist." Jamal raised his eyebrows so his eyes looked even bigger.

I sat forward in my chair and waited for him to explain. I was aware of the rumors about the chair being less than welcoming to students of color but hadn't heard anything specific.

"I got a letter saying they were going to revoke my fellowship because my thesis topic was, quote, not suitable for undergraduate credit, end quote. I thought you approved it, Professor Rousseau. You know, I'm about out of energy to keep fighting this." Jamal slouched in his chair, abandoning his usual erect posture, and looked as if he had had a long bout with insomnia.

"I did approve it. But it's too big of a topic for an undergrad thesis, and I encouraged you to scale it back."

"And I told you why I couldn't!" Jamal rose and stood, jiggling one heel. "I can't cut out anything. I need the lit review, the case studies, the follow-up. All of it."

"Yes, but I approved it because you are a mature student, you have the background, and I believe you can pull it off. Being older, you're serious about your work, unlike some of the students who are fresh out of high school."

Jamal whirled to face me. "So what's the problem?"

"The problem is Dr. Kensington. I put the topic through, and she disapproved. She can't disallow you from doing it academically, but she does have a lot of influence on where the money for the department is spent. Now I'm arguing with the fellowship committee, most of whom are terrified of Alexa because they are about to be considered for tenure. And she can be, well, a bit critical." Saying 'a bit critical' was like calling Mount Everest a foothill.

"Man, that is so unfair! I work with those kids at the Boys and Girls Club and at the chess club. Listen, I used to be one of those kids. I know their language, and I know how it can hold them back. You think I study linguistics to keep my head in the clouds?" He stared at me, brows drawn together, sinews standing out on his folded arms, dark eyes burning into mine.

"Tell me about the chess club." Maybe talking would calm him down.

Jamal sat again and started tapping one hand on the arm of the chair. "I started a chess club for kids from Lawrence a couple years ago. Knights and Kings. Got a storefront, and it's always full. Lots of brothers come by and play with the little guys." Jamal smiled. "Written up in the *Globe* once when two of our players placed way up in a tournament, the New England Masters."

"Oh, yeah. I read that story. My youngest sister was a top-level junior chess player. She was one of the only girls."

"That reporter couldn't believe a bunch of kids from the Boys and Girls Club were smart enough to play chess. Hmm." Jamal shook his head and smiled again.

"How long ago were you in Japan?" From comments he'd made in class, I'd realized he'd lived there at some point.

He tilted his head to the side and looked at me with narrowed eyes, as if trying to figure out if I was changing the subject. "It's been almost fifteen years. Navy," he said. "Two years over there. Found I loved the culture."

"Me, too." I taught English conversation in Japan for two years after college. "At least the traditional culture. You know, the Zen temples, the food, how they pay attention to details."

"I almost brought home a young Japanese woman to marry, but at the last minute her parents told her our cultures were too different, that it was doomed to fail. Frankly? I think they didn't like my skin color." He gazed at the bonsai tree.

I nodded.

"Now, what about my fellowship, professor?"

"Well, I'm going to do my best to intervene with the committee. I'll see what strings I can pull." I was unsure of my actual prospects for success, but you never knew. If any student deserved a fellowship, it was Jamal.

Jamal thanked me and left for another class.

The man was the most unusual undergrad I ever met. He must be at least my age, was devoted to his studies, and talked with passion about his work with young black people. And he was nice to look at, with a gorgeous voice to boot.

Five other students dropped by to talk about the midterm, to discuss paper topics, and, in one case, to present an implausible excuse for not finishing assigned work on time. At four o'clock, I shut the door to my office and stood at the window. I focused on the bonsai and looked at its new growth, kneeling so the plant and I were at eye level. I closed my eyes for a moment.

"Now, Elm…" I addressed the plant with open eyes. "You know we're going to be doing some pruning soon. I want you to know it's nothing personal. You and me, we're creating art here. You've had a nice, cool, low-light winter, and now you're doing some growing. You know the drill, right? I trim, you complain, and then we're both happy with the results."

A noise outside the door caused me to whirl in that direction, and when the sound didn't recur, I took a deep breath, glad no one had caught me talking to a miniature tree on my windowsill.

"So get ready," I continued. "Not today, but next week probably. And in a couple months, you can go back outside. Won't that be nice?"

I decided to put in a couple of hours on my book. If I wanted to move from associate professor to full professor at Agawam College, I had to keep up with publishing. Once midterm exams got underway next week, I'd be in grading hell for days. I might as well do some writing now. Plus I had a date with Zac Agnant tonight. I sighed.

We'd been dating since last summer, but he'd suddenly gotten very serious.

I shook my head and switched on my computer. The slanting light cast a stretched-out shadow of the tiny elm on the burnished wooden floorboards as I got to work.

Zac and I faced each other in a booth in the Dodd Bridge pub, remnants of the best fried clams in the state on our plates. In my pocket, I fingered the tiny red Swiss Army knife Zac gave me at the start of the night. No occasion, just a fun little present from my boyfriend.

The fun disappeared a few minutes ago, though, when he resurrected the argument we kept having. The topic? Commitment. That is, *him* wanting commitment, walking toward me with arms open. And me, wary, backing away from it. From him.

"If you can't decide, maybe we should start seeing other people." He raised his eyebrows and challenged me with his eyes.

Ouch. That felt as cruel as the frigid weather outside, despite my own behavior a few nights ago. But that wasn't really seeing someone else. It was just a one-time thing.

I downed my glass of Ipswich Ale without looking at him and marched out of the pub, feeling like he'd slapped me. Let him pay the damn tab. I hurried up Meetinghouse Hill, glancing behind me when the wind swirled a pile of last fall's leaves.

I crossed High Street. Small-town life in Ipswich had some drawbacks, but being able to walk home at night from the pub wasn't one of them. I kicked at a pebble in the road, ruing Zac's opinion along with my own temper.

I'd been looking forward to spending a cozy night with him, and instead I'd ended up alone. Again.

I started up the steep incline of my street. The woods across the road were straight out of Grimm's fairy tales. The dark filled with obscured moving shapes rustling in the wind that was forecast to bring snow later. I knew the shapes were sumac, northern spicebush, and tall maples, but, in my imagination, Orcs and red-eyed wolves watched me. Pulling my beret farther down on my head, I trudged up the hill and made it into my condo safely. I collapsed on my couch with a glass of Scotch. Wulu jumped up next to me. I stroked his curly black cockapoo fur.

Zac. Why did he have to be so difficult? I wasn't ready to get married and have babies yet. What was his big hurry?

Why wasn't I ready, though? I was heading toward the far side of my thirties. Maybe I didn't want to give up my bad habits. I had quite a history of letting myself be drawn in by men like Jamal, who I knew were either off limits or bad for me, but who were exciting and dangerous. A shrink would probably say I had abandonment issues because my father disappeared when I was nineteen then turned up dead a week later. Or maybe I wasn't ready to admit to myself that Zac, my sexy Haitian-American videographer boyfriend, was the best thing to happen to me in years.

I pulled the little Swiss Army knife out of my purse and turned it over in my hand. It was exactly like the one my dad always carried on his key chain. The one I always coveted, the one that went with him to his death sixteen years earlier. It was a sweet thing of Zac to do, giving me that. It wasn't my birthday. It wasn't the anniversary of our meeting. He was way too sweet. Thinking of my slip-up with Jamal, I clearly didn't merit such thoughtfulness. I threaded the knife onto my own key chain and returned my hand to Wulu's warm head.

I'd have to thank Zac sometime. Just not tonight.

By some miracle, the sun shone the next day at noon, although a breeze chilled the air. I met Ralph Fourakis, my colleague and friend, at the end of his Modern Greek class and walked with him to the Lebanese lunch truck that parked on the campus common every midday. I bought a falafel sandwich and a bottle of water. Ralph ordered a shawarma with a soda.

We walked to a wooden bench in the sun. Several students played Frisbee on the patchy lawn. One brave soul, his eyes closed, sunbathed shirtless on his jacket.

I left Ralph a lot of space on the bench; he was both tall and bulky. Combined with his heavy black glasses and hair, he could look a little scary but was a gentle bear at heart.

We ate in silence for a few minutes then I squinted up at him. His wild hair in the sunlight created an aurora like Einstein's. I outlined Jamal's predicament for Ralph. "I don't get what Alexa has against Jamal. It's a big thesis topic, but I know he can do it."

"Ah, she's just a hard ass. Maybe she was the third child growing up and didn't get enough attention or something or didn't have enough power in her family. I don't know, Rousseau."

"Think I have any chance of swaying the fellowship committee?" I picked at the edge of my sandwich.

Ralph stretched out his legs and laid both arms along the back of the bench. "Well, I can try to help you. But you know the Ogre populated it with the newly hired and non-tenured among us. They don't want to cross her." He laughed. "We were there ourselves recently, remember."

He and I had secured tenure a month earlier, despite Alexa's attempts to railroad us in our efforts.

"Morning, Professor." A rich voice spoke behind me.

Startled, I sat up straight and turned to see Jamal coming around the end of the bench, followed by two young boys. I greeted him then wondered if he heard us talking about Alexa.

Jamal introduced his Little Brother, Tyrone, and Nicky, Tyrone's friend, who looked about nine. "They don't have school today, so I'm showing them my school." Jamal beamed at the boys. "Guys, this is Professor Rousseau. She speaks a lot of languages and is a good teacher."

I held out my hand to Tyrone, who stepped right up and shook it. When I extended my hand to the smaller boy, he hesitated and looked at Jamal, who nodded and motioned for Nicky to shake hands.

"Jamal, boys, this is my colleague Ralph Fourakis. He teaches languages, too. Ralph, Jamal Carter."

"You mean like Spanish and Creole?" Tyrone asked.

Ralph laughed. "That's good, those are languages. I teach Greek and German, though. My Spanish isn't too good." Ralph stood and shook hands with Jamal.

In a quiet voice, Nicky asked Tyrone, "What's a colleague?"

Tyrone turned his head away from the adults. "I don't know, I thought it was a kind of dog. Maybe it's somebody she calls a lot?"

I smiled at the boy's sensible interpretation of a word he'd never heard before. Ralph, my "call-y." Children's creative take on language was one of the things that got me into linguistics in the first place.

"Okay, guys, let's go." Jamal ruffled the top of Tyrone's head. "I want to show you the Science Center before we leave."

I watched them walk along the paths of the quad toward the new multi-story building at the other end. The little group stopped suddenly, and I peered at the scene. A tall woman talked with Jamal.

"Uh-oh," I said to Ralph, pointing. "Isn't that Alexa?"

"You need new glasses? You bet it is."

Alexa bent down and said something to the boys then straightened up. Jamal began gesturing at her with one hand and drew the boys around behind him with the other arm. Alexa stood stiffly. She started to walk away, and Jamal took hold of her wrist. She twisted away, and, even from this distance, I thought I could see the rage in her face.

I whistled. "This isn't good, Ralph."

"No, it isn't. Should we do something?"

"Too late now. She's walking away."

Jamal stood in place, holding the boys close. He stared at Alexa as if at a monster.

I left Lockhart Hall at 9:30 after my evening class the next day. I pulled my tur-quoise wool scarf closer around my neck as what I hoped was the last cold wind of March stabbed at me. A small red car crunched on the ice when it exited the parking lot. The muffler backfired like the one on my friend Elise's Rabbit. She didn't have any reason to be on campus, though.

Maybe she'd been looking for me or attending a play. Not that I'd ever known Elise to attend plays or performances of any kind, for that matter.

Alexa Kensington's light pushed into the dark from the fourth floor of the building. No one else walked the paths of the campus. Students cleared out as soon as they could after class was over.

I hoped I could persuade Alexa not to cancel Jamal's fellowship. I hurried along, wondering if she was racist, as Jamal claimed. The toe of my leather boot caught on a brick. I staggered and fell, my gloved hands reaching out for the ground. My right knee grazed the uneven stones and I swore—that joint didn't need any more dam-age than the years of running had already wrought. I looked around to see if anyone was passing by, but the walkways were empty.

The shadow of the branches in the wind caught my eye as I stood up. I walked fast between low hedges to the deserted parking lot. I glanced up at the building. A silhouette looked down from Alexa's window. It was awfully late. Didn't she have a life? At least someone else was around. The campus felt eerie at this time of night: during the day, students and faculty were always on the move between buildings.

I climbed into my small truck, creaked the door shut. I loved the reliable old set of wheels, but it was getting on in years. I pushed the lock button and started the truck. Letting the engine warm up, I rested my head on the steering wheel, not look-ing forward to the thirty-minute drive home. Wishing I didn't have to get up early and drive right back here for morning classes. Hoping Jamal wasn't in trouble with Alexa. Wondering what that incident with the children was all about.

I turned on the headlights. In front of me, I saw the still icy ground between the lot and the building illuminated as if on a movie set. The fir cast its shadow behind on the remaining bits of snow. My hand froze on the gearshift.

No. No! It couldn't be. I shifted back into neutral, turned off the ignition, and stared at the scene. I climbed out, leaving the lights on and the door open. The chilly wind clawed at my chest and my eyes. My hands numbed. I couldn't think. I moved forward at a pace that felt like slogging through a knee-high swamp. The ding-ding-ding from the vehicle sounded distant, from another reality.

A reality that did not include my star pupil slumped against a tree trunk. Papers spilled out of his messenger bag onto the ground, dry fir needles drawing scattered brown lines on the white surfaces. Jamal's arms sprawled at his sides. His head tilted at an unnatural angle onto the collar of his open leather jacket. His eyes focused on nothing.

CHAPTER TWO

I sank into my office chair after class the next morning after barely getting through the hour. Jamal's customary seat by the window had slammed my heart with its emptiness. The students had been quiet and worried. The school had sent out an email blast about the death. Several students had been in tears.

Now I gazed unfocused at the tiny elm on the windowsill, seeing the scene again. My desperately wanting to help him. Touching the skin of his cheek. Seeing the hole in his shirt and the stain surrounding it.

Frantically jabbing 911 on my cell phone. The police and campus security arriving at the same time, including my unpleasant Uncle George, who was head of the night division of campus security. The motionless form of Jamal being loaded into the ambulance, which drove away slowly, no siren, no lights. The waiting, the questioning. The chilling sight of Alexa Kensington standing on the periphery, as frozen and emotionless as an ice mannequin.

A knock on the door startled me into sitting up straight. My heart raced. I relaxed when I saw Ralph's unruly hair around the edge of the doorway.

He asked how I was.

"Oh, you know. It's pretty much awful." I took a deep breath and waved my hand at the other chair. "Sit down."

Ralph leaned down to give me a friendly hug but stayed on his feet. "Gotta get to Mythology in a sec. It's awful news, the death. Do they have any leads?"

I shook my head. "Jamal's killer is out there!"

Ralph murmured reassurances, offered to take me out for a drink at the end of the day then disappeared down the hall.

I dug my cell phone out of my pocket and pressed my best friend's number. No one answered. "Why doesn't Elise pick up?" I asked the bonsai, stroking its tips.

"You talking about me, *Gaijin*?"

"I'm not a foreigner here," I protested, even though we'd been using that nickname—"foreigner" in Japanese—with each other for years. Elise and I had met in Tokyo, where we'd both taught English conversation to businessmen. We'd become good friends. When I'd landed the position at Agawam College, we'd ended up living in the same town.

"I've been trying to reach you all morning."

Elise slouched into the room and sat in the upholstered chair. "Well, some of us have to work, you know." Elise looked paler than usual, if that was possible and her spiked hair was yet a new shade of black. She sat with one arm thrown over the arm of the chair and a leg up over the other side, a red Chuck Taylor high-top sneaker waving in the air. Long fingers dressed with multiple silver rings worried the edge of the red silk *furoshiki* she wore as a scarf around her neck. A sliver of silver dangled from each ear.

"Then what are you doing here?"

Elise shrugged and said, "Oh, took the afternoon off. You know."

I stared at my friend with a growing sense of dread. She didn't know yet. "Elise, didn't you hear?"

"Hear what?" She examined a black-painted fingernail.

I wanted to grab her and shake her. "Jamal..."

Elise sat up. Now I had her attention.

She and Jamal had become friends after I'd introduced them a year ago. They'd started meeting, usually over beers, to practice their Japanese together.

"He... he's dead. He was killed!"

"What?"

"Last night. I found him, under a tree..." I shook my head, tears welling in my eyes.

Elise moved to the window and set her hands on each side of the sash. She turned slowly to face me, a grim look frozen on her face. Then her eyes widened as she looked beyond my head to the open doorway.

I turned to see a police officer in the doorway. Her navy blue uniform was crisp and snug, with a dark t-shirt showing at the neck. The duty belt around her waist held a dozen attachments and looked heavy.

"Natalia Flores." She looked at me. "Are you Professor Rousseau?"

I told her I was.

Elise bounced on her heels. "I gotta go, Lauren."

"Excuse me, but I am here to speak with both of you."

"No, I, uh, have an appointment." Elise tried to edge through the door.

"Officer Flores, this is my friend, Elise Chase." I wondered why the officer wanted to speak with Elise as well as me.

"I'm afraid you're going to have to cancel that appointment, Ms. Chase." Flores stood with feet apart, legs slightly bent, face alert. "I gather you've heard the news?"

Elise nodded, jerking her head toward me. "She told me. Just now."

"You don't watch local news?"

"Lady, I haven't owned a television in twenty years. And I choose not to burden myself with radio chat crap, either."

"How often do you come to campus?"

"I don't have to talk to you, you know."

"True. However, I'd appreciate it if you'd answer the question."

"I've been here a couple times. It was a free world last time I checked." Elise stuck her chin in the air and raised her eyebrows.

I looked back and forth at the two women. "Elise and Jamal are friends, Officer Flores. Were friends, I mean."

Elise glared at me.

"When was the last time you saw the victim, Ms. Chase?"

"I can't remember."

Flores stared at her. "Are you sure?"

Elise nodded.

"And you, Professor?"

"Well, let's see, it might have been in class on Tuesday. Today's Friday? No, it was Wednesday on the quad. He seemed fine. He was fine!"

"May I go now, Officer?" Elise dredged the last word with sarcasm.

"I expect I'll have more questions, so please respond to your phone in the next few days. And I'd advise you not to leave town. But yes, you may go now."

Elise mocked a salute then laid a hand on my shoulder, her expression softening for the first time. "*Gambatte, da yo.*"

I nodded, whispering, "You hang in there, too." My throat swelled at the kindness. I watched Elise as she left. It was hard to believe she wasn't saddened by the news about Jamal.

"Professor? Lauren?"

I turned my head up toward Officer Flores. "Do you suspect Elise or something? That'd be crazy. They were friends."

"We have to check everyone who knew him, who might have known something. Anyway, I wondered if there were any students he might have had conflicts or relationships with that you're aware of. Or anyone else on campus."

I stared at Flores then said, "You'd better sit down. And shut the door. This could take a while."

⌒✖⌒

I sat cross-legged on the floor of my living room that evening. I rubbed the throbbing spot on my left temple. It felt like a week since last night. The blue Chinese bowl on the coffee table contained a spoon and brown-twig remnants of my dinner. Kashi, the dining choice of single women. The scotch in my glass—the drinking choice of many single professors—slid over the shell of an ice cube. Bocelli sang Bellini's "*A te, o cara*" on the CD player. I hummed along.

I hadn't called Zac yet. I was wiped out by the events of the last twenty-four hours, and I wanted his company. I imagined his hand stroking my back, heard him cracking a bad joke to try to make me laugh, smelled his scent that always made me want to drag him immediately into the bedroom. I reached for my cell phone and pressed his number. By some miracle, he was home.

After I explained what happened the night before, I endured several minutes of commiserations along the lines of "You poor thing" and "Oh, *bebé*."

"Can you come over, Zac?" I asked, in what I hoped wasn't too pitiful a tone.

"I would be there in a New York minute, Lauren. But the tire on my scooter went flat on my way home today."

"I can come over there," I said, then thought about the energy involved in packing an overnight bag and driving a couple of towns away. I wasn't sure I was up for it, but having his company trumped being alone tonight.

"Sure. Have you eaten?"

I heard a gap in the transmission. I knew what that meant. Call waiting was breaking in on his end with a beep. The phone company genius who thought the person on the other end wouldn't know what a gap of silence meant had to be clueless. I referred to it as the Call Interrupting service.

"Hang on a minute, will you?"

He was gone before I had a chance to agree. I waited. I didn't know any of his friends or much of what he did outside of work when he wasn't with me. I suddenly realized how odd that was.

We'd been going out since the fall.

"Laur? That was my boss. I have to go back to work. They just got some footage critical to something or other."

"How will you get there? I thought your scooter wasn't drivable."

"I'll take my bicycle. It's not far. Not like going all the way to Ashford."

"Be careful." I hung up. I rose and paced the length of my condo and back a few times with leaden legs then sank onto the couch.

The tulips I'd bought to hurry up spring were splayed and leaking pollen onto the top of the bookshelf. I stared out into the dark sky, seeing Jamal motionless under the tree. My fingers were cold. As cold as Jamal's would now always be.

Wulu jumped into my lap for a caress then promptly fell asleep under my hand. The doggy daycare next door must be going overboard on exercise. I leaned back against the end of the couch, humming, then stopped abruptly. The indigo smell of the African cloth that acted as slipcover brought back a flood of memories of my Peace Corps days in Mali. But not so many that I forgot where I was right now.

I jabbed the Off button on the CD player. Jamal's killer was out there somewhere. And there was nothing I could do. Why would someone kill him? There was a lot I didn't know about Jamal. And his dynamic with Alexa: that had to be more than the fellowship thing.

Officer Flores had taken notes on what I had observed about Jamal's interactions with the department chair and fellow students, as well as with Elise. Elise—I hadn't understood her reaction to Jamal's death. She'd looked grim. Then Natalia had shown up. Natalia had asked me about Elise's recent behavior. Lots of questions. And she hadn't given any information in return.

I was exhausted. A train announced itself through town then clacked its way south to the city. I wished I could put my questions on a train and send them out of town. Way out of town.

I managed to reach Saturday. One more week until spring break. Then at least I wouldn't have to be on campus every day. It was painful to be there. To see Jamal's classmates, heads down, taking the midterm exam with a somber air, Jamal not among them. To not hear his resonant tones bantering with me and with Tashandra, Li, and the others.

I hadn't seen or heard from Elise since yesterday, despite having left a couple of voicemails.

Life felt tense and unpleasant.

I wiped the sweat off my forehead as I continued my workout on the elliptical strider. I turned the page of the *New Yorker* and started to read a David Sedaris essay (always good for raising the spirits). The rain outside threatened to freeze. The lunch in the sun with Ralph felt like weeks ago. What a long month. Few outdoor running opportunities meant I was forced to go to the Y. It smelled of stale sweat, but working out my muscles and heart also worked out my psyche and my caloric intake. Better than a shrink and Weight Watchers put together.

I finished my forty minutes of cardio, wiped down the machine, and strode over to the weight room. I slowed when I saw Natalia Flores carving her biceps with slow, deliberate fifteen-pound curls. Her tight t-shirt showing the perfect definition of her shoulder and back muscles. Her light brown skin glowed with the effort. The officer watched herself in the mirror and stopped the exercise when she caught sight of me behind her.

She nodded at me in recognition.

I picked up the eight-pound weights and began my own routine, standing in front of another wall-sized mirror. The eights were a reach for me, but I knew I had to push myself to get stronger. Plus what *they* said: muscle mass increased metabolism. Increased metabolism meant I could eat more without applying the food directly to my hips. That was a good thing. And I did feel sort of buzzed after a half hour of lifting, almost as if the stepped-up metabolism kicked in instantaneously.

Flores finished a set of stretches and walked past me toward the door, pausing to say, "So, Professor Rousseau. You know, I met a Jackie Rousseau recently. Related?"

I smiled. "My sister. Where'd you meet her?"

"Oh, uh, friend of a friend." Natalia cleared her throat and drummed her fingers against her leg. "Well, gotta go. Nice to see you under more normal circumstances."

"See you around," I said and watched her trim figure as she strode away.

Hmm. Officer Natalia Flores. I'd have to ask Jackie about her.

I spent the rest of the day on mindless chores. I accomplished a couple loads of laundry and a halfhearted vacuuming. I graded a set of quizzes from my Beginning French class. I took a look at my taxes then looked away—I wasn't up to tackling the IRS in all its senseless bureaucracy.

Late afternoon had snuck up on me, and I hadn't eaten for hours. And I hadn't had any fresh air or exercise.

After downing a turkey sandwich and a glass of Chardonnay while standing at the kitchen counter, I grabbed reflective gear and Wulu's leash and set out for a walking tour of the town. I needed to clear my head.

An hour later, we found ourselves in front of Pulcifer's Boat Shop. It perched askew at the side of the river in a section of town once industrial but now half abandoned and run down. I had walked by here many times but never investigated it up close. The building stretched wide, facing the road, and was two stories high, sided in old dark wood. The entire shop looked like it might slide into the river with even the smallest nudge, like the ones its former owners probably used on new boats that were freshly sanded, varnished, and polished.

I felt drawn to the wreck, curious about it. Since Jamal's death, anything dark and mysterious was creepy, too. Decrepit lifts listed over the water below. Rusted chains hung down and clanged in the wind. Two old-looking, long, wide cars were angle-parked in front.

I approached the black car. My curiosity was edged by prickles up my spine. It looked familiar. Although rusted and dinged, it bore current inspection and registration stickers. Canvas and a chain-link cloak covered the other vehicle, its tires flattened on the dirt. A relic from long-gone prosperous times, like the boat shop itself.

Wulu pulled on his leash and dragged us up to the dingy windows and the doorway. Peering in, I saw dusty tools and a wooden cupboard with dozens of small, square drawers. In the rear, the skeleton of a pre-born ship reached up into dark rafters. A wave of cold rolled through me, and I shuddered. Wulu emitted a tiny growl.

I leaned on the glass door as I looked in. It gave way. Wulu yipped and pulled us both away from the doorway. I closed the door with a soft click and hurried back to the street, fast, whispering, "Come on, Wulu." I thought the edifice was abandoned, left to deteriorate. The door should have been locked. As I stopped and looked back, a shape moved at the top of the stairs, but I couldn't make out anything else. I walked past the structure and looked up at the second floor. A light from a river-view room at the back made only a small dent in the darkness.

CHAPTER THREE

I sat across from Zac at a small table at the BrewWorks in the evening. "Thanks for coming out with me, Zac. I didn't want to be home alone again tonight." I reached for his hand and squeezed it.

"Hey, sugar. No thanks necessary. I do care about you, you know. I'm sorry I've been so busy at work. And you've been through a lot. Finding a body." He shook his head. "More than a girl should have to go through."

I winced at being called a girl, even though I fully agreed nobody should have to be the one to stumble across a corpse. Particularly one of someone they knew and liked.

We clinked our pint glasses together and tasted our drinks at the same time.

"This is too cold for an Imperial Stout," Zac said, frowning. "As usual."

I swirled a bit of ale against my tongue and savored the thick, bitter quaff. "Here, taste the IPA. I'm so glad Bill got the job as brew master here and started making cask-conditioned beers on a regular basis." I looked across the cavernous brewery at a blackboard posted up high, each of the draft selections written in different colored chalk. The IBU for each was also listed—our brewer friend's doing, I was sure. Not too many people cared about international bitterness units. I was happy Bill was one of them.

"Speak of the devil," Zac said as a tall, slender man with trim dark hair and a Van Gogh beard made his way toward us. "Yo, Molina."

"Hey Zac, Lauren. Good to see you again." Bill shook hands with Zac and leaned down to give me a kiss on the cheek. "Thanks for coming in." He pulled over a chair from a nearby table and straddled it. "How're you liking it?"

"Well, you gotta figure out some way to warm up the stout, man," Zac said.

"I know. Management says it's too hard to keep it at a different temperature. It's a losing battle, I'm afraid. Yours, Lauren?"

"I love the cask. Wish I could stock it at home."

Bill lifted his eyebrows and chin and laughed. "You'd have to drink a hell of a lot of it! Once you tap an unfiltered real ale and it gets oxygen into it, you only have a few days before it spoils." His eyes gleamed, and he seemed delighted at the prospect. "Think you could put away nine gallons on a weekend? I must say, my Scottish granddad probably could have."

A man in a white shirt and tie came out from the kitchen. He stopped and stared at our table.

"Oops, there's the boss. Gotta run, kids. Enjoy," Bill said as he rose and ambled back to the bar area.

"So, Zac, any progress?"

"Well, we got the footage from the parking lot cameras. It's pretty dark—a couple of the lot lights were out, which is odd—but I'm working on lightening the area around the tree."

"The latest budget cuts were across the board, so Facilities probably doesn't get around to replacing lights as often as they should." I shook my head. "So much for the Safest-Campus-North-of-Boston routine they feed parents of prospective students. And no other news from the department?"

"I'm not so sure they'd tell me, Lauren. I'm just the video guy, you know. And a civilian, to boot."

After our meal and another pint, I dropped him at his apartment. A long, hot kiss pulled me to accept his invitation to stay the night, but I felt unsettled.

"I'll see you for Easter brunch tomorrow, Zac." I drove home. I needed to be alone until then.

"Damn."

I peered through the window again. No Zac. I checked my appearance in the mirror. Again. Pink Chinese-style blouse. White slacks. Sandals. The Haitian bracelet Zac gave me and the dangly earrings of pink disks that were my birthday present from Jackie. A perfect outfit for Easter brunch. Except my date was late. And, it being one of those early Easters that fell in March, it was cold and raw out. Not exactly sandal weather.

I checked the window. Definitely not spring. The Japanese maple and the lilac both sported buds, but they were not green. The tall maples across the street reminded me of my Aunt Louise: spare, austere, skeletal.

I rooted around for my cell phone as it vibrated in the depths of my handbag.

"Zac? Where are you?"

"Sorry. I'm tied up at work."

"Why are you at work?" I paced from the window to the kitchen door and back as he elaborated on how he was called in and couldn't refuse.

"I know it's a new job. But it's Easter, Zac!" I looked out at the bleak day.

"Please tell Jackie I'll be late."

"I'll tell her, but she won't like it." I jabbed the End button with particular intensity, and the phone fell to the ground. I pulled on my spring jacket and a purple silk scarf, slung my bag over my shoulder, and slammed the door. I paused at the door of my truck and cursed then returned to the house and grabbed the pastry box.

I drove to Jackie's at a faster speed than usual. "Why are they making you work on Easter?" I monologued to my absent boyfriend. "Or maybe that's what you're telling me? Maybe you volunteered for the shift because you love your work more than you love me? Nice. I told you Jackie's brunch was important to me. Didn't I? I wanted you to be there with me. Right? I need some support. Do you care? Apparently not! Do I care?" That thought shut me up. The hell with him.

Bearing the coffee cake, I walked into Jackie's small antique colonial. Fragrant cooking smells filled the living room. It was a typical Jackie production. The table ought to be groaning out loud from the weight it supported: a fat poached salmon fillet nestled into its coat of sour cream-dill sauce dotted with slim disks of green-rimmed cucumbers and pink-rimmed radishes. Triangles of fruit turnovers glistened with a crispy sugar coating. A small sliced ham. Several dozen huge strawberries with dark chocolate skirts. A Boston-Italian Easter bread, braided and baked around whole eggs in their colored shells and dusted with multi-colored candy sprinkles.

"Hi, Mom." I balanced my box in one hand as I embraced her with my other arm.

"Been baking, have we?" Mom's eyes twinkled.

"Mother. You know Jackie cooks. And I don't."

"Hey, sister." Jackie wiped her hands on a blue-striped apron that clearly sported a morning's worth of residue. Her concession to a holiday outfit was to put on a pink t-shirt with her black jeans in place of her usual black shirt. "Ooh, Emily's coffee cake? You know I love that bakery."

"Emily's it is. Why should I try to bake when Emily does it so much better? Although your turnovers are as good as anything the bakery makes."

Jackie looked behind me. "Where's your man?"

I lifted my chin and spoke to the corner of the ceiling. "He's going to be late. Again."

"Oh, honey," Mom said. "Well, you know men." She smiled and shook her head.

I took another look at my mother. "You look nice." She wore a dress-length tunic over loose pants in shades of lavender and periwinkle. Bangles encircled her wrist, and a violet flower was clipped to her hair. "Is that another one of your outfits from India?"

"Yes, dear. That was such a lovely trip. Smelling of flowers everywhere, and all those sexy carvings."

Jackie snorted and turned back to the stove. "Most moms take tours of exotic art when they retire. Ours goes and looks at erotic art." She lifted a steamer full of asparagus and rinsed it in cold water in the sink.

I poured myself a glass of Pinot Gris from the bottle on the counter. "Who else is coming?"

"Aunt Louise and Uncle George, plus Luke. Luke's coming, right, Mom?"

Mom nodded, smiling.

"And a friend of mine might come for dessert," Jackie said. She whisked together a vinaigrette and rolled the asparagus in it before lining up the spears on a square dish.

When at last my angular aunt, her florid husband, and our mother's boyfriend, Luke, arrived and all were seated, I gave Jackie an eye. My sister sighed and nodded. I was used to being the only Quaker in the family. I discovered as an adult the faith community of Friends. It suited me like no other church. I extended my hands to each side and asked for a moment of silence. We sat with joined hands for a few moments, although George fidgeted and coughed.

Jackie sighed again. "Now can we have a proper toast instead of some goofy Quaker prayer?" she asked, surrounding the final word with finger quotes. "Here's to spring, to greenery, to rebirth." Jackie raised her glass of wine.

"To our health," Mom added as we clinked glasses.

"And to Dad," I chimed in. My father died six years before, but, on occasions like this, the pain of missing him was sharp.

"To my brother, may he rest in peace," Louise said, raising her glass.

We were nearly done eating when the doorbell rang. I perked up and looked expectantly at the hallway as Jackie disappeared around the corner. I was disappointed to hear two female voices instead of Zac's deep tones.

A moment later, Jackie reemerged. I was startled to see her accompanied by Natalia Flores. She wore a white silk shirt and purple microfiber slacks snug around her waist and hips. A slim phone was clipped to her waistband. Instead of a braid, her dark hair was pulled back in a purple scrunchy and hung straight and long down her back. Both women looked pleased and furtive. Jackie's cheeks were pink, and Natalia's eyes were bright. I glanced at George and could almost see smoke coming from his ears. He glared at the two women.

Jackie put an arm around Natalia's waist. "Family, this is Natalia," she said. "Natalia, this is my mother, Miriam." Jackie then introduced everybody else at the table. George avoided her eyes and grunted something noncommittal. When Jackie got to me, Natalia stopped her.

"Hi, Lauren. We should stop running into each other like this."

Jackie glanced at her then at me with a smiling frown.

Natalia turned to Jackie and said, "I didn't get a chance to tell you, I met your sister in the gym the other day. She saw me at my worst, at the end of my workout, sweat and all. "

"I'd kill to look that bad," I said. "You're in great shape." I explained to Jackie that Natalia and I had a talk after Jamal's death, too. I stared at the ruins of the meal in front of me. The room quieted.

"Jacqueline," Mom said with a bright smile. "Get a chair for your friend." Addressing Natalia, she said, "You're in time for dessert and coffee."

I slouched in my chair as I picked at my strawberries and sipped my tiny glass of the Bahia coffee liqueur Natalia brought. I wished Zac were there. Mom chatted with Louise. Luke looked on in silence, aglow with his affection for my mom. Jackie and Natalia talked together in a low voice, Jackie's arm on the back of Natalia's chair.

George drummed his fingers on the table. His puffy face looked redder than usual, and his small eyes seemed lost between the vast expanse of forehead and excess cheek flesh. He was a portrait in contrasts with his wife's lean, tidy figure.

He stared at my glass. "I thought Quakers weren't supposed to drink."

I flushed and nodded. "That was certainly true in the past. Now? Some don't. Some do."

He snorted, downed his somewhat larger glass of liqueur, and stood.

"Come on, Louise. We're leavin'," he said, cutting his words with scorn, his South Boston roots in full evidence. "I'm not sitting here with these perverts, even if she is your niece." He put his beefy hand on his wife's chair.

Louise sat up straight, took a deep breath, kissed her sister-in-law on the cheek, and stood. "Please forgive us, Jacqueline. It appears we're going."

"Damn right we are! Hurry up. I'll be in the car." George clomped out of the room and slammed the outside door.

"It was a lovely meal. Very nice to have met you, Natalia. Goodbye, Luke. Lauren, say hello to your fellow when he arrives, will you?" Louise found her purse and walked toward the hall. She turned back toward the table for a moment. "I'm so sorry. Really."

A moment later, Zac strolled into the room. I looked up with a start.

"Hi. Happy Easter." He smiled and walked over to my chair. His Haitian dreadlocks were tied back in a rubber band, and his pink Oxford shirt and green tie fit the occasion. "What was all that about? I heard your Aunt Louise say she was sorry then her husband honked the horn and she rushed out."

"Homophobia strikes when you least expect it," Mom said. "Or, to tell the truth, when you had been expecting it for a while. Poor Louise. I don't know how she puts up with such a man."

Natalia gazed straight ahead and kept her hands quiet in her lap. Jackie rubbed her shoulder, while Luke nodded his head at Miriam.

Zac shrugged and leaned down to kiss the top of my head. He sat next to me in George's vacated chair, leaning back and stretching. "Can you possibly forgive me, Jackie, everybody, for missing the entire meal? I got called in on a robbery, and since I'm the only video analyst, I had to stay until I worked the footage for them."

I also looked straight ahead, wondering that he didn't seem to care if I forgave him. I was the one he stood up. Damn him.

"And how did it go, dear?" Mom asked, focusing her inquisitive eyes on Zac. Natalia, apparently relieved the focus was off her and Jackie, also looked in his direction.

"Well, in the video from the parking lot camera, I was able to lighten and clarify the license plate of the car that was parked outside the convenience store, and, last I heard, they'd found the car and its driver. The bad guys, as the cops say. Technical term, you know." A smile lurked behind Zac's eyes, but then he turned to me and said in a serious tone, "*Bebé*, I'm sorry I didn't show. I couldn't, you know, but I'm sorry. Peace among us?"

I looked at those liquid brown eyes and felt a hunger for him that surprised even me, Lauren of the large appetites. "Of course, Zac," I said, feeling all eyes on us. "So, you need some food?"

"I'm starving. I kept envisioning eating Jackie's cooking and got here as soon as I could. Miriam, Luke, how is everybody?" He looked at Natalia and continued, "And, since nobody seems to want to introduce me, hi, I'm Zac."

Jackie, on her way to the kitchen, turned and said, "Oh, sorry, man. This is my friend Natalia Flores. Natalia, Zac Agnant. Lauren's, uh, friend."

"Nice to meet you," Natalia said. "I'm curious, do you happen to work for a police department? You mentioned robbery."

"Yep. As of a month ago, I am the Millsbury PD video analyst. As a civilian, you understand. It's a good gig."

Jackie set a plate of food and a wine glass in front of Zac.

"Do you have the dTective app?" Natalia asked. "I'm an officer in Ashford. We're too small to afford a system, but we could sure use it."

Zac's eyes lit up. "That's exactly what we have! Are you part of the regional consortium?" He took a sip of wine. "My boss, the chief at the station, started it. If you ever have video tapes or digital footage you need analyzed, I think we can work out a deal."

"If that's the regional electronic and computer crimes task force, we are." Natalia sipped her coffee. "I'll be in touch, if you don't mind. I didn't realize Millsbury was part of the RECC, but it's good to know." She put a hand into her pants pocket then brought it out empty. "Oh. I usually have my card on me, but I'm off duty and..."

"No problem. Jackie's got my email address, right?"

Jackie said, "I got it, *bofré*," nodding her head.

"Hey, girlfriend, where'd you learn *Kreyòl*? And I'm not your brother-in-law." He winked at me. "Yet."

Mom, raising her eyebrows, asked, "Is there news I haven't heard of?"

"No, mother. No news." Anger rushed through me. I eased away from Zac's body as he tucked into the food. Why would he say something like that? He knew I wasn't ready for marriage. I gazed at his long fingers as he ate, and the anger turned to lust. I longed for those hands to be feeding my body to him instead.

Mom poured wine for Zac, Luke, and herself, then fixed her eyes on my beau. "Now, how are you finding the Media Composer documentation, Zac?"

He paused in his eating. "Ma'am?" His eyebrows rose.

"Lauren didn't tell you? I am—that is, I was—the technical writer who wrote the user's guide and the help system for that application. Not for dTective. That sits on top of Media Composer. I wondered if you found the information helpful. We were always looking for user input, you know. To improve things."

"No kidding! I'm a big believer in RTFM. Really. And in my world, that means Read the FINE Manual, not the other interpretation. At least the fine books from your, what, former company? I thought Laurie said you were retired."

I winced at the nickname but kept my reaction to myself. Just one more issue to raise with Zac later. I hated nicknames.

Mom's laugh was heartier than her petite presence might indicate. "Oh, yes, dear, but I retired only last fall, and my documentation lives on. I'm glad you can use it, that's all."

Chapter Four

Zac put his arm around my shoulder and nuzzled my hair. "You forgive me now, *bebé*?" We had walked for twenty minutes in near silence on Toil-in-Vain Road after a brief stop at my house to grab a sweater. I'd changed from the unsuitable sandals to sneakers and put a leash on Wulu. I'd wanted to salvage what I could from this holiday, and the party at Jackie's had broken up mid-afternoon.

After ascending the first hill, I slowed at the beaver pond on the downslope and reached for Zac's gloved hand to keep him with me. The ice was starting to clear, but there were no signs yet of new chewing activity on the trees at the perimeter. I twisted to look up at him. Then returned my gaze to the pond. "Yes. But—"

"But nothing. You either forgive somebody or you don't." He returned his hand to the pocket of his jacket.

"Look. I don't get as much time with you as I want. Today's a holiday. I felt lonely and abandoned." I heard my tone drip hurt as I resumed walking. "And it's been a tough week."

"I know, Lauren. Hey, wait up." Zac caught up with me and wove his hand under my elbow. "It's something we're going to have to work out. I don't think it's going to be easy, either. Maybe you should find somebody else."

"Don't be an idiot." I shook my head, clamping my arm tight against his, feeling his muscles strong in my side even through my coat. Slowing my pace, I took a deep breath. Why did I feel so needy all the time? I had a job I loved, I had a beau who cared for me, I was healthy. Why couldn't I feel satisfied with what I had?

As we continued up the next hill and down toward the salt marsh, we talked about the personalities at the brunch, about the dearth of news in Jamal's case, about Zac's twin sister Pia, who lived with her daughter in Haiti and who was about to remarry.

"So that'd be interesting if I could help out the local force, work with Natalia," Zac said. "She seemed pretty curious about my work."

"Uh-huh," I murmured, watching a hawk circle high.

"Are she and Jackie hanging out together now?"

"Sure looks like it. That's good. Jack's been by herself for a while. Although she doesn't tell me too much about her love life."

We stopped at the bridge over Toil-in-Vain Creek and watched the water swirl on its way to the tidal river ahead as it hit the bridge supports. Wulu barked at a passing seagull and tried to chase after a kingbird that landed on the railing then flew off. I huddled into Zac's arms, away from the wind coming off the marshes. "Tide's in. The banks are mudflats when it's out; when it's really high a boat can hardly pass under here. One time I saw a couple of guys lie right down in their boat as it passed under so they didn't get their hats knocked off."

He pulled away, reaching for his camera. "You spend a lot of time out here, don't you?" His smile was warm.

"Oh, yeah. One of the few places to run where there's almost no traffic. The advantage of a dead-end road. And the hills are a good workout." I gazed at the moving water, glad I had pushed for this walk. I was starting to feel better when I realized Zac was no longer beside me. A movement over my shoulder caught my eye.

Zac was on the other side of the bridge, waggling his fingers at me as he held a small black camcorder in his hand, his eyes focused on the folded-out viewing screen. "Smile, honey. Smile, Wulu. It's my new HD Canon—like it?"

I rolled my eyes then smiled and waved. There was no escaping being filmed with this man around. "Come on. There's more to this walk." I strode to the other side of the bridge and took a right at the rock that read, "End of Road. Turn here." Zac followed, shooting me, the dog, the marshes, the hawk, and two bufflehead ducks I pointed out to him on the creek.

The only house on this extension of the road was a weathered blue wooden structure. The small two-story colonial nestled in the tall fir trees that punctuated this edge of the marsh. It didn't have a Historical Commission plaque on it, but I'd bet it was built before 1720, making it one of the town's many First Period homes. Although I ran out here several times a week, I only saw people in the house during a few weeks in the summer. A glass-walled sitting room jutted out from one end, with model sailing ships and carved wooden shorebirds sitting on a shelf under the windows. When the city people were here with their grandchildren in August, the place had a busy, comforting air. Abandoned at the end of winter, it looked stranded and desolate. I shivered and shook my head.

I'd never had this kind of reaction before I'd found a dead body—Jamal's. I scolded myself. Not every unoccupied building had to be sinister.

I strolled farther down the road to where it opened up to the marshland. Tilted ice heaves poked jagged edges up from the first of the ditches running through the marsh. I looked around for Zac—this would look great on film—and saw him standing just past the house, looking from his viewfinder to the real scene and back. "What's up?" I called.

Zac motioned me toward him, looking at the camera. He pointed to a speck on the screen then started walking toward the house.

I moved past him, pulling Wulu with me. A shred of something red was caught on a tree near the back of the house. "Is that what you saw?" I had to push back bare branches to reach the tree then stopped.

"Do you recognize it, Laur?" Zac reached my side and laid his hand on my shoulder.

I stared. And stared some more. I was back in my office. The last time I saw Elise. A red silk *furoshiki*. A scarf that now hung on this branch, behind a house on a road I wasn't sure Elise even knew existed.

"How did that get here?" My voice rose in alarm. "That's Elise's favorite scarf. See, it has the *Same Komon* pattern. She brought it back from Japan with her."

"Maybe she came out here for a walk."

"A walk?" My voice rose higher. "That girl doesn't walk! She used to, but now she drives everywhere. And why would she come to the back of this house?"

Zac swore. I whirled away from the tree to see him examining three broken panes next to the door handle at the back of the extended room. Glass lay mixed with ice on the ground, and the wooden door was open an inch. He drew his cell phone out from his pocket then swore again when he couldn't get a signal.

"Elise. She's in trouble. I know it." When I reached for the door handle, Zac stopped me. "What if Elise is in there?" I tried to push past him.

"Why would she be?" He pulled a blue bandanna from his pocket and handed it to me. "Anyway, if this is some kind of break-in, well, I've been at the station long enough to know you should protect evidence. You seem determined to go in there, so use this on the door handle. I'm right behind you."

The door swung in with a creak. "Whoa, Wulu!" The dog darted through the doorway ahead of me. I tugged him back outside as he yelped and strained for the house. "He must smell Elise in there."

"Here, give him to me," Zac said. "I'll tie him up. We don't want him to cut his feet." He rejoined me, and we picked our way over more broken glass. To our left was the kitchen, with sixties-era avocado-green appliances and minimal cupboards. The counters and wooden table were bare but for a coating of dust, befitting a house vacated last September. A very small gray mouse zipped along the baseboard.

"Do you think we should call 911?" I whispered. Was someone in the house? Was Elise?

"Not yet. Let's check out the place, and then we can report the damage. I'm sure it was only kids smoking pot who wanted to get in out of the snow or something."

The stairs cracked as I followed Zac up to the second floor. The wallpaper featured faded garden scenes and a diagonal line of somber framed figures preceded me up the stairs. I was passing a particularly severe-looking couple in stiff black clothing when Zac stopped.

"Look." He pointed to the treads above him. The dust was disturbed. "Somebody's been up here recently."

I pushed past him to look then took the rest of the stairs two at a time. At the landing, I was met by three closed doors in a small hallway. Cold air blew in through a crack in a window at the end. Heart throbbing in my chest, I yanked open one of the doors to see a tiled bathroom with clawed tub. No Elise. The door to its right opened to a bedroom looking out onto the marsh. The only furniture was a double bed covered with a lace spread and an upholstered rocker near the double window with the view. I slammed the door and opened the last one. In a large bedroom, two neatly made twin beds lined up in parallel several feet apart, and a bunk bed stood against the opposite wall. A bookshelf held paperback books and boxes of Clue and Monopoly, with a wicker basket of toys on the bottom shelf. On a bedside table, a faded rubber lion perched next to a cowboy-motif lamp with the light springing out of the head of a rearing black stallion.

My heart pounded in my ears as I searched the room, even lifting the bedspreads to look under the beds. I sensed danger but couldn't locate it. I heard Zac's voice say, as if from a distance, "Honey, it's all right. Nobody's here. Let's go." His warm hand on my neck felt suffocating, controlling. I twisted away then spied a small door under the eaves. I wrested it open to see an ascending stairway. I raced up the narrow passage.

At the top was a rough attic floor. Hundreds of nail points impaled the underside of the wooden roof, and several antique trunks stood in the far corner. A small window in the gable streamed southern light onto a circle of old sofa pillows surrounding a pie tin littered with the browned ends of a dozen hand-wrapped joints and a couple of roach clips. Several empty Budweiser cans stood sentinel over a crew of Miller bottles on their sides.

Zac followed me up and stood behind me. I sighed and called in a weak voice, "Elise?" I didn't expect an answer. She wasn't here. So Zac was right. This was only a teen hangout. But why Elise's scarf? Why the sense of foreboding? My neck hairs stood on end. So many whys.

I waved Zac down the stairs. "I'll be right there." I looked around the attic one more time, squinting as if I could conjure up Elise's presence. I turned toward the stairs. Then turned back. Silver glinted next to one of the cushions on the floor. I bent and picked it up. An earring.

The long thin shaft of silver Elise had been wearing in my office. She'd been here after all.

⤜∽⤏

Zac put his arm around my shoulder as we stood in front of Elise's saltbox.

We had reversed our steps from the house on the marsh and dropped Wulu at my condo. After finding Elise's earring in the attic, I'd needed to make sure she was all right.

The saltbox was a small house in the oldest section of town, with a weathered Historical Commission sign on the front reading, "Nathan Chase House, built c. 1695." Elise was fascinated by the thought that she might be living in a house built by one of her ancestors but was never able to find a direct link between Nathan and her father's family. The house was weathered, too. I remembered Elise saying it was sold as a fixer-upper and that she was trying to save the money to fix it up.

"I don't know how somebody with a PhD, a steady job, and no children doesn't have enough money to hire somebody to work on her house." I shook my head. "But Elise somehow always seems short on cash."

"Are we going to stand here until it gets dark, or should we see if she's home?" Zac said with a squeeze to my arm.

"Her car's here. I expect she is, too, but I don't see any lights." I knocked on the plank door. The strap hinges were rusty, and paint was missing in patches. I looked through the window closest to the door, but the curtain was pulled. "Maybe she's sleeping or something. Although it's awfully early for that." I was turning back to Zac when I felt a pressure against my ankle.

"Milo!" I reached down to stroke a small orange tabby cat. The cat wore a collar with a metal name tag dangling from it. He rolled over and rubbed his back on the step.

"What are you doing out?" I looked up at Zac. "He isn't supposed to be outdoors. Although he loves escaping, so that's why she got him the collar and tag." I scooped up the beast and walked around to the back of the house. "I'm going to see if the back door is open and put him in."

I knocked at the door of the screened-in back porch then tried the latch. It opened, so I carried Milo inside, shutting the outer door behind us. The porch, with faded paint and patched screens, held gardening supplies on shelves at one end—empty pots, a half-full bag of potting soil, a pair of purple gloves, plus trowels and clippers hung neatly on the wall—and a small round table and two chairs at the other. A pair of rubber boots and a set of muddy rubber clogs were lined up near the door. Nearby sat a green recycling bin half full of wine bottles, an empty fifth of bourbon, and two orange-juice containers. Nothing was out of order, but why was

Milo wandering around outside, alone? What was Elise's car doing home when she didn't answer her door? I pictured the red scarf blowing from the marsh tree.

I rang an Asian temple bell hanging next to the inner door then knocked again. "Elise?" I called, trying the door. It did not budge.

"I'm sure she'll let you in when she wakes up or comes home, kitty cat." I gave Milo a last scritch then slipped out, making sure the door shut behind me. As I walked toward Zac, who waited on the driveway, I wondered if I heard a door shut. I whipped my head back, staring. Elise did not emerge. I sighed. If my friend didn't feel like talking to me, that was her business.

"Didn't find her?" Zac stretched out his hand for mine.

"No. I hope she's all right." I pressed the fingers on my other hand to my forehead. "Maybe she doesn't want to see me. I don't know."

"Don't be obvious about it, but look up there." Zac made a small gesture toward a second-story window next door.

I looked up then raised my eyebrows at Zac.

"Not sure, but I think somebody might be watching us," he said. "I saw light bounce off something like a lens. You know?"

I didn't like the thought of somebody tracking our movements. At all. But I hadn't seen anything except blank window glass. I shook my head. "What I do know is this has been the longest Easter of my life." I looked up at him. Strain pulled at my eyes, and my face was so heavy I could barely smile. "I want to go home and do nothing."

"You want company? I'm pretty good with a back rub." Zac's hand was strong and warm as it squeezed mine.

A hot streak of longing rushed through me, and I returned the squeeze. Nothing would suit me better than a hot toddy, a hot back rub, and whatever might follow.

A rustle in the yard chilled me. I turned. Traces of a border garden in front of the back fence featured a stone Buddha presiding in stern peace. Tufts of tall perennial grasses in shades of ecru waved in the cold breeze. The water wasn't running in a small waterfall in the corner of the yard, but the cascading rocks were free of leaves and debris.

A rock garden had been raked into wave patterns around several stones pushing up like islands. Elise's yard had been on the Garden Club's Hidden Treasures tour last summer and had looked spectacular.

Now at the tail end of a long New England winter, it was no longer so tidy, its stark emptiness ominous, like a scene from a monochrome horror movie.

CHAPTER FIVE

The fog in my eyes was reluctant to register the red digital numerals telling me it was 7:00 a.m. "Lower than normal temperatures this morning and a moist cold front could bring frozen precipitation by midday," the announcer said. I groaned and shut off the radio. *Time to get up.* I turned and spooned with Zac's smooth back.

A low laugh resonated in his body. "You could set that thing to play to some nice music, you know, *bebé*? Why let the bad news about New England weather be the first thing you hear when you wake up?"

I pressed my nose into his back. "I need to know what to wear," I mumbled.

He laughed again, louder, and turned to face me. He ran a hand over my cheek and hair. "But you always look good. Is it so difficult to choose an outfit?"

"Yes," I muttered into his chest. "Now. Coffee. Need coffee."

"Yes, ma'am." He kissed the top of my head and started to roll away.

Suddenly bereft, I reached out for his arm and ended up with a handful of hip. "Or it could wait?"

He rolled back and stretched out, facing me. "Do we not need to get to work today?" He raised a seductive eyebrow over a half smile.

"Well, not urgently." I pressed closer to him. "You?"

Monday morning wakeup was nice. But Monday classes were rough. No news about Jamal's killer and no contact from Elise didn't make it any easier.

I'd left a couple of messages, but she hadn't called back.

I started to pack up to head home when the phone on my desk rang. It was Alexa's secretary, Nahid, saying Alexa wanted to see me. Now.

I said I'd be right there and hung up. I finished stuffing my papers and books for the night into my briefcase, locked my office door, and went up the two flights of stairs to Alexa's much more spacious, much more expensively decorated office. The door was ajar.

"Come in, Lauren." Alexa beckoned to me from where she stood in front of her desk. I walked in and stopped. Natalia Flores and my student, Helmut, sat in chairs in front of Alexa's desk. Natalia sported an inscrutable expression, while Helmut and Alexa looked faintly triumphant.

"What's going on?" I asked. What *was* going on? Alexa did not ask me to sit, so I stayed standing near the door.

"I'll get right to it, Lauren. I know you are familiar with the college guidelines on sexual harassment."

Thoughts raced through my head. Was Helmut accusing me of something with Jamal? *Oh, crap.* What did he know? I looked at him. He squirmed a little and looked at Alexa.

Alexa cleared her throat.

I stared at her. "Of course I am." And waited.

"It appears you were conducting yourself in an unprofessional manner with, uh, the deceased Mr. Carter."

Oh, double crap. The heat rose in my face, and I knew I was approaching beet-red status. I took a deep breath and stood up as straight as I could. I had to stonewall this. My career was ruined if I couldn't. "What makes you think that, Dr. Kensington?"

"There have been reports. Including from Mr. Herzog here."

"I don't know what these reports consist of, but I can assure you I have done nothing wrong."

"We'll see about that. Officer Flores?"

Natalia rose. "Dr. Rousseau, we'd like to speak with you further about Mr. Carter's death."

"Why? I didn't have anything to do with his death. I just found him." I couldn't believe this. I looked at Helmut. He wouldn't meet my eyes. He was lying. He couldn't know anything. One of my worst, most unmotivated students was trying to destroy me. Or maybe Alexa talked him into her little scheme. Well, let them try.

"We'll decide that. Is now a convenient time?" Natalia didn't seem as friendly as at Easter.

"Sure."

"Sit down, Lauren," Alexa ordered, gesturing to a straight chair.

"No, thank you." I folded my arms and met Natalia's eyes.

"There have been various sightings of you with Jamal—dancing, at the pub, and, um, 'fondling' him," Natalia said, looking at a small notebook.

Fondling? Jeez. That must have been Helmut's contribution. "I was his profes-sor. I was his advisor." I frowned. "We spent a lot of time together for those reasons. And only those reasons. Nothing happened. You didn't get a complaint from Jamal, did you? Before he was killed?" I didn't acknowledge I had, in fact, gotten in deeper than I should have. I wasn't suicidal. I looked at Alexa.

"No, we didn't," she said.

"Am I a suspect in the murder?" I asked Natalia. "Is that why you wanted to talk with me?"

"We have to investigate everyone who associated with Jamal."

I looked at Alexa again. "Am I being formally charged with sexual harassment?"

Alexa, looking at Helmut, shook her head.

I, in turn, looked at Natalia. I didn't care if she was my sister's girlfriend. "So if I'm not being accused of either murder or sexual misconduct, I can go?" I knew my face was red and didn't care.

Natalia nodded. Alexa avoided my eyes.

I left as fast as I could. That was the closest call of my professional life. Jamal was never going to tell our story now. And unless someone saw him leaving my house that day, I was safe. Or should be.

After a long day of teaching, office hours, and committee meetings on Tuesday, I needed to get the stink blown off, as my nephew used to say. After I got home, I suited up for a run and headed out.

I shook off the memory of the meeting in Alexa's office the day before, resolving to enjoy the fresh air and scenery. I ran past the brick cottage at the bottom of the second hill on Toil-in-Vain Road, sweating despite the chilled air. The house was set back in a forest of monster-sized rhododendrons. Pens for ducks, chickens, and roosters nestled under the pines to the right. The white-haired man who lived there walked his two basset hounds slowly on the road several times a day and usually smiled and greeted me as I ran past, although he never stopped to talk. Neither did I. This was New England, after all.

The last house before the creek was the big white one perched at its edge. I often greeted the young couple who lived there when I ran past, as they raked leaves or shoveled snow, but didn't know them by name. The cloudy afternoon light tinted the clapboards a gray matching the color of the water. A turkey vulture dipped its wide dark wings as it circled above the narrow bridge.

I slowed at the blue house across the creek. The upstairs bedroom window caught my eye. Something seemed odd, and the uneasy feelings from Sunday flooded back.

Elise's scarf on the tree. The apparent youth hangout in the attic and Elise's earring on the floor. Not finding Elise at home later. I stood and stared at the house then found myself drawn to the back entrance again.

I tested the door and found it open. I climbed the stairs to take one more look. In the children's room, I stared at the twin beds. The matching chenille bedspreads were now rumpled and askew, and a threadbare stuffed dog on the far bed lay supine, one floppy ear flung over its eyes. I moved around the near bed and stopped with a sharp intake of breath.

In the narrow space between the beds, Elise lay crumpled on her side like a discarded sack of clothes.

Chapter Six

Elise's feet were bare, and her dark pants showed streaks of dirt. Her face was paler than ever. The red-striped legs of an antique Raggedy Ann doll covered Elise's ear, and its embroidered mouth grinned at her face. Near her head, a syringe lay next to her bag.

"No!" I dropped to my knees and pressed my fingers into my friend's ankle. A faint pulse pressed back. "Elise! Wake up!" I said, grabbing the foot and shaking it. Elise didn't respond. I reached for my phone then remembered I'd left it at home. Frantic, I looked at Elise once more, dragged one of the bedspreads off the bed, and laid it over her. I raced down the stairs. A green rotary phone hung on the kitchen wall, but, when I lifted the receiver, no dial tone greeted me.

My heart raced. *What should I do?* Try to wake her up? Carry her out of there? Run to the nearest house? I'd never been confronted with such an emergency and never felt so confused.

I took a deep breath and considered the options. Since I skipped Girl Scouts the day they did CPR training several decades earlier, I decided my only strength was in my legs and raced back over the bridge.

My heart sank when I saw neither of the cars that customarily parked in the curving drive of the white house, but I banged at the door and rang the bell anyway. When no one answered, I ran on, past the conservation land on the right then past the house and parcel for sale. On the verge of tears, my breathing growing ragged, I pushed on as fast as I could.

My hand was raised to knock on the front door of the brick cottage when a voice behind me made me jump.

"Can I help you, dear?" The owner emerged from the open garage with both dogs ambling behind him.

"Oh, yes, please. My friend, I found her." My throat tightened. "Can you call 911? Please?"

"Why, certainly. Uh, where might your friend be? And what's wrong with her?" His voice was kind.

Feeling like I might soon drown in a full-blown cry, I forced myself to calm down and said, pointing down the hill, "In the blue house. Right over the bridge. Upstairs. She's alive, but barely. I couldn't wake her!"

"Come in, now. We'll call, and then we'll drive down there. Sit," he said, turning to the dogs, who cocked their heads and shuffled back into the garage.

"Thank you, sir." I followed him into the house. We entered a kitchen, where a sink full of dirty dishes contrasted with clean counters and a scrubbed stovetop. "I'm sorry to bother you like this."

My host pressed buttons on a black telephone sitting on a cracked linoleum countertop. He handed me the receiver. "Here, you talk."

I gave the dispatcher my name. I described Elise and the house, explaining why I left. I promised to go right back there and hung up.

"I'll drive you," the man said, escorting me outside to a tiny silver car. When we got to the blue house, I wanted to run upstairs to Elise, but the dispatcher had said to wait outside.

We stood near the car as sirens approached. My heart beat too fast. The man paced up and down the road in front of the house. An ambulance screeched to a stop. A flood of activity followed. I watched, anxious. The EMTs had just brought Elise out on a stretcher when a police car pulled up.

"Afternoon," a man said as he climbed out. He wore an old sweater with wrinkled slacks and looked tired. "I'm Chief Flaherty."

"I'm Lauren Rousseau." My eyes left Elise's unmoving form reluctantly. We shook hands.

He gazed at me. "Say, are you that professor who—"

"Found a body on the Agawam campus? Yes."

"And now you found another one?"

I looked back at the stretcher. At least Elise sported an IV, an oxygen mask, and blankets under the stretcher's straps, so she must be alive. For now. "I was worried about my friend, and—"

"Did you break into the house?"

"No! We were out here on Sunday. On Easter," I began.

"Who's we?"

"My boyfriend and me. We were taking a walk. He saw a scarf on that tree, right there." I stopped, staring at the tree, remembering the red scarf draped on the branch, as limp as Elise's foot was twenty minutes earlier.

"A scarf." Flaherty ran his hand through a grizzled haircut that looked like it might be self shorn.

"It was Elise's. She wore it all the time. Then we saw the door had been broken into, and I thought maybe—well, I don't know." What I thought was that I'd better not tell him all my worries about Elise. Not right now. "Anyway, we went into the house, but she wasn't there."

"Did it occur to you to call your friendly local police station to report a break-in?"

"I called. The next day." I turned back to the ambulance holding my friend, trying to hide the blush that bloomed when I remembered why I forgot to call that night.

"And why didn't I hear about it?" His expression was stern.

I shook my head. "Maybe the officer lost it? I don't know, sir."

He raised his eyebrows.

I saw the ambulance start to move, and all my anguish for Elise flooded back. "I need to follow her. Do you know where they're taking her?"

"Probably to Mercy Hospital in Millsbury."

"So can I go now?"

"Yes. But I'll have more questions for you later, Professor." He took my phone number. "Hope your friend does all right."

"She's going to be fine." I hoped that was true. I looked around for the man who helped me. He had pulled his car out of the way of the ambulance now speeding, siren blasting, over the bridge.

He waved me over. "Need a ride home?"

"Oh, thank you. I have to get to the hospital." Relief rushed through me. "I don't live far from Town Hill."

"I'll run you up there. I have all the time in the world."

"I'm so sorry," I said after I fitted myself into the car. "I never introduced myself. I'm Lauren Rousseau."

"I'm Phillip Pulcifer. Pleased to meet you."

"Oh! The same Pulcifer as the boat shop?"

"Well, yes. In a way."

I waited for him to go on. When he didn't, I said, "I walk by there a lot. Does someone live upstairs?"

The man regarded the marshes in the distance then sighed. "That's my brother. Samuel. It's a long, sad story, don't you know."

I kept quiet, hoping he would go on.

"He isn't very well, mentally. Our uncle left him the boat shop in his will. Samuel had been his apprentice. But since Uncle Silas died, the building and business have gone downhill. People still bring Samuel boats to repair, but he doesn't seem to do a very good job. And he stopped making new boats."

"Can I ask why he has those junk cars out front?"

"He used to modify old car engines into boat engines. It's an eyesore, but he won't listen to me." Phillip's tone turned grim. "Some scumbag lawyer talked him into a reverse mortgage, too. That's how Samuel pays his taxes and buys food, I think. But he'll barely speak to me now," Phillip continued, his voice now low and sad. "Our sister's daughter Lexie is the only one he talks to. He thinks I have demons. I tell him the building is going to fall down and crush him in a strong wind one of these days. That's the demon he needs to worry about."

I stood by Elise's side in a chilly bay in the Mercy Hospital ER. My friend was as pale as the linen jacket I changed into before coming to the hospital. The spikes of her hair lay dark and limp on the pillow. An IV and several wires tethered her to a pump and a beeping monitor. Nurses in purple scrubs and doctors in blue bustled in and out of adjacent curtained bays, but the space in which Elise lay was an island of ominous quiet. I had to claim Elise was my sister to get in to see her. And I was, really, with all we had gone through together. I smoothed back her hair. We weren't as close lately, and I didn't know why.

"Come on, *gaijin*," I whispered to her. "We need a chance to work this out, girl-friend. Don't give up on me now."

One of the blue-clothed figures marched into the area. "Who are you?" she said while examining a slim laptop computer.

"I'm her sister. Lauren."

The doctor looked me up and down with frank skepticism. "Right."

Ignoring this, I asked, "How is she? Do you know what happened to her?"

"You're the *sister* who found her, aren't you?"

"Yes. I don't know what's wrong with her."

"It was an overdose. She's lucky to be alive. Heroin, most likely." The doctor checked a machine and typed something on the laptop.

"Really? Heroin?" I wondered why. Elise had so much going for her. I knew the Japan thing had been tough on her, but that had been a long time ago. I realized I was staring at Elise and the doctor was staring at me.

"Can you give us any information about how long she's been doing this?" She felt Elise's neck and wrist.

"Oh, no. I didn't even know she was! I mean, she'd been getting kind of flaky lately. Lost weight. Didn't ever seem to have enough money despite having a good job. But heroin? I had no idea."

"Well, it's out there, and it's cheap. You can get a hit for the price of a six-pack of beer. And Lawrence is the major hub around here. Couple towns away." The doctor shook her head. "Anyway, she'll be all right. Physically. But she's going to need intensive rehab." With that, the doctor was gone, rushing on to some other patient in need.

Leaving me to whisper, "Why, *gaijin*? Why?"

"We've talked about *katakana* and how it's the syllable-based writing system used primarily for non-Japanese, non-Asian words." I wrote several sequences of the blocky stylized characters on the whiteboard in my Linguistics 101 class the next morning. "Who can tell me what word these might represent in some European-based language?"

"You mean, not just English?" a student in the front row asked.

"That's right. Most *katakana* signs you see in public are from English, but not all." Li, a slim beauty in the front row, raised her hand and waited to be recognized. Several other students stared at the board and tried to sound out the syllables. I nodded at Li.

"The first one looks like it should be 'beer' but it's actually *biru*, short for building—*birudingu*—right?"

"That's exactly right, Li. And the *katakana* for beer is what?" I gestured toward to the whiteboard.

"*Biiru*. Long vowel." She looked pleased with herself.

I wasn't surprised. She was one of my best students. Then it hit me. Now she *was* my best student. Now that Jamal was gone. I took a deep breath and continued.

"That's right. Who has the next phrase?"

A radiator kicked in with several clicks and a hiss. Trees were dripping last night's rain off the branches outside the window, and the sun cast me in a spotlight as I waited.

I called on Helmut, who looked bored but was waving his hand with a lazy motion. "Is it 'old disco dance'?"

"No."

Helmut looked annoyed while a couple of male students in the back row snickered.

I called on the girl behind Li. "Tashandra?"

"Um, hard disk drive?"

"Excellent! Read out the *katakana*, please."

"*Haado disku doraibu.*"

"Nice job."

Tashandra graced her desk with a smile and aligned the edges of the papers on its surface.

"All right, everybody." I looked at the wall clock. "Your homework is on the class web page, and I'm adding one more thing: bring in your name written in *katakana* according to Japanese phonotactic rules. Remember the mid-term exam is Friday. "

Tashandra lingered after class, fussing with her backpack, retying her shoe, until all the other students left and I was ready to leave, too.

"Professor Rousseau?"

"Yes?" All I wanted to do was get back to my office and call the hospital. But she was friends with Jamal. Maybe she wanted to talk about his death.

"Can I, like, ask you something?"

"Of course, Tashandra. What is it?"

The young woman looked through the window for a moment then faced me. "It's that I, um, think I might have, like, seen something."

I stopped breathing and stood with both hands on my briefcase.

"It was when I was walking with Jamal one day after class. This guy, like, wanted to talk with Jamal. I don't know what it was about, but Jamal wasn't very happy with him. The guy was, like, threatening him!" She looked up at me. Her eyebrows drew together in the middle, and her eyes held fear.

"Really? Threatening him? Did you hear what it was about?"

"Yeah. No. I just heard the tone of voice, you know? And then they went off somewhere, you know, together."

"When was this?" Was she being a drama queen, or was this real?

"I think it was the week before he died." Her eyes welled up. "He was being so nice to me, Jamal, and we were going to study together. You know, for the midterm."

"I think you should tell the police, Tashandra. About what you saw and heard."

She widened her eyes and shook her head.

"No, really," I said. "This could be important. Do you think you could describe the man?"

A slow nod. "I even drew his face later."

The surprise on my face must have been evident as Tashandra went on. "Yeah, I draw a lot. I wanted to be an art major, but my grandma said it wasn't practical. She raised me up."

"And what is your major?"

"Business. I have to be able to support myself." The young woman smiled. "Maybe I'll start an art school or something."

"So you drew this man who was threatening Jamal?"

"Uh-huh. It's in my notebook."

"And where were you when this happened?"

"Over by the student union. Near the bookstore."

"Listen, I think we should take your drawing to the police, Tashandra. This man might have information about whoever killed Jamal." It might even be Jamal's killer, but I kept the thought to myself.

She worried a strap dangling from her pack between her fingers, rolling it over and over. "Oh, I don't know. I mean, like, are they going to think I was involved in something bad?"

"You weren't, were you?"

"No!" Tashandra backed up a step.

"We both want to help Jamal. Make sure nobody else gets killed." Finally I had something to act on, to do. I had to get her to cooperate.

"Of course I want to, you know, help him." She looked up, her eyes flashing. "But, Professor, I don't think you understand what it's like to be me. Nobody I know goes to college. Nobody in my family ever did. My daddy's incarcerated, and my mama's dead. The police aren't nice to people in my neighborhood."

In fact, I didn't know what it was like to be a young black woman living in a neighborhood like hers. In my world, most police officers were friendly and helpful.

"Listen, I can give you a ride down there right now. We'll go together. When's your next class?"

"It's at one. And it's a three-hour lab. But I have study group now. I'm already late."

"Well, we at least have to call. Now."

"Okay. Okay, call them. It's that, where I come from, the police don't always believe you. But I'll, you know, talk to them if you think I should."

"I think you should." I scanned through my phone then pressed Natalia's number. When nobody answered, I left a message for the officer, pausing to get Tashandra's cell number and including it.

"I'm glad you told me, Tashandra. Officer Flores is a young woman. I think you'll like her, and you can trust her. You'll talk to her when she calls you, right?"

She nodded. "Do you want to see the picture?"

"Yes, please."

The young woman extracted a spiral-bound notebook adorned with doodles and drawings and flipped through to a page near the back. A drawing in fine-point black ink of a man's face stared up at me. He was Caucasian, with a dark Van Dyke type of beard and narrow glasses. He wore a neck scarf wrapped with European style. He looked professorial and a little familiar. Maybe he taught on campus or was a colleague of Ralph's from another college. The details in the drawing of his facial bones and expression brought the man to life in a way I couldn't really describe but that impressed me.

"This is excellent. You have quite a talent."

"Thanks. I like doing it. Seems like I've always been drawing."

"Some people do make money with their art. In fact, police departments sometimes hire artists."

"Really?"

"Yes. When you talk to Officer Flores, you could ask her."

She looked dubious.

I fixed my gaze on the student and decided I needed a little insurance. "Tell you what. Can I make a copy of the picture? You know, in case you lose the notebook or something?"

She agreed. She walked with me to my office and waited in silence while I used the combo printer-copier-scanner attached to my computer.

Tashandra took the notebook back and slung her pack onto one shoulder. "I'll see you, then."

"See you Friday. And thanks."

I stood in the doorway, arms folded. I watched the flow of undergrads in the hall, many ambling with phones glued to their ears, others rushing to class or work or an early-spring game of Frisbee on the quad.

Who was the man in Tashandra's drawing? I wished Elise was conscious. I wished I knew who killed Jamal. I wished I had my quiet academic life back, when the worst of my worries was a boyfriend who wanted more commitment than I did.

CHAPTER SEVEN

Later in the afternoon, I set down the box I carried. Taking a deep breath, I knocked at the door of the boat shop. I pushed the door open a few inches and called, "Hello? Mr. Pulcifer? Hello?" My curiosity about the boat shop was intense even before I met Phillip. I needed to try meet Samuel Pulcifer and understand his story. And having him take a look at my father's model ship might be the opening.

A gruff voice from the top of the stairs responded, "Yeah? Who is it? That you, Phillip?"

I ventured in a few more feet. "No, sir, I'm a neighbor. I wondered if you could help me with something."

"No neighbors of mine that friendly. Nobody likes me." The voice drew closer until a thin figure appeared on the landing. "What do you want, missy?"

"I have an old model ship. I'd like to get some information about it, if I could, please. Do you have time?"

"Time's all I have, young lady. Wait a minute, I'll come down." He disappeared then reemerged to walk down the stairs, holding the railing. He was tall, like Phillip, but much thinner, and seemed to need the support.

"Here, come into the office." He shuffled his tattered gray slippers along the floor.

I followed him to the back of the building, looking around. Time and neglect gnawed at a once-thriving business. I sneezed, passing rows of hand tools. Webs clogged corners and hung from stacks of yellowed plans. To my right stood the ship's skeleton I'd previously spied through the front window. It was even more impressive close up, with its tall curved ribs and beautifully rounded edges. The late-afternoon sunlight shining through dusty windows surrounded the structure with a haze.

Samuel turned into a doorway with a rusted metal Office sign above the opening. The office was clean and lit by two lamps. A set of framed pen-and-ink ship portraits hung on one wall. The wood on the wide oak desk in front of Samuel shone with years of elbows and hands rubbing its surface. A rotary telephone sat on one corner.

I must have looked surprised at the contrast between the cluttered musty shop and this tidy, dust-free office.

"What, looks a little different than the rest?" he asked. "Sit."

I carefully transferred the ship from the box to the desk then sat, per instructions.

"They all think I'm crazy," Samuel said. "I'm not, but does even one of them ever come by to see me? No!" He arranged and rearranged several piles of paper until they were perfectly aligned then straightened them some more. "Even Phillip stays away now…"

He barely knew I was there.

"Wants me to sell. Won't do it. It's my shop, dammit." He slammed his fist on the desk with sudden vehemence. "So, what do you want?"

I put a hand out to steady the model ship.

Samuel's eyes blazed then fell on the boat and softened. "Oh, that's a beaut. *The Star of Greenland*. 1918, if memory serves." He took a pair of glasses from his shirt pocket, put them on, and reached out and took the boat into his knobby hands, turning it and examining it. "Nice work. Oh my, very nice work." He finally looked up. "Who are you, again?"

"My name is Lauren Rousseau, Mr. Pulcifer. I live on Upper Summer Street. My father made this model. A long time ago."

"Does he have any more?"

"This is the only one I have. He passed away six years ago, I'm afraid. I think my mother might have a couple more, though."

"Whatever you do, don't sell them!" Samuel's eyes pierced mine and held them.

"No, sir."

His face filled with disgust, and he looked back at the ship. "You're like all the others. All you want is money."

"Oh, no, really. I have no plan to sell the ship. Please believe me. I just want some information about it."

Samuel stared at the model, his hands continuing to stroke it gently. "Well, you're all out there in la-la land, anyway," he said in a soft voice.

I thought it was more likely that he was. "Oh, I forgot!" I dug in my bag and brought out a box of mint Girl Scout cookies. "I thought you might like these. They were my father's favorites." I set them on the desk next to the ship.

"That's kind of you, young lady. Thank you. My Lexie used to sell these. My niece." A smile played around the edges of his eyes as he picked up the box. "She's all grown up now. Only relative who cares about me."

"You're welcome," I said. "Will you talk to me about the model?"

"Why don't you leave it for a few days? I'll take a look at it. Do some research."

"I don't know. I don't have much of my father's, and I cherish this. "

"I'll take care of it for you. Yes, this is a beauty." He ran a finger down the mast.

With the amount of affection he gave the boat, I wondered if I should kiss it goodbye. "All right. I'll stop back again in a few days."

"Yes, yes," Samuel answered, waving dismissal. "Goodbye."

On my way out, I glanced at the tools and pieces of machinery now rusted and unused. The air tasted sad and abandoned.

At the corner, I looked back. The setting sun backlit the building, casting an aurora. A breeze clanked the chains hanging from the old metal lifts. A tattered green plastic tarp flapped its ineffective protection against the next rain.

6∞9

When I walked into Elise's hospital room several hours later, I was startled to see Natalia sitting next to the bed. Elise was conscious and sitting up in bed. Natalia frowned at me.

"Hey, this is a nice change," I said to Elise in a sunny tone. "You're back, *gaijin*."

"Sort of. I feel like crap, though," she said in a low-volume voice. She looked thin in the hospital gown. She was still hooked up to a bag of fluid hanging from a pole, but the other tethers to machines were gone. "She's not helping, either." She cocked her head toward Natalia.

"What's going on, Natalia?" I asked. I slid between the other side of the bed and the window and squeezed my friend's hand.

"Hi, Lauren," Natalia said. "I need to follow up on my questions about Jamal's death and figured Ms. Chase here finally wasn't going anywhere for a while. We'd had a little trouble locating her recently." She put a pen to the small notebook she held.

I had, too. I hoped Elise wasn't in trouble, beyond the obvious. "How's it going?" I asked, holding Elise's eyes with my own.

"Not so great."

Natalia cleared her throat.

"Do you mind if I stay?" I asked. "Since I just got here?"

Natalia frowned again. "Stay. But be quiet. So, Ms. Chase, I was asking you where you were on Thursday, March 20, in the evening."

"And I was telling you I don't remember. It was a while ago."

"It was last week." Natalia's face was without expression.

"I guess I was at home, reading. Or maybe out with a friend." Elise studied the bed.

"With this friend?" Natalia gestured at me. "Or another one?"

"I don't remember!" Elise said with sudden force. "I don't remember." This time her voice was low and shaky.

"Do you know of anyone who might have reason to want Mr. Carter gone, either temporarily or permanently?"

"Not really."

"Had you had any disagreements with him? Any arguments?"

"Not really."

"Where did you get your heroin, Elise?" Natalia asked.

Elise looked up at the sudden change in topic. Her eyes widened. "I can't tell you! They..." she began then clamped her untethered hand over her mouth.

"Was it from Jamal Carter?" Natalia pressed.

Elise shook her head. Anguish filled her eyes. She reached with a quick movement toward the over-bed tray and grabbed a pink kidney-shaped basin. She retched into it as a nurse swept into the room.

"That's enough. Both of you, out!" the tall, athletic-looking man commanded.

I looked back as I left the room to see him gently wipe Elise's face with a cloth.

I parked in front of Elise's house the next afternoon, wondering if there was a link between her involvement with heroin and Jamal. Maybe somebody near her house would remember something odd going on. It was the last thing I felt like doing, knocking on strangers' doors, asking questions. But if it got me information, it would be worth it. And it was something proactive I could do.

Then I realized nobody was going to talk to some stranger. What was I thinking? I watched a gray cat wander along a hedge across the street, turning with a sudden move to check out a chipmunk taunting it from a rock wall. "Milo!" I said out loud. That cat wasn't Elise's. But I had no idea who was taking care of Milo. I could ask about him first then see what else people might reveal about Elise.

I started on the far side of her house and worked my way down. Knocking on doors up and down the street didn't seem to get me anywhere. Neighbors either didn't answer the door or didn't recall seeing anything odd going on.

As my last attempt, I rang the bell for the downstairs apartment of the two-family home next door to Elise's. The air was already warming after last night's chill.

I saw a battered wicker rocker and a low table with an ashtray full of cigarette butts on the covered porch.

Getting no response, I rang the upstairs bell. I heard movement then the door opened. I gave a little wave and smiled.

"What can I help you with, young lady?" A tiny black woman with a grizzled cap of hair pushed the door open.

"Good morning, ma'am. My name is Lauren Rousseau. I'm a friend of Elise, who lives next door."

"Oh, yes. I have seen you around here."

Really?

"Such a nice girl, don't you know." The woman gestured toward Elise's house.

"Yes, ma'am. She had an accident recently, and I was wondering if you were taking care of her kitty. Milo."

"No, I'm not. But what a shame. Is she going to be all right?"

"Yes, they think so. She's run into some trouble, and I'm trying to help her out."

"How can I help you?"

"I thought if you had seen any suspicious activity..." I sounded like a bad cop movie. She didn't see anything. Probably half blind.

"Hmm. I don't know if they were suspicious, but she did have several visitors the other day, dear."

"Really? Do you remember the time?"

The deep lines around the woman's eyes crinkled as she smiled and nodded. "Oh, yes. I keep close track of the goings on around here. You'd be surprised at what people do when they think nobody's looking. Can you keep a secret?"

I nodded. What kind of secret could a little old lady hold?

"Well, I have me a little telescope, more so a spyglass. When I see something interesting, why, I write it down in my notebook." She beamed at me. "Old ladies don't have much to do, and I don't get around like I used to. So this keeps life interesting." She gestured with a brown hand knobby with arthritis.

"Would you mind describing those visitors for me?"

"Not at all, my dear. Come upstairs and sit. I'll check my notebook for you."

I followed her up a staircase well past its prime. The wallpaper was faded and dented in places. The apartment was clean but worn. A stack of library books kept company on the coffee table with crocheted coasters in orange and red. I sat in the chair she gestured to and sank into the middle of the seat. She sat in a recliner next to the window overlooking the street and picked up a notebook from the round table at her right side that also held several sharp pencils, a crossword puzzle book, and a shiny spyglass, telescoped out.

"This is where I spend much of my day, you see. My daddy left me this glass. Oh, he was a big one for watching life go by." She picked up the notebook and turned to a page marked by a ribbon. "Let's see. A pileated woodpecker worked on that dead tree on Thursday. Gorgeous bird. The FedEx man brought a big box to number fifteen across the street. That young girl on the other side got a beautiful bouquet delivered."

I wondered exactly how many neighborhood events I was going to hear about.

"Here it is. Monday at 2:00 p.m. Two men. A white fellow and a colored man." She laughed. "What my nephew Thomas says I'm supposed to call a 'brother.' He wasn't too dark, though. Maybe one of those Brazilians we have so many of in town now. Anyway, Elise let them in, and after an hour she came out with them. They were waving their hands around, so I opened my window a little and heard them arguing."

"I am impressed, Mrs.—what is your name, please?"

"Virginia MacDonald. Just call me Virgie, dear—everybody does, and I'm no missus, you know. Never married. Don't be surprised by the Scottish name, neither. My great-granddaddy's owner was a MacDonald, so all the slaves got the same name."

Many aspects of this font of information surprised me. I thanked her and left.

I thought I knew Elise. I thought I knew her friends. Who were these men visiting Elise? Why were they arguing?

I left my evening class after lingering to answer questions from two of my keener students. Night students were a much more varied bunch than the usual daytime undergrads. Like Jamal—older, more diverse ethnically and racially, more interesting. They chose to be there, despite the stress of holding down a day job as well as attending class after work. And if any of them asked a question I couldn't answer, they seemed to respect me for saying, "I'm not sure. I'll look it up and post it on the class web site." Most of the undergrads I taught were straight out of high school and wanted their education delivered in black and white. They didn't yet get it that learning goes on for a lifetime and that even their teacher might not know the reply to a challenging or insightful question. Not that I got too many of those from the typical student. I missed Jamal.

I headed to my office through the empty halls. I stopped when I heard voices to my right coming from behind a classroom door. I strained to hear. One was Uncle

George. Huh? I didn't think Security had an office here in Lockhart Hall. What was he up to?

George burst into the hall, scowling and shaking his head, muttering to himself. He slammed the door then saw me. "What are you doing?" he growled.

"Nice to see you, too, George. I teach here, remember?"

"Late, isn't it?"

"Night class? Revenue producer for the college? Edict from the Dean mandating us all to sign up to teach evenings on top of days?" I couldn't believe a higher-up in Campus Security didn't know about the Night School project. Especially someone in charge of the nighttime. I didn't really care for the program, myself. None of the faculty had any choice in the matter, and, despite the interesting students, it was still an extra load.

"Yeah, yeah. Just brings in more riff-raff, that's what I think. More of those damn, you know..." he began then caught himself and stomped away. He paused and turned. "Don't be hanging around here. Might not be safe. You know."

I stared at his back as he disappeared around a corner. By 'riff-raff,' did he mean murderers...or people of color? The door he had come through shut with a tiny click. I thought I saw a shadow behind the frosted glass. I shivered. I pressed my back to the wall and clutched my teaching materials to my chest then edged down the hall, keeping my eyes on the door. I didn't want to turn my back on it. As I rounded the corner, George's words echoed in my head. I quickened my steps to my office then hurried to the parking lot. I locked the truck door and sat for a moment, trying to put it all together. That click reminded me of something, but what was it? A thought danced around the edges of my memory, but I couldn't catch it.

I drove toward Ashford, ruing my slow reaction to George's comment about riff raff. I regretted letting him spout his bigotry yet another time. Easter had been bad enough.

I was only five minutes from home when I smelled smoke in the air. I realized the sky was lighter than at the college. Sirens grew louder. I crested the hill overlooking the river and gasped. A tower of smoke filled the sky, with a wide wall of flames at its base.

The boat shop! I raced toward the river and pulled over a block before the cluster of fire trucks and police cars. An ambulance sat at the ready.

The sight up close was terrifying. Primeval. The entire building was lit from within. The borders and mullions of windows upstairs and down were outlined by the reddish-yellow flames behind them, like grotesque Halloween pumpkins. Fire danced along the outside walls near the roof. The metal structure at the end of the building stood unused, an anachronism ready to lower boats into the water.

Samuel Pulcifer. Did he get out in time?

Firefighters wrestled with hoses streaming water onto the flames, which continued unabated. Quiet onlookers lined the sides of the street and the antique bridge spanning the river, some extending cameras to capture the moment, others talking in low voices, pointing and shaking their heads.

I walked as close as I could to the yellow police tape. I asked an older gentleman, "Excuse me. Do you know if the man who lived there got out? Mr. Pulcifer?"

The man turned and stared at me. "How do you know Samuel?"

"I talked with him a couple of days ago."

"Really?" His tone indicated disbelief. "I didn't think he talked with anyone, don't you know. Pity. We went to school together, but the last few years..."

Just then, in slow motion, the burning structure listed toward the river and gracefully, horribly collapsed. To the crackling and roar of the conflagration was added the hissing of embers falling into cold water. A low murmur from the onlookers turned to cries and a collective gasp. A couple of young teenagers cheered then were hushed by adults near them. The smoke billowing up turned dark and ominous.

Chapter Eight

I closed my eyes and stood with my hands at my sides. In the face of the intense flames, I tried to pray for Samuel Pulcifer, holding him in the Light, as Friends did, for safe passage and healing. The heat and commotion drew me back, though, and I couldn't stay in that moment of inward silence. The metal beams of the lifts now sizzled in the river.

Two small boats moored nearby had barely escaped the collapse. What had been a productive business in the town several decades earlier had become a pile of burning timber. That beautiful skeletal ship, the antique tools, Daddy's boat—all gone. Perhaps Samuel Pulcifer gone with it.

Now that the height of the boat shop was gone, I saw that the fire had spread to a smaller structure on the far side. The building housed a gourmet deli and market, one of the few thriving businesses in the area. The firefighters seemed to be devoting most of their energy and water on saving it. With this one they had a chance.

I turned to go and spotted a tiny silver car parked near the yellow tape. I peered back through the smoke and darkness into the group of emergency vehicles. Phillip Pulcifer gestured. He seemed to be arguing with a police officer.

As I watched, a man who looked like he might be the fire chief joined the dyad. At Phillip's apparent pleading, the chief shrugged then shook his head, lifting his hands. It was like watching a silent movie, overlaid with a soundtrack of flames and pops. Phillip turned and stormed toward his car, lifting his foot to stomp down the plastic tape barrier.

"Mr. Pulcifer? Phillip!" I waved at him.

He looked up. His hand on the car, he waited for me. "It came to this," he said as I approached. "It came to this." The set of his mouth was grim, his eyes steely.

"What do you mean? Is your brother safe?"

"Samuel." Phillip stared at the fire. "Poor crazy Sammy."

"Did they know if he got out all right? Phillip?"

"Fire chief says he doesn't know. Samuel's car was gone. They don't know if he was in the building or not, and it went up so fast they didn't get a chance to search inside. They won't let me near it. Police are going to send out an alert about the car. I guess it'll take a while to know."

"Did anybody else drive his car? I mean, if the car is gone, he's probably in it, right?"

"You ask a lot of questions, missy." Phillip folded his long legs into his tiny vehicle.

Missy. That's what Samuel Pulcifer called me, too. I watched Phillip drive away. I did have a lot of questions, and most of them didn't have answers. Like when was the last time Phillip spoke to Samuel? Phillip seemed fond of his brother but also wanted him off the property, ostensibly for Samuel's own good. It had to be a valuable property for development, right on the river as it was. And I had to figure out how to get some answers, that was certain. I felt drawn to Samuel in a way I couldn't explain.

Heading slowly to my truck, I passed a large van with WBZ-TV Mobile News written on the side and a satellite dish perched on top. Through the open side doors, I saw a young man seated at a bank of displays. The center monitor looked a lot like Zac's system.

"Are you editing the fire video live?" I asked, leaning in.

The man nodded. "Avid NewsCutter."

"That's like Media Composer, right? My mother wrote the manual."

"That's great," the man said, not taking his eyes from the screen or his hands from the keyboard, in a tone that actually said, I don't really care, lady. On screen, the burning boat shop collapsed again and again in a hellish loop. It reminded me of the awful days after September 11, when the news media couldn't stop replaying the falling towers. Zac had said his senile grandfather had gotten very agitated, thinking every replay was a new attack.

As I left, a slender woman in a black dress, red jacket, and heels climbed out of a car. A reporter on the late news, she carried a notepad and, like a magnet, instantly attracted a cluster of officials. She was followed by a shorter woman in jeans who held a heavy camera on her shoulder. Driving the short distance home, I was agitated, too. I knew it was a single fire, but that was enough.

I soon saw the reporter again, on the news at eleven, interviewing the fire chief, who said the boat shop went up fast because it was an open structure made of old, dry wood. The cause was under investigation. They did not know if the resident got out or not. The only new thing I learned was that the popping sound was likely from engine oil, varnishes, and other flammable substances in the building.

I opened my kitchen window and smelled the smoke on the cold air.

Maybe Samuel had been out driving to the market and the fire had been caused by bad wiring, leaving him safe somewhere. Maybe he'd been taken away by someone who'd started the fire. Maybe he hadn't been able to escape the flames and smoke. Or hadn't wanted to.

⟊⟋

I stood with Ralph in the parking lot of the Boys and Girls Club in Millsbury after Friday classes. The style was early institutional grim, but painted balloons and stylized children's shapes in shades of blue and orange added a note of cheer. The sun was finally out, teasing us with a taste of spring, and the light made the building look more welcoming.

"Thanks for coming with me, Ralph." I leaned against the bed of the truck.

"No problem, Professor. I needed to get out of my office, anyway."

"Jamal was really devoted to working with the kids here. You should have heard him talk about his work. His face lit up, and he was so, I don't know, animated."

Three boys emerged from the building with a basketball and whoops of boy-noise then ran around the back of the building. Thwacks of bouncing followed.

"So I want to find the boys we saw Jamal with. I want to give them something of his. Maybe they'll tell me something."

"What were their names?" Ralph asked. "Ricky? And?"

"Nicky, I think. And Tyrone was Jamal's Little Brother. Had been for a couple of years, I think."

"Okay, Rousseau. What are we waiting for?"

"Let's do it."

The scene inside was busy and noisy. Two table-tennis games were in progress along one wall of the cavernous space, with kids cheering on their friends. Computers at the other end of the building were mostly operated by two children each. A pair of girls laughed about something, heads close, beaded braids touching. A brightly colored rug in primary colors, beanbag chairs, and a full bookshelf took up one corner of the room. Kids practiced yoga on mats in the middle of the floor, and a group of young-teen artists worked on a wall mural featuring the Monster School.

After passing through the main doorway, we waited at a reception counter until a woman emerged from a windowed office area.

"Can I help you?"

I introduced myself as one of Jamal Carter's professors. "I'm looking for Tyrone and Nicky. Tyrone was Jamal's Little Brother. I'm afraid I don't know the boys' last names. This is my colleague, Dr. Ralph Fourakis."

"Oh, Jamal. That's a terrible loss. Awful." The woman shook her head. "We miss him around here. He was one of our most dedicated volunteers. Loved the little guys."

"I have something of Jamal's I'd like to give Tyrone. And Nicky, his friend, too."

"Oh? Well, I'll have to give it to them for you. You know, nobody who hasn't been CORI'd can spend time with the kids."

My heart sank. I wanted that contact with Tyrone, as if it would bring Jamal back, even for a moment.

"What's CORI?" Ralph asked.

"Criminal Offender Record Information. It's a check we do on adults who work with children. Make sure they don't have a background that would put our kids at risk. You know."

At the counter, she bent over a book filled with scrawled childish signatures. "Yes, they're here." She turned to survey the room. "Look, there they are at one of the computers. Now, that was Jamal's influence. He always told Tyrone and Nicky they had to do their homework first before they played, and they actually listened." She laughed quietly. "Even on Fridays. What do you have for them, by the way?"

"Jamal had recorded them talking for his research project. I made copies on a CD for each of them. Thought they might like to have a memento of their time with him."

The woman nodded. "I'm Brenda Watson, by the way. Nice to meet you." As she held out her hand for the CDs, Tyrone raced up, an arm's length ahead of Nicky, and grinned, breathless. Brenda greeted them with a smile. "Well, look who's here."

"Hi, boys," I said. "Do you remember me?"

They both nodded without speaking, remembering Jamal, I imagined.

I introduced myself, reminding them I was Jamal's teacher.

"Yeah, and he teaches languages, right?" Tyrone said, pointing his chin at Ralph.

"Exactly. How are you holding up without your buddy, Tyrone?"

The boy glanced away then shrugged. "It's bad. He used to help me with stuff. And we played a lot." He was somber faced. "I heard somebody killed him."

"I'm afraid so. The police are working on it, but they haven't found anyone yet."

"My uncle's in the force," Nicky piped up. "Maybe he can catch him."

"I hope so," I said. "What's his name?"

"Uncle Charlie."

I smiled. "Is he your mom's brother or your dad's brother?"

"My dad's. Oh, yeah..." Nicky nodded with his whole body. "His name's Officer Charles Almeida."

"Thanks, I'll look him up," I said. "Listen, guys. Remember when Jamal used to talk with you and he recorded it?"

Both kids nodded.

"Well, I made a copy of those meetings for each of you. I thought you might like it. Something to remember him by." I pulled two CDs in paper sleeves out of my bag.

Tyrone reached out with a stubby hand. He whispered, "Wicked," and held the CD in both hands, staring at Jamal's printed image.

"Can we listen now?" Nicky asked, bouncing on his toes.

Brenda nodded. "I'll get you some headphones."

"Thank you very much, Mrs. Rousseau," Tyrone said in a practiced, polite voice. He continued to gaze at his benefactor's picture as if he held Jamal's soul in his hands.

"Yeah, thanks," Nicky chimed in.

We said goodbye and made our way toward the door. I turned and saw the boys back at the computer. Each had one headphone pressed to his ear. They were talking intently.

"Guess you picked that one right, Rousseau," Ralph said then slowed at a wall of framed pictures—mostly of white men in suits. Two were of men with skin tones more in keeping with those of the majority of the children around us, and one was of a white woman in a tailored jacket. "Well, well, look who's on the Club board."

I was face to face with the visage of Alexa Kensington. Questions roiled my brain. I never expected this. I glanced up at Ralph. He was watching me.

"What?"

"What what? You're the one who's been lost in space the last five minutes. I didn't even know Jamal, remember?" Ralph's smile was at once gentle and serious.

"I might have found what I was looking for. How much do you think the board members interact with the children?"

"Appears the boys were happy with your gift," a voice behind us said.

I turned. "Oh, Ms. Watson. Tyrone seems sad. He must really miss Jamal."

"Those two were close, all right. It was good for him to have a brother as a Brother, if you know what I mean." Brenda's eyes bore into mine. "Adopted as he is. You know."

I cocked my head. "I don't, actually."

Brenda looked around the room then back at us. "I like that kid, and it's a shame. Tyrone's parents are white—they had been his foster family—but they don't seem to take much notice of him, and they're always late paying the after-school program fee, low as it is. Well, I've said too much. He'll be lucky to find another Big Brother as attentive as Jamal. God rest his soul." She turned to go.

"Wait, Ms. Watson? Brenda?" I reached out a hand for her arm. "Alexa Kensington." I pointed at the picture on the wall. "What is her involvement here?"

Brenda trained her eyes on the ping-pong game. Her face lost its animated expression as she said in a level tone, "Dr. Kensington is on the Board of Directors."

"Does she ever spend time with the children?"

"Excuse me, Ms. Rousseau. I need to get back to my work. Thank you for bringing the CDs to the children. I'll walk you to the door." Brenda extended her arm as if to sweep us out through the exit. She avoided my eyes.

In the parking lot, I looked at Ralph. "I would so like to know what that was about. She really didn't want to talk about Alexa."

"Well, maybe she's not supposed to. Or maybe she doesn't get along with our esteemed Chair—God knows we don't, either—and doesn't want to risk her job. Or maybe she knows something and doesn't want to tell outsiders. Like us."

I nodded. Lots of maybes. I opened the door of the truck. "So, how about continuing this discussion over a beer?"

"Hey, twist my arm!" Ralph smiled and hoisted himself into the passenger seat. "Ow!"

"What's the matter?"

"Arm hurts. From the twisting, you know."

As we drove away, a silver Mercedes passed us going the other way. I pulled to the side of the road, watching the rearview mirror. "That was Dr. Kensington herself. She turned into the parking lot. Should we go back?"

"Listen, Rousseau. You have no further business there. She's probably going for a board meeting or something."

"At four in the afternoon?"

"Whatever. She's our boss, remember. Leave it alone. For now, anyway."

Despite the warm afternoon, a cold unease spread through me. Something wasn't right.

CHAPTER NINE

I spent the first Saturday of spring break catching up on laundry and cleaning my condo. I read half of a mystery novel I usually never had time for, squeezed in a visit to Elise during which I refrained from interrogating her, and spent the night with Zac. All uneventful. I made an effort not to think too much about Jamal.

It had worked for a while.

I sat quietly on a long wooden pew Sunday morning. Outside the tall, antique windows of the Millsbury Friends Meetinghouse, branches covered with leaf buds ready to pop danced and bowed in a breeze. I watched the movement then closed my eyes again. I came to Meeting hoping to absorb some of the collective wisdom of a group gathered in silent prayer. If an attender felt moved, he or she rose and shared a message, but this congregation usually preferred the stillness of silence.

Despite the quiet, my thoughts pulled away from a quiet center. I saw Jamal and Alexa in conflict. Jamal's face in death. Elise's odd behavior. The flames consuming the boat shop.

I opened my eyes again to scan the people in the room. I saw no one who could help me answer all my questions. Who killed Jamal? What did Alexa have to do with the children? Where was Samuel? I didn't know why I thought anybody here would be able to. I needed to let go of those thoughts, or I'd never find any peace of mind. That was why I was here, after all.

I glanced at Cynthia, an angular, white-haired woman across the room. She was one of the elders of the Meeting and often seemed to have a few words that cut with wisdom straight to the heart of conflict or cares. I took a deep breath, settled a few kinks out of my shoulders, and closed my eyes again. Maybe I'd talk to Cynthia in private later.

Harold Swenson stood and began to speak. He meant well but always droned on too long. My centering was disrupted again. I once almost left the room when Harold began to speak about one of his experiences and its meaning. He rambled on about it for fifteen minutes, allowing no one the quiet space to absorb his words or their message. He obviously needed to talk, but I needed to find a way to clarity. I shook my head, resigned to sit and listen.

6∞9

After Meeting, I stopped into Shaws and picked up a couple of packs of sushi on my way to the hospital. Elise had to be tired of institutional food. We could eat lunch together.

I stared at her room. Not only was it empty, the bed didn't even have sheets on it. The flowers I brought her before were gone.

"She's been transferred," a low voice behind me said.

I turned and stared at the same nurse I'd seen the first time I'd visited Elise. "What? When?"

"This morning." He folded his arms.

"Where?" My voice rose. "I saw her yesterday. She didn't say anything about being transferred."

"A spot opened up in a rehab facility."

"Which one? Where is she?"

"I'm sorry. I can't tell you. Privacy issues. We can only communicate with family."

"But I'm her best friend!" I stared at him. "She doesn't even have any family." Not really, anyway.

"Sorry, ma'am." He gestured toward the exit. "I'm sure she'll call you. If you're such good friends."

I stood in the fog on a sidewalk in Lawrence the next morning.

I hadn't heard any news about the police finding Jamal's killer. Elise had not called me, and I hadn't a clue where she'd gone.

I felt restive, unsettled, and the whole week of spring break stretched out in front of me. I decided to use part of it to learn more about Jamal's life outside of school.

The door in front of me sported a logo with chess pieces and the name Knights and Kings. Two preteen boys approached, so I held the heavy door open and followed them. Several dozen children sat at tables in a big room, also on spring break, apparently. Timers ticked as the players bent their heads over green and white vinyl chess mats. A girl in dreadlocks and a pink shirt moved a rook then slapped the top of the timer. A diminutive red-haired boy scratched his head, pushed up his glasses, and smiled triumphantly, taking a black queen with his own white one. A man moved a magnetic chess piece on a grid of a chessboard hanging on the wall, showing two children a move.

"May I help you?" A deep voice spoke behind me.

I turned toward a man whose arms were folded across his chest. "What a wonderful place," I said.

"Yes, it is." The tall man, whose skin and bulging eyes evoked Jamal's, held out his hand. "I'm Thomas MacDonald. What brings you to Knights and Kings?"

I shook his hand and introduced myself. I looked around the room. "I'm not sure, really. I teach at Agawam College and..." I examined the man's face. "Are you related to Jamal?"

His look hardened. "Jamal was my brother." He stressed the name in a bitter tone, the corners of his mouth pulling down. "Half brother, actually. Why? How did you know him?"

"I was his professor. I'm the one who found him, when he was killed. I'm trying to—"

"Ma'am, nobody here knows anything about his death. The police have already talked to us. I'd advise you to get information from them." When the two children sitting closest to us looked up in surprise at Thomas' raised voice, he lowered it, then said, "His name isn't Jamal, either. It's William. William's the name our momma gave him. I don't know why he had to go changing it just because he decided to become Muslim."

"I'm so sorry. The police don't seem to be getting anywhere. Jamal... William... was my best student, really. I wanted to see if there was something the police were missing."

Thomas' gaze burned with the same interest as Jamal's but with far fiercer intensity. He cleared his throat, surveyed the room, then motioned me into a small office in the corner, shutting the door after us. Tournament trophies lined shelves, and one wall displayed a framed photograph of Thomas with Senator John Kerry, both beaming at a team of young chess players, all in white shirts or blouses and wearing medals around their necks.

"Sit down."

I sat on the edge of a chair and looked up at Thomas, who was looking anywhere but at me. I didn't know if he was going to help me or not, but I had to try.

"He talked about this place," I said. "He told me he started it. He spoke with love."

"I am not sure if William knew what love was." Thomas shook his head. "He pretty much cut off our family. Never brought any of his girlfriends home. Left Momma alone. And now she's gone. Sure, he started this place, but he left it behind, too." He straddled a chair, facing me. "Look, Will was kind of troubled. We were running the place together, and we argued. He decided he'd rather go his own way than stay here and work it out. That's all."

"What kind of troubled?"

Thomas didn't speak.

"Please? See, a friend of mine was also friends with Jamal. She almost died from a heroin overdose last week."

Thomas turned his head with a quick movement and looked at me with narrowed eyes. "Oh?"

"She and Jamal had argued about something, too. He told me he had been clean for years, so I'm sure she wasn't getting it from him, but—"

"Listen, Professor. My brother was brilliant. He could be sweet. He loved to dance—did you know that about him? And he could play him some chess. But he had problems, too. He wanted money from me. Wanted his *investment* back. As if we have any extra cash around here!"

"Do you know why he needed money?"

Thomas shook his head in disgust. "And then when—"

Someone knocked twice then the door opened a crack. "Thomas, we need you out here. Session's over, and parents want to speak with you," a man's voice said.

Thomas rose. "I'll be right there," he said in the direction of the door. To me, he said, "I told you too much as it is. Good luck. Don't come back, unless you want to give us money or tutor some kids. We could use both." He motioned to the doorway.

"Thanks for your time, Thomas. I appreciate it." I put out my hand to shake his.

He kept his arm extended toward the exit. "Goodbye."

Damn. Damn, damn, damn. I walked along the sidewalk, staring at the heaved and bumpy pavement without seeing it. Thomas almost told me something. But what?

I slammed the door of my truck. Jamal was a lot more complex than I realized. And it seemed I wasn't very good at investigations. I wanted to clear the air of my life: find out what happened to Jamal, figure out what had been going on with him and Alexa, sort out Elise's life for her. "Yeah, Lauren. As if," I told my reflection in the rearview mirror. I wondered if I was still trying to solve my father's death. In my opinion, nobody really had. But that kind of amateur shrinkship didn't usually get anybody too far.

A loud noise from my stomach made me realize how hungry I was. I scrabbled first in my bag then in the glove compartment for a granola bar, a pack of peanuts, any shred of snack stashed for emergency purposes. Nothing. I unearthed a takeout container from a forgotten lunch box under my seat but, upon examination, decided I wasn't hungry enough to eat petrified broccoli in black bean sauce. As I drank from my Ashford Recycles water bottle, I realized I was reluctant to start the drive home. But where else could I go?

On the sidewalk, a man strode past the truck. I watched him in the rearview mirror. What was familiar about that guy? From the back, he looked slim, neatly dressed, with gray streaking a dark head of hair.

The man turned into the doorway of a small restaurant a couple of doors down. The sign overhead read "Tigedigena" on a stylized map of Mali.

Here was lunch, after all.

As my eyes adjusted to the dim light, artifacts similar to those from my Peace Corps days emerged. A two-foot-tall wooden mortar with a pestle bigger than a baseball bat. Three *djembes* in a corner, ready to be drummed on, next to the wooden xylophone called a *balafon* and a *kora*, the twelve-string half guitar, half harp that gave Malian music its unique sound. A wreath of dried habanero peppers, or *foronto*, hung on the wall. A Malian flag proudly stretched flat next to it. Plus an assortment of dark wooden booths and tables and a short bar at the end of the room. Scents of fish grilling, onions frying, and the aroma of extraordinarily hot peppers flooded me with memories.

A woman behind the bar, her robust figure draped in brilliant emerald batik, waved at the room. "Sit anywhere you want." Her accent was as familiar as the decorations in the restaurant: the English learned as a third or fourth language, after the native Bambara or Fulfulde was overlaid with school French.

The man I followed in was seated at the end of the bar, which was otherwise unoccupied. I took the stool at the other end. Examining the menu gave me a chance to glance at his face. Then I forced my eyes back on the laminated card. I didn't see the descriptions of ground-nut stew or leaf sauce with fish, though. In my head, I saw the picture from Tashandra's notebook. This was the same man. And in the neighborhood of the chess club.

"Been in here before?" His voice was soft, but it startled me.

I looked up. "No," I answered, "but I read about it somewhere. I lived in Mali for a couple of years."

"That's very cool. I am hoping to get there myself. I drum with some guys here, so I get to know the culture. And the food, of course."

I couldn't quite place his faint accent but thought it might be French. I studied the menu, still without seeing it. I wondered how he knew Jamal.

And what they had been arguing about.

"All set?" the proprietress asked.

I smiled at the Malian's use of the all-purpose expression typical of the greater Boston area. "I'd like Poulet Yassa, please. And do you have Castel?" Food from a hot climate demanded cold beer, even if it was the first day of a chilly April in Massachusetts, and even if it was a lighter lager than the ales I preferred.

"Of course we do, ma'am. And you, Pascal?" she asked the man.

Now I knew half of his name.

He ordered the leaf sauce with fish, plus a Coke.

"Do you live around here?" I asked him.

"At present I do, yes. And you?"

"I'm over near the coast. I had an, uh, appointment nearby, so I thought I'd see how the food was here. Old times' sake. You know."

A man in a mud-cloth shirt walked in and hailed Pascal. "Yo, Martin."

And the rest of his name. I pulled a paperback mystery out of my bag and pretended to read as they talked in low voices. Pascal Martin. Martin Pascal? I wished the man would leave so I could talk to Pascal a bit more. I wanted to ask him how he knew Jamal. What they had fought about. A tic vibrated in my lip, and my knee jittered. It was possible he was Jamal's killer. But I had to find out, and I was sure I was safe in here.

A plate laden with steaming chicken, onions, and rice arrived in front of me. I inhaled the scent of lemon and oil and thanked the proprietress. "*Iniché*!"

"*Ntse! I ka kene wa*?" The woman laughed heartily, grabbed my hand, introduced herself as Fatoumata Kone, and started the round of ritual Bambara greetings. They bounced back and forth between us; we inquired about how the other passed the night, how the other's parents were, and so on, ending with salutations of "*Herebe*" (peace among us) and "*Here doron*" (peace only).

I blushed as I saw the two men staring at me. "It's a Bambara thing. I lived there." I loaded my fork with a piece of chicken, pausing with eyes closed for a moment of silence before I ate. I long ago stopped worrying what people might think of me when I prayed before eating.

Pascal's friend sat between us with his back toward me. He continued the conversation as Pascal ate, which seemed to be mostly about the drumming circle and the vagaries of its various members. I tasted my way through half my plate, finished the beer, and asked for a takeout container. The men talked, Pascal gesturing with the knife in his right hand, his left busy with his fork. Pascal occasionally glanced over at me but made no attempt to bring me into the dialogue.

I really wanted to find out something, anything, about Pascal. "Excuse me." I leaned toward them. "I heard you talking about drumming. What nights do you play? Can anybody come and listen?"

The other man turned and frowned at me. "Sure." He turned back to Pascal, as if closing a virtual door. Tight.

So much for that. I paid the tab, thanked Fatoumata, donned my jacket, and gave a little wave as I walked toward the door. Pascal nodded then returned his gaze to his friend.

I had found out nothing about him except his name and his penchant for African drums.

I pulled into traffic and glanced in the mirror. Pascal stood at the curb, staring after me.

CHAPTER TEN

On the drive home, I pulled over once my route led me off the highway and onto country roads. I turned on my smartphone. Google came up with several hits for a Pascal Martin. I clicked one and stared at the screen. I pressed the numbers for Officer Flores and got her voicemail.

"Natalia, I have some information you might be interested in." I didn't want to go into much detail in a phone message. "About the drawing my student did." I pulled back onto the road. The cold fog was as thick as a dirge, and the sky was dim, despite it being early afternoon. I drove at a slow, careful speed, thinking about Pascal Martin.

At my condo, I called out, "Wulu, run?" He didn't appear. He was always up for going out under any pretense. "Wu? Where are you?"

It was too quiet in here. Where was His Dogness? Wulu napped, sure, but never this deeply. I sat very still, listening. A cardinal chirped nearby, loudly, but otherwise the apartment was quiet. Wait. Why was it so cold in here?

On silent feet, I followed the source of the cold air into my office. I cursed. The room was trashed, and the window was wide open at the bottom. File drawers gaped. Papers covered the floor. The back cover of the desktop computer was off, and the tooled leather box where I kept my CDs was on its side and empty. The contents of my briefcase were dumped on the chair.

And the batik-covered cushions on the window seat had been sliced open, the stuffing ripped out and scattered like forlorn clouds come to earth.

"Wu!" I shouted, opening the closet. I raced from door to door in the small condo, even opening the clothes dryer, but Wulu was not there. When I returned to the office, the cardinal called again from the tree outside the window. Who would have done this? A fury made my cheeks blaze with heat.

I dialed 911 and reported the break-in. I tried to reach the Animal Control officer but had to leave a message. Zac didn't pick up his phone, either, so I left a message. I usually didn't. I'd have liked his company, though, and hoped he'd call back.

Who would break in and take my dog? Destroy my things? I cast about for ideas as I paced the living room, waiting for the police. What could this person want from me? I was just a teacher. I checked the bedroom, but it was intact. Even my grandmother's gold bracelet was in the jewelry box. I slipped the bracelet onto my wrist and turned it as I compared the tidy bedroom with the hurricane-aftermath office.

Somebody thought I had a file or papers they wanted. But what? I resumed pacing but stopped short in the hall at the sight of Wulu's purple leash hanging from its hook and let out a shuddering sob.

I dashed to the phone when it rang.

The Animal Control officer hadn't spotted Wulu anywhere but said she'd keep her eye out.

I slumped onto the floor, sinking my head into my hands. The last time I sat here, Wulu was in my lap. Then I sat erect, telling myself to hold onto the rage I'd felt a minute ago. I was not going to become a victim.

After the police came and went—a young officer who checked the place, secured the window, and filled out a report form—I sat at my table and pressed Jackie's number.

She was suitably outraged by what happened. "I'm worried about you, Laur. You should come over here for the night."

"Thanks, Jackie, but I'm going to stay here. I'm spooked, but I'm okay." Well, maybe I was okay. "Maybe Wulu will come back on his own. I have to be here."

"Well, don't go anywhere. What if he's lurking around the corner?"

"Jack! I'm an adult." A rush of irritation rose up whenever somebody told me what to do. I said goodbye and hung up.

I wondered if she could be right. This burglar, this dognapper, might still be around. It didn't matter. I had to look for my dog. I changed my clothes, stuck my phone in my pocket, and went for a run after all. Instead of heading out Toil-in-Vain Road, though, I jogged with determination through all the nearby streets, calling Wulu's name.

I slowed to a walk. I hoped Wulu leapt out the window when the intruder opened it. The alternative, that the ransacker stole Wulu, was too painful to consider. Although, after an hour, it looked like I might have to.

Walking the final block home, my heart a lump of lead, a wild thought arose.

Had somebody been looking for Jamal's thesis? He had been murdered, after all.

That seemed too crazy, though. Why come to my condo when the more likely place would be my campus office? And why take Wulu? None of it made sense. I resolved to find a picture of Wulu and spend the rest of the night plastering the neighborhood with posters.

Somebody had to have seen him.

⟡

By Tuesday, I knew I needed help, so I called Ralph. He was a good friend and an uncomplicated one. And he was on vacation, too. I set two cups of coffee on my coffee table, next to a plate of bakery muffins, and opened the door.

"*Herete*," I greeted Ralph. That was close to the extent of the Greek I knew.

"*Kalimera*." He leaned down to give me a kiss on the cheek. "You look terrible."

"Good morning to you, too. Come on in. Sit. Eat."

He obeyed. "Looks like you didn't sleep very well."

"I got through the night... but barely. I heard every small noise as either a threat or as Wulu returning on his own." I sat on a cushion on the floor. I looked up at Ralph, who already had his mouth full. It was the second day of vacation, and I knew almost nothing about Jamal or his killer. Nor had I done any of my actual work. And now I didn't even have Wulu.

"Thanks for coming by, Fourakis." `

He said he didn't mind then asked where Zac was. "He's your boyfriend, isn't he? Shouldn't he be here protecting you?"

I stared at my empty lap, which should be holding a little black dog. "That's complicated, Ralph. Anyway, he was busy last night." I was surprised he even asked. Ralph usually liked to keep emotional business at a distance. He was my uncomplicated academic friend, and I wanted to keep it that way.

In fact, Zac had called back, but by then I had wanted to be alone.

"My life is crazy. I'm furious about Wulu. I keep thinking about Jamal's death. Elise is in rehab somewhere but hasn't called me. I have to grade midterms and prepare classes for next week. Plus work on my paper for the conference in May. But it's hard." My lap was forlorn without Wulu. I pounded the cushion beside me. Whoever took him was going to pay. "I thought maybe we could talk about who could possibly have wanted Jamal out of the picture. Permanently."

"Offer me food, I'll do anything, Rousseau." Ralph's weathered jeans, with a hole in one knee, along with his faded green college sweatshirt, made it clear he had been doing anything but academic work. "It's only day two of spring break, Professor. I haven't exactly immersed myself in academia this week, either, between the garden and my home-brew project. Hey, it's called a break for a reason, right?"

It didn't feel like much of a break to me. "What do you think? How about Alexa? Do you think she's capable of killing somebody?"

Ralph raised his considerable eyebrows. He licked the corners of his mouth and brushed the crumbs off his stomach. "I think probably about anybody is. But then, I teach mythology. Zeus, Hera, Poseidon—they were all killers. Alexa? I don't know.

Did you ever find out anything else from the Boys and Girls Club? I mean, what's her history there? She is on the board, after all."

I shook my head. "Hard to get anybody to talk. I called again, but Brenda Watson is pretty much covering her behind. Doesn't want to reveal much. I'm not sure how to go about getting inside information."

"Ask the policewoman—I mean, officer—you met. You know, the one dating your sister. What's her name?"

"Natalia. Natalia Flores. Yeah, I guess I didn't tell her about our visit to the Boys and Girls Club. That's a good idea, Ralph. Got any others up your sleeve?"

"Got any more muffins?"

I looked at the empty plate. "Wait a minute."

"What?"

"I'm thinking about who could have trashed my office. Elise is at rehab. Plus, she wouldn't have taken Wulu. George has been acting true to form. But he's Security. He has keys to my office—wouldn't he have looked there? You don't think Alexa would come here and do something like that, do you?" I almost told Ralph my suspicions about Jamal's thesis being the target of the attempted burglary but decided to keep it to myself for a little longer. It would sound too crazy.

"Well, that would be pretty strange. I must admit, Alexa is a strange lady."

"It was probably some random bad guy." I might never find out. "Like that guy Pascal."

Ralph asked who Pascal was as he stretched out his legs.

"He's the one Tashandra, my student, saw arguing with Jamal." I explained I'd seen him in Lawrence Monday and followed him into the Malian restaurant. I also told him I'd thought Pascal was ignoring me, but that he stood outside watching me when I drove away.

"So? It's a free world, right?"

"Ralph, I searched for his name on the Internet as I drove home."

"Uh, you know using your phone to do that kind of thing makes you drive like an eighty-five-year old, right?"

"Yeah, yeah. I stopped the car, looked him up then drove on. Satisfied?"

Ralph nodded, smiling.

"Anyway, he's—" The doorbell rang. I stared at Ralph. "I'm not expecting anybody."

"Do you want me to get the door?"

"No, but I'm glad you're here."

I rose and checked the peephole then opened the door. "Natalia... Wulu!" Wulu leapt from Natalia's arms to mine. I hugged the dog tight then laughed as he licked my cheek. A rush of cold air surrounded us.

"Where was he?" Relief filled me like a pool of sunlight, and I couldn't stop smiling at Natalia. "Come in. Please."

Natalia, in uniform, stepped into the condo. "We were doing a patrol out on Toil-in-Vain. After the incident with your friend, we thought we'd check out the house, make sure there were no more intruders. I heard a noise coming from the shed, and look who we found."

Holding the dog, I said, "But that's a couple miles from here! He wouldn't have gone so far by himself."

"The door was jammed shut with a rock. Somebody put him in there. No food or water, either."

Wulu gave a short bark and looked up. I rubbed his head and set him down.

"Poor doggins. Your dishes are full and waiting for you."

Natalia remained standing by the door.

"Come on in, really," I said. "Oh, this is my colleague, Professor Ralph Fourakis. Ralph, Officer Natalia Flores. Natalia, coffee?"

Natalia nodded and sat on the couch next to Ralph, shaking his hand. "I think you were on my list to call after Mr. Carter's death, but it's been pretty busy."

"I didn't know him at all. Just met him once on the quad. If there's anything I can do to help, though, let me know."

"Thanks. How did he strike you, when you met him?"

Ralph described the sunny lunch that already felt like a year ago, even though it was only a couple of weeks prior.

"He seemed really fond of those little boys he had with him. And then when he ran into Alexa—whoo, fireworks!" Ralph shook his head.

"Lauren mentioned that to me."

"Yeah, and it was like he was protecting the boys. Didn't want the Chair anywhere near them."

"What do you think the business between her and Jamal was about?" I asked Natalia.

"I couldn't say, really."

She couldn't tell us... or didn't want to? I watched Wulu munching. Anger at his abductor started my heart racing.

"Natalia, are you going to be able to find out who trashed my office and took Wulu? Fingerprints, witnesses, anything?"

"Do you have any ideas about what someone might have wanted from your files?" Her somber brown eyes fixed on mine.

"The only thing I thought of was that somebody wanted the draft of Jamal's thesis. I was supposed to be reading it. But it's in my college office, not here."

If only I'd gone over there last night. But what if Wulu had come back and I'd been gone?

"Which has a lot better security than a condo in an old house, Rousseau," Ralph said. "Might be why they looked here first."

Natalia nodded then asked, "And what's in his thesis that would be so compelling?"

"I hadn't started reading it yet. He was studying the speech of the kids at the Boys and Girls Club where he volunteered. Comparing African-American Vernacular English and General American. Trying to make a case for learning the standard dialect as a way to get ahead in the world. Not exactly groundbreaking science, but his research was careful and in-depth. I'm sure it's a well-written paper."

"When had he given you the draft?" Natalia sipped her coffee. "Do I need to see it?"

"It's an academic paper. I shouldn't think you'd need a copy. He gave me the draft about two weeks ago. It was right before he was killed." The image of finding Jamal dead filled me with sadness. Then I sat up straight. "Hey. So I never heard how he died."

Where had my brain gone? I hadn't even wondered about the murder weapon. This had gotten bad.

"Don't you read the newspaper?" Ralph asked, leaning forward.

"In the last week or two? Not a chance."

"He was shot, right?" He looked at Natalia then back at me.

"That's correct. Haven't found the weapon yet, though." She set her mug down. "While I'm here, Lauren, let's talk about this Martin guy. I called you back yesterday, but you didn't pick up."

"I know. I was out looking for Wulu. When I listened to your message and it wasn't about him, I wasn't up to calling back. Sorry."

"Yeah, you were going to tell me what you found out," Ralph prodded.

"You talked to Tashandra about Jamal arguing with some guy, right?" I looked at Natalia. "I told her to show you her drawing."

"Yes. That girl's got talent. I'm going to see if I can get her an internship with our graphic artist. But your message said something about seeing the man."

I described the restaurant scene again and his watching me from the sidewalk. "He was an odd guy. Then I drove straight home... well, almost. I pulled over to check him out on the Web."

"And?" She cocked her head.

"After deciding he wasn't the Belgian journalist or the Pascal Martin who works for Microsoft in Redmond, I saw a reference to a *djembe* player by that name. West African drumming. The Pascal Martin I saw was talking about drumming with a guy at the restaurant. So I followed the thread, poked around some, and saw an old news report linking him to a heroin ring. Can you look into it?"

She nodded, writing something in her Blackberry.

"Elise did too much heroin. Maybe she's connected with Pascal somehow," I said.

"I'll check it out." Natalia's Blackberry rang. As she checked the number and turned away to answer it, the color rose in her face. "Uh, tell you later," she said into the device. "I'll be off in an hour. Okay, soon." She clipped the device back on her belt and cleared her throat, not meeting my eyes. "Where were we? That's interesting information about Pascal Martin."

I nodded, wondering if the call was from Jackie. Wulu finished eating and, with a contented dog-sigh, curled up in a ball next to my feet.

"Wonder what the connection is with Jamal?" Ralph stared at me. "Did he ever mention an interest in drumming?"

I shook my head.

"We'll be looking into it, don't worry, Dr. Fourakis," Natalia said. "Lauren, your windows are all secured?"

"As far as I know. I made sure all the storms were closed tight and the windows locked. What else can I do?" At the thought of a stranger going through my belongings, seeing where and how I lived, invading my privacy, I felt jumpy. Unclean. Violated.

Natalia rose, thanked me for the coffee, and said she'd be in touch. She checked her large utility watch as she hurried out.

"Thanks for finding Wulu!" I remembered to call after her, getting a wave in return.

"Notice she didn't say much about anything? Not even about finding who trashed your place." Ralph finished his coffee.

"I noticed. I don't think she likes me very much, you know? The only tidbit she let out? They haven't found the murder weapon yet. Seems like nothing is getting done. Besides finding Wulu, of course. And that was accidental."

CHAPTER ELEVEN

I sat in my college office several hours later with the door locked. The halls were spooky with no one around, and, after yesterday, it felt a lot safer to hear the snick of the bolt as it locked.

Jamal was dead.

I'd been avoiding reading his thesis because the thought made me too sad. But he'd been such a good student.

Maybe I could get it published under his name with the other undergraduate honors theses. The deadline was at the end of April. At least I was able to find the thesis draft under a stack of exams.

I shivered as I sat with the stapled sheaf in my lap. The afternoon sun streaming onto the paper did little to heat the air. The college was prudent to turn the heat way down during vacation. The bonsai took it fine and probably preferred the cool air. I, on the other hand, forgot to wear my gloves and scarf—it was finally April, after all—and I wished I was wearing more layers. I began to read.

Pages later, I stared at the printed words. His thesis was grounds for an investigation.

Jamal hadn't gone to the police. Had he felt so disenfranchised, so powerless?

This was a linguistics thesis with a difference; it included an entire preface devoted to an exposé of child abuse. Alexa Kensington. Her name right there in black and white.

No wonder he'd been so protective of Tyrone and Nicky. He hadn't wanted Alexa near his charges for a reason.

He had written under guise of his thesis rather than talking to me about his concerns. Maybe he hadn't really trusted me, either. Or he'd wanted to have it in writing first.

I got up and stroked the tiny elm then wandered around my office, seeing nothing, thinking. I wondered if Jamal's accusations were true. I didn't like Alexa, but I pondered if she was capable of such awful actions. I sank back into my chair.

The handle on the door rattled. No one knew I was here. Several knocks sounded. I got up and gave a quick look out through the window, even though I knew the way down held twelve feet of sheer brick facade without even a vine of ivy to grab onto. If whoever was at the door was threatening, I had no place to go.

I took a deep breath and walked to the door. "Who is it?" I said to the gray painted wood.

"Lauren?"

Speak of the devil. I wished I were anywhere but here. But I already made my presence known. I closed my eyes for a moment, trying to center, then opened the door.

Alexa faced me. She was in jeans and a turtleneck, but they were designer jeans, and a colorful scarf draped over the shirt. She wore dangling earrings in a matching shade of green.

"Alexa," I said. Realizing Jamal's thesis lay atop the stack of papers on my desk, I moved to stand with my back to it. I hoped the tic starting a furious beat at the edge of my eyebrow wasn't obvious.

"I saw your truck in the parking lot." Alexa's color was high, and she sounded breathless. "I'm surprised to see you here on your break."

"I wanted to clean up my office." I tried to keep my voice casual. What did she want from me?" You know, without interruption."

She walked in and surveyed the cluttered space. "Looks like you have a ways to go." She raised an eyebrow.

"I was just getting started."

She stopped in front of a framed picture of Holt Beach, which I'd taken from the boardwalk on a sunny winter day. "Ah, Holt. Lovely place."

"You know it?" I thought she was from the lower Midwest somewhere.

"I have family roots in the area."

"Was there something you needed?" I wished I could say what I was thinking. Did you do those things Jamal thought you did?

"I..." Alexa cleared her throat. "That is, the student association asked me to do something to commemorate Mr. Carter. I was wondering if you would be willing to handle it. Since you were his advisor."

I watched her. It was unusual to see her flustered and uncomfortable. Maybe I could drag this out. "Oh, really?"

"Yes. I am quite busy at this time." She picked imaginary lint off one sleeve.

"I would love to." Why was she trying to palm this off on me?" But I am really in over my head with exams and student projects. And, remember, I was asked to deliver an address at the East Asian Linguistics conference next month." I hoped I didn't have to start worrying about my own memorial service.

"Yes, but—"

"I know how important keeping our presence up at conferences is to the department." I kept my eyes on her. She stressed this in every department missive and meeting. I waited. "And to the college. Right?"

Alexa narrowed her eyes at me. And nodded.

"So I'm afraid I'll have to decline," I said. "I'm sure you can work with the students to come up with something suitable."

"I see. He was so important to you, I thought you'd want to be involved." Alexa's eyes moved to the window, and she fell silent for a moment. "Everybody deserves a remembrance when they die." She blinked hard several times then looked at me and continued. "I had a neighbor. An old man. When he died, nobody came." She ran her finger across an elm leaf in a gentle caress.

Wow. Maybe this woman had feelings after all. "He didn't have family?"

"Apparently not. I paid for his burial, got the local minister to say a few words at the grave. We were the only two there." Alexa gave her head a little shake and faced me. "Will you at least deliver a memorial statement about Jamal?"

No. I was suddenly back at my father's memorial service.

Which had taken place even though the circumstances of his death had never been clarified. I had tried to speak, to tell the crowd what he'd meant to me, and had then found myself being revived. I had passed out from grief, exhaustion, worry.

I didn't intend to go through that again but wasn't going to tell Alexa why.

"No, I really can't. I'm sure your words would mean more, because you're the head of department." And they would. This might be a chance to see if I could do better at a memorial than the last time, but my obstinacy won out.

"All right, then. I'll see you next week at the faculty meeting." Her face broadcast displeasure. She turned to go then paused, addressing the door. "I should have a copy of Jamal's thesis, if you can locate it. You know, so I can speak more clearly about his work."

"I'll see if I can find it, Alexa."

When the door clicked shut, I locked it again. "Oh, wouldn't you love a copy," I whispered. I tucked the thesis securely into my knapsack. "Oh, wouldn't you just."

I walked with Wulu in the oldest part of the cemetery on High Street after I got home that afternoon. I carried the knapsack containing the thesis securely on my back.

"Anybody else would call the police," I told Wulu as we roamed the antique part of the graveyard. "But I'm afraid they're going to discredit Jamal if I tell them his ideas. Alexa Kensington may be unpleasant, but she's a respected academic. Nobody's going to believe a dead student's accusations."

Wulu barked, which made me smile. He always agreed with me.

The days were finally longer than the nights, and the weather warmed up a little during the afternoon. The air was starting to smell, at last, of spring. Grape hyacinths and yellow and purple crocuses bloomed in sunny spots along the iron fence. They made me smile, too. It was about time.

Gravestones featuring many of the town's old names—Chase, Pulcifer, Choate, Heard—tilted this way and that. The oldest ones were of thin, dark-gray slate with the angel of death carved into the top; others featured grinning skulls. I slowed to read the dates on a number of the stones. It seemed people either died young or lived long lives—no in between. My thoughts wandered to what my gravestone might read. I couldn't imagine ending up described as "Faithful Wife." I supposed it might read, "Linguist, World Traveler, Spinster."

Wulu and I climbed granite steps until the hill flattened out. I wrapped the leash twice around my hand as we walked on the cemetery road. Wulu was eager to explore, and I was determined never to lose him again. Newer sections here appeared to be reserved for ethnic groups. In one area, all the stones were inscribed with Greek names and flowery dedications; another's tall monuments featured names ending in -eski, -owski, or -czyk.

I started when a car honked behind me. "Hey!" I backed onto the grass, pulling Wulu with me. I had thought we were alone up here. I whirled and saw a wide black car approaching. I cursed. Now we were alone with a car coming after us. The vehicle drew closer.

Maybe I should have called the police after all.

Wulu let out a series of his loudest, fiercest barks. We started running until I recognized the car as Samuel Pulcifer's. I pulled Wulu to a stop.

As the car pulled closer, Samuel stuck his head out through the driver's side window. Scraggly white whiskers poked out from his chin, his hair was disheveled, and the shirt he wore under a v-necked sweater was misbuttoned, so one side of the collar stuck up farther than the other.

"Mr. Pulcifer! Thank God you're alive." I stared, mystified by his being there. And relieved it wasn't my ransacker coming after me. The relief made me shaky.

"Want a ride, Missy?" Samuel creaked.

He was definitely alive.

But where had he been in the last week? I hadn't heard anything of his fate after the fire.

And I was curious. I took a deep breath. "Why not? Come on, Wulu." I wrenched open the passenger door, sat on the cracked Naugahyde of the bench seat, and lifted Wulu onto my lap. He uttered a little growl in Samuel's direction and cowered back into the door. The car smelled of motor oil. A layer of dust and pollen coated the broad dashboard, which was littered with bits of rusty hardware. A film coated the inside of the windshield, making it hard to see through. I hoped Samuel didn't have big travel plans.

"Where might you be headed?" he asked.

"We're not going anywhere in particular," I said, watching him, my hands stroking Wulu's back. "But how are you? I'm so sorry about the boat shop."

Samuel gripped the steering wheel, looking straight ahead as he drove slowly among the gray and pink granite markers. "Yes, well, some things come to pass, don't they?"

The words of a prophet. "What do you mean?"

He remained silent for a moment then said, "Your father's model. It went with all the rest. Too bad. It was a beaut."

As I had thought. "That's very sad. It was the only one I had. But I'm glad you're safe. I was down there that night, and nobody seemed to know if you were inside or had gotten out. Not even your brother."

"Phillip."

I waited, but that avenue of conversation went no further, either. "So you had time enough to get out safely? How did the fire start?"

"I got out. My car was gone, wasn't it?"

"Yes, but no one knew if you had driven it or if someone had set the fire and then taken your car. It was quite a blaze."

"Yes, it was." Samuel nodded and gestured with a knobby, yellowed, trembling hand. "What were you doing looking at my place burning, anyway, Missy?"

"The whole town was looking, Mr. Pulcifer. The flames were huge, and then the whole thing collapsed into the river." I shuddered, remembering the sight.

"Indeed." Samuel drove at a crawl down the hill and out onto Town Farm Road then pulled over. "Well, young lady, I'll be seeing you."

"Oh!" Apparently dismissed, we got out. "Thanks for the ride?" I watched the car drive off, my hand raised in a wave that went unheeded. "Wulu, what on earth was that all about?"

Wulu barked in the direction of the car.

CHAPTER TWELVE

I leaned into the stretch, right leg extended, on my front steps. Running usually cleared my brain, but not this Wednesday morning. At least the sun was out.

A motorcycle horn beeped, sounding like the cartoon Road Runner. "Those doughnuts for me?" Zac parked the Honda and picked up the paper bag from the porch then greeted me with a kiss and a smile. He'd called the night before and asked if he could come by. Said he had something to show me.

"As long as I get one, too. I earned it. Hey, how old is that thing, anyway?" I pointed to the cycle.

"Uh, let's just say it was built before I was born. But it gets me where I need to go, and MPG is in the high nineties. Can't beat it, right?"

I nodded as I wiped my brow and unlocked the door. "I'll make coffee."

Zac greeted an excited Wulu then extracted a laptop computer from his bag and started it up on the dining table. "I'm ready when you are, sugar."

I brought mugs of French Roast and sat next to him. I sniffed his hair as I placed his coffee in front of him. He smelled of fresh shampoo and a faint touch of incense. All was suddenly forgiven. His over commitment to his work. And my own ambivalence toward him.

The screen held several boxes on the left with lists of icons and words, a large area on the right displaying video, and a horizontal box along the bottom showing several colored lines. A couple of the icons looked like little movie cameras, and two were clearly tiny loudspeakers. Most of the labels on the tabs across the top didn't make much sense to me—like, what was a Bin? Help was the only one I could make sense of.

"So this is your special system?"

"Yup. The dTective program runs on top of the basic video editing software for the kind of work we do at the station. Just think, I could be editing an Oscar-winning movie on this, or a prime-time TV show—it's the same program lots of them use—and instead I'm fighting crime in my local neighborhood." He raised his eyebrows and smiled.

"My hero," I said, kissing his ear. I wondered if there was maybe a little more to editing a major film than just having the software.

"See, I can move through the video slowly like this, or I can play it in a loop." Zac clicked the mouse on a line in the video display and dragged it to the right. The video played, and a corresponding blue line moved in the box at the bottom.

"That's what they call the Timeline," he said, pointing to the horizontal box, "and those are the video and audio tracks."

"You have sound from security cameras?"

"Sure. When they're posted outdoors, it's pretty bad quality, but it can help inside."

"So what are we looking at?" I leaned in so our arms touched.

"You know the deli next to the boat shop? They'd had a couple of break-ins lately, so they put up cameras outside. Look here." He pointed to the screen. "The cameras are digital, not videotape, though, and fairly low res."

I asked what low res was.

"Low resolution." His fingers were busy on the keys.

"Does that matter?"

"The higher the resolution, the more information you have. And I need it if I'm going to be able to clarify images. But high res takes up more storage space, and small businesses like this don't want to pay for it. I'll see what I can do. Anyway, here..." He pointed. "See how the air is getting murky? The flames were on the other side of the building at first, but there's a lot of smoke in the sky." The scene was of the deli parking lot abutting the boat shop. The outdoor lights lent only dim illumination to the small lot and grew less useful as the smoke increased.

I pointed. "What's moving?"

Zac raised a single eyebrow and winked, nudging my leg with his knee.

I laughed. "How do you do that with only one eyebrow?" I pressed my leg back into his.

"Don't you want to see?" he asked, moving his hands on the keyboard and the mouse. "Civilian Video Forensic Analyst Agnant at your service, ma'am," he said in a warped imitation of a police show from the sixties, smiling. "Watch. The fingers never leave the hands!"

His fingers were slender and deft. With a rush of heat, I wanted them exploring my skin, instead. But when I reached out for him, he held up a hand.

"Watch." He paused the video, and, as I watched, the scene became lighter. It suddenly had more contrast, too. Two figures stood in profile between the looming boat shop and a wide, low shape resolving under Zac's touch into Samuel Pulcifer's vehicle. One of the figures looked like Samuel himself. At least, it had the same height and stooped back.

My heart rate increased even more. As of yesterday, I knew Samuel survived the fire. Now it looked like we might see how and with whom he got out. I squinted and leaned in close but couldn't quite make out the other person, who wasn't tall enough to be Phillip. "Can't you do something with the other figure?"

"Doing my best. Hang on a minute." He concentrated on his work.

As the figure became more distinct, I gasped and sat back. "How can that be?"

"What?"

"Zac, I could swear that is Pascal Martin!"

"Oh? Old flame of yours?"

I watched in silence for a moment while he manipulated a few more coordinates then explained who Pascal was. As much as I knew, anyway. "Does Natalia know about this, Zac?"

"Since I didn't even know about this Martin character, no. Besides, this is the first chance I got to work on this footage. Chief gave me permission to work 'at home.'" He surrounded the last two words with finger quotes. "Because I said my scooter was in the shop. Decided your home was as good as mine. Thought maybe I could score some points with you." He turned, abandoning the screen. He wrapped his arms around me, locking my lips in a long kiss. "You've been awfully busy, *bebé*." He looked me in the eyes and smoothed my hair with one hand.

"Well, yeah." I stroked his cheek with longing.

He rose with an extended hand. "Shall we?"

"But shouldn't we call Natalia?" I frowned, drawn to the screen as much as to the tug of his hand.

Zac bent down and nibbled my ear. "The video will keep," he whispered.

"I can't believe they're kicking Elise out of the detox center so soon."

I'd gotten a call from Elise an hour earlier, saying she had finished with rehab and needed a ride home. I had been basking in the afterglow of 'the video will keep,' but I hadn't been willing to refuse Elise.

I kicked at a pine cone in the path in front of the Northeast Detox and Rehabilitation Center. "Four days can't be long enough to make any difference. And they sure moved her out of the hospital quickly."

Zac squeezed my hand. "Funding cuts, I guess. Give the bed to somebody who needs it more."

"I guess. Well, let's do it."

At the front desk, a worn-looking older man with an infectious smile showing a jewel in one of his front teeth greeted us. He said he'd call the supervisor and gestured toward a couple aging institutional chairs.

A woman in a green blazer and tidy slacks appeared from around a corner. Her short black hair was trim, and her glasses matched her blazer.

"Dr. Rousseau? Thanks for coming. Alice Rodrigues. Director." I stood, and we shook hands. "You'll be keeping Elise at your home, I understand?"

I raised my eyebrows. "At my condo? Why? Can't she go home?"

"Didn't Elise tell you? She is signing herself out. She hasn't completed the course of treatment her doctor recommended and is definitely not ready to be living alone. She'll go right back to her previous habits."

"But she said she was done here!" I loved Elise. I did not think I could live with her without coming to blows. Especially if she was an active addict.

"She is done with us. We are not done with her." Rodrigues pushed up her glasses and put her hands on her hips.

I looked at Zac. He frowned and shook his head. I turned back to the director.

"Look. I can't take care of her. I work, and…"

Rodrigues pursed her lips. "She wouldn't tell us if she has family. Does she?"

"Not around here. Her mom's in California, but last I heard, she's pretty much of a drunk. Not quite what Elise needs." Having Elise live with me wasn't quite what I needed, either.

"No. Well, I can't legally detain her, but if she goes home alone, she's basically guaranteed to start using again as soon as she can find some drugs. Opiates, crack, anything. She's very vulnerable. Just so you know."

"Can I have a minute?"

I stepped outside and stood in the weak spring sunshine. I closed my eyes, trying the find the answer. Actually, I realized, I was trying to find peace with the answer I already knew I'd give.

After Alice Rodrigues left to fetch Elise, I sank down next to Zac. "What am I doing?"

"You're being a faithful friend. But it's not going to be easy." He squeezed my hand.

Although I was grateful to have his support, my concern for how both Elise and I would do was topped only by my annoyance with her. Zac wasn't going to be taking care of Elise, I was. She was asking a lot of me.

"Hey, *gaijin*!" Elise put on a smile as she strode toward us, the kind of smile not involving her eyes, which were too bright. Her voice shook, and her clean hair looked odd, forming a cap on her head instead of her signature spikes. She carried a plastic bag in one hand and her carrier bag over her shoulder. Rodrigues followed close behind with a sheaf of papers.

"*Gaijin* yourself." I rose to hug my friend then looked at the director. "What do I need to know?"

Rodrigues answered by addressing Elise. "As we discussed, you are not fully detoxed. You need lots of water and healthy food. You need counseling. You are in trouble legally—your court date is, let's see, next Tuesday. This was your first Class A possession offense."

I tried to catch Elise's eye. I guessed the center didn't know about her deportation from Japan. It had happened a long time ago, and no one around here knew but me. She clearly didn't tell the authorities, and they didn't uncover it. Which surprised me. But it was a drug charge, despite Elise maintaining her innocence at the time. She would not meet my gaze.

"You'll be on probation for a while," Rodrigues said. "And a second possession will be much more serious."

By this time, Elise was tapping her hand against her leg and gazing through the front window.

"You almost died, Elise," the director continued. "If your friend here hadn't found you, if the EMTs weren't carrying Narcan, Dr. Rousseau wouldn't have anybody to take home. So stay clean, all right? Good luck."

We shook hands all around, except Elise, who kept hers in her pockets. As we walked out, Elise suddenly turned back.

"Timmy, I'll miss ya!" She approached the man at the desk, who looked surprised then pleased.

He held out his arms for an embrace. "Take care, girlfriend. Don't go using. It'll mess you up, hear? Call me anytime. I'll take you to NA with me."

"Yeah, maybe. *Ciao.*"

As we squeezed into the truck, with Elise in the middle, I wondered how compliant she would be. If she wouldn't even stay in the detox center the full amount of time, how likely would she be to stay drug free? Was it going to be hell having my old friend sleeping in my guest room? On the other hand, maybe I could help her.

Maybe I could find out what had been going on between Elise and Jamal. Maybe Elise could help me solve Jamal's murder. Maybe.

"So, *gaijin*, what's going on?" Elise and I sat with mugs of chai after Zac drove away on his bike, promising to call later. She sprawled on the couch with her legs stretched out, looking through the window. Wulu curled up next to her, looking hopeful, but she ignored him.

"Nothing I want to talk about."

I watched my friend. "You know, you're going to have to talk sometime."

She shrugged.

"I'm the one who rescued you. And speaking of which, here's your damn *furo-shiki*." I got up and grabbed the red scarf off a hook in the entryway. I tossed it to her. "And I'm the one who got you out of detox against their advice. Why won't you tell me—me!—what you're going through?" My neck was hot, and my pitch was a few dozen kiloHertz higher than usual. I shouldn't have to remind her how far back our friendship went.

Elise stared at the cloth in her hands and caressed it as she wrapped it around her neck. Taking a sip of chai, she slammed the mug down on the coffee table. "Damn. Hot!" The gesture sloshed liquid onto the finish I had worked so hard to make beautiful.

I grabbed a napkin from the dining table and threw it at her. "Here, wipe it up." I paced to the hall and back, hands in my pockets. "I mean it, Elise. What's with the heroin? Why wouldn't you finish rehab?"

She looked down, finally stroking Wulu. "I can't talk now, *gaijin*. Later, all right?"

I sighed. "I'll be down the hall. Don't go anywhere."

She dismissed me with a wave and closed her eyes.

I stared at the stacks of midterms on my desk. It was already Wednesday. I'd gotten nothing done this break except try to track down a killer. I'd wanted to call Natalia about seeing Pascal Martin on the video, but Zac had said he'd do it, and it was his job, after all.

I resolved to focus on the exams until they were done. I put in a Baaba Maal CD and got to work.

The light outside the window had dimmed and I had one more paper to do when Wulu yipped and ran in.

"You hungry, small dog? Just a few more minutes, okay?" I looked back at my desk, but Wulu kept barking. "What?" The dog ran to the doorway and back. I got up and followed him.

"Elise? *Gaijin*?" I called when I saw the unoccupied couch. The kitchen, open to the dining area, was clearly empty, and when I ran to check the bedroom and bathroom—no Elise. "Damn her!" I looked at the front door. It was closed but unlocked.

I had locked it after Zac left. I'd been very careful since the break-in.

I opened it and looked up and down the street. I couldn't see Elise. Or the scarf. I was not surprised.

After locking the door again, I sank onto the couch and put my head in my hands.

Why in the world had I put the music on? I should have come out here and checked on her. Where had she gone?

As my cell phone rang, I sat up and grabbed my purse, rooting around until I found the phone, managing to answer before it stopped ringing.

"Lauren, listen," Elise said.

"Where are you?"

"I had to get out. Please don't come looking for me. I'll be fine."

"*Gaijin*, I'm sorry I was hard on you. I'm worried. Please come back? Please?"

"I can't." Her voice softened. "Thanks for caring, *gaijin*." The phone shut off with a whispery click.

CHAPTER THIRTEEN

I stared at the phone. Now what do I do? I called Zac but got his voice mail. "Oh, yeah, he was going to work," I told Wulu, who was wagging his tail in front of his dinner bowl. I decided not to leave a message. I thought about calling Natalia, but didn't want to load Elise with additional troubles. She was sufficiently screwed as it was. I poured Wulu's food into his bowl and some cereal into my own. Looking through the front window, I munched and thought.

Maybe Elise had gone home. Certainly what I would have wanted to do if I'd been through what she'd been through.

A few minutes later, I was at the door, equipped with jacket, pocket flashlight, and cell phone. I tucked my hair into a beret and leaned down to pet Wulu.

"No, Wu, you stay home this time. I'm just going across town. Be a good guard dog. I'll be back soon." I locked the door and, slipping on fleece gloves, set out.

Elise's house was dark, as was the sky at 7:30. I crept along the edge of the gravel driveway, mindful of any small noise. If she was in the house, I didn't want to spook her. And I didn't really want her neighbor Virgie MacDonald watching me, either. It was a windless evening, and even my breathing sounded loud.

Elise's car was there... a good sign. I peered through the kitchen window at the side of the house, but the only lights I saw were the LEDs on the stove and the microwave. I tiptoed through the torii-style gate. Looking at the back porch, I remembered how Milo was out the last time I was at the house. He didn't seem to be around now, though. Good. Coyotes were reputed to live in the nearby woods. Milo would be a tasty morsel for them.

A rustle near the fence at the rear of the yard made me start. I turned slowly but saw nothing. Patting my chest to slow my pounding heart, I turned back to the porch door. Elise didn't want to stay with me and definitely didn't want me looking for her. But if she OD'd again, I wouldn't be able to forgive myself for not trying to help her now.

I tried the porch door, and, as before, it was unlocked. The loud creak as it opened sounded like it came through a bullhorn. I propped it open so it wouldn't creak as it closed then shone my light around the porch for a minute. No Milo, not even any cat dishes.

Elise had called a neighbor from the hospital to feed the cat in her absence. Which meant Elise must have come here.

So where was she? Sleeping it all off? Or unconscious in her own home?

I knew Elise hid a key under a small stone gargoyle in the far corner of the porch. I headed toward the dark corner.

A hard object whacked with force on the side of my head. I cried out. A sharp pain radiated from where I was hit. What was happening? I struggled as something dark came down over my head. Whoever was attacking me grabbed both my hands from behind and wrapped what felt like a thin cord around my wrists. My heart raced. I stomped down behind me, trying to find a shin or an instep, like I'd learned in self-defense class. A forearm squeezed across my neck.

"Who are you? Let me go!" I croaked, the pressure on my larynx making it hard to speak.

"Keep out of it," a whisper replied.

I was trying to place the faint accent when all went dark.

Someone shook my shoulder and called my name. I opened my eyes, going from dark to piercing light, which hurt my eyes, so I squeezed them shut. That hurt, too. I realized the jackhammer I felt was my own head pounding. A flood of fear rushed back over me.

"Lauren?" Natalia's voice was close as I heard a snipping sound. My hands were freed. "Dr. Rousseau?"

Whew. I let my eyes creep open. I was still in Elise's porch. I squeezed and opened my tingling hands. My heart started to slow down with the relief of safety.

"What happened?" Natalia asked.

"I was going to ask you." I tried to sit up, but, when things got dim again, I lay back down on my side. I kept silent for a moment. I remembered hearing the noise in the bushes. Exploring the porch. Being attacked. "I was looking for Elise. Somebody hit me on the head, put something over me, grabbed me."

Natalia held out a navy blue pillowcase.

"Tied my hands, said..."

"Said what? Man or woman?"

"I don't know. They whispered. So it could have been either."

"They?"

"No, I mean he. Or she. And the voice sounded familiar. Sort of."

"How tall was this person?"

"I never saw who it was. But he must have been at least as tall as me, because, after my hands were tied, he put an arm around my neck. Next thing I knew, you're here." I looked up at Natalia. "Why are you here, anyway?"

A siren drew near. She patted my head with great care, parting the hair around a painful spot. "Quite a goose egg. Skin's not broken."

Red lights flashed outdoors, and an EMT strode through the door, red bag in hand. He looked at Natalia.

"Hey, Silvio. That was quick."

"I don't need an ambulance! I need to find Elise." I pulled away from Natalia's touch, setting off another wave of pain. "Were you looking for her, too?"

Another officer poked his head into the porch. Natalia told him we were all set and would be out shortly.

"Little bit of a long story," she said to me. "Why don't you tell me why you were here alone, in the dark, while Silvio checks you out?"

I related the saga of getting the call from the detox center, bringing Elise home, and how she slipped out of the condo. Meanwhile, the EMT, dark hair jelled into little curls on top of his head, smiled with white orthodontist-model teeth as he put an ice pack on my head. He checked my pupils and vital signs, helped me sit up, and draped a blanket over my shoulders. When I assured him I knew both the correct date and the name of the current president, he agreed to let me go, cautioning me to take it easy and call my doctor if I got a bad headache or became dizzy.

"I wanted to see if she had come home," I said to Natalia. "The woman at the center seemed pretty sure Elise would start using again if she didn't finish the program there. I don't want to lose my friend."

"Did it occur to you it might be dangerous to poke around a dark house by yourself? Didn't think of getting anyone to go with you or at least let them know where you went?"

I looked at the officer with disbelief. "I've lived alone for years. Here and abroad. I'm used to doing things by myself. Plus, Elise is my friend." Natalia was such a tough character, maybe she didn't want to see other women acting the same way.

"Heroin addiction changes people. They can get desperate. Different. Maybe not as loyal as they had been. And suppliers can be brutal."

"Well, I did try to call Zac before I left." So there, I continued in my head.

"Let's get you home," she said, helping me to my feet. "Did you drive here?"

"No, I walked over. But aren't you going to see if she's in there?" I turned my head to look at the door into the house then winced as a pain shot out from the bump on the left side of my head.

"We looked in windows, tried the doors, knocked and so on. We don't have a warrant, though—we can't just break in."

"She must be in there! Or at least she's been here—Milo's dishes aren't out."

"Milo?"

"Her cat." I explained about the neighbor feeding Milo.

"That only shows she has been here, not that she is still here." Natalia gestured to the door. "Come on, I'll give you a lift. And listen—next time you want to play detective, call me. That's my job. Got it?"

I nodded then said, "Wait." I was really being the absent-minded professor. Must be the bump on the head. "Maybe you can't go in, but I can. I know where she keeps a key." I moved toward the gargoyle in slow motion, not wanting a repeat of pain. The statuette sat on the floor in the corner of the porch, its strange head supported on both hands, elbows on the base, a jester hat curling off its head. The look on its face was half menacing, half comical. When I leaned down to lift it, I got the pain back, anyway. And then I stared. Nothing.

"A key, huh?" Natalia's skeptical tone grated on my nerves.

I leaned the sculpture back down and rose slowly, holding the side of my head. "She's always left a key there, in case I needed it." My disappointment was heavy.

I hadn't had such a bad day since the night I'd found Jamal.

Natalia headed for the door, beckoning me. I followed her but would have preferred to follow the magnet that pulled me back to the house, to Elise. Where was she? Was she safe? What if she was inside, alone, near death, like last time?

"*Bebé*, I would have gone with you! Why didn't you call me?" Zac's cheeks were pink from the ride over on his motorbike.

He'd come as soon as I'd called, which had been right after Natalia had dropped me off, with stern admonitions to stay home and apply ice.

"I called you. You were at work. I was worried about Elise, so I went over there. I didn't expect to get hit on the head!" I turned away from the door with a rush of impatience.

He followed me into the condo, shed his leather jacket, and came up close behind, wrapping his arms around me. He brushed his lips over the bump on my head and murmured, "Poor Lauren."

I wrested myself from his embrace. Not looking at him, I walked into the kitchen. "Tea? With whiskey?"

He stood rooted, arms at his sides, looking at me with disbelief. "You get whacked on the head by some criminal, and you won't let me get close. I don't get you, Lauren." He shook his head and jammed his hands into his jeans pockets.

I didn't know what to do. He drew me in, and yet I prickled when he wanted to protect me. Take care of me. It was like walls closing in, like something I couldn't control. I wondered if it had been a mistake to call him.

"I don't know! I don't seem to want anybody to tell me what to do. Especially now—the police tell me what to do but won't give me any information. The college tells me what to do. And when you do, too—I feel like I'm suffocating. No, it's more like prickly heat or a sweater that's too hot, too itchy." I knew this was an extreme reaction to his affection, but I couldn't seem to help myself.

His mouth took on a grim set. "And what am I supposed to do? Are we lovers and partners? I care for you. It feels like... like love. But you won't let me love you." He looked away, running a hand over his dreds, then looked back at me. "I was so worried when you called me tonight. I wanted to come and be with you. Looks like I'd be better off at home. Alone." He drew keys out of his pocket.

Feeling the rush of longing and lust that always rose up when I was near him, I opened my arms. "I want you to stay. I'm difficult. Fully acknowledged. I don't want to be alone, though." He was such a good man. Did I even deserve him?

"Let's have that tea. With whiskey. Then you tell me all about it. If you want to," he added quickly.

"Tea and whiskey it is."

As we nestled on the couch, warm mugs smelling of Jack Daniels and cinnamon on the table, I related the events at Elise's.

"You must have been scared."

"You bet. When the hood came over my head, when whoever it was grabbed my hands and tied them—I was terrified." I relived the sheer terror. "I even tried to do an instep crush, but I missed."

He smiled and squeezed my shoulder. "Did this person say anything?"

I explained, as I did with Natalia. "And the voice sounded sort of familiar. I'm going to have to sit with it for a while. You know?"

"You mean, like when you don't focus on something, it sometimes gets more clear?"

I nodded. "Ow. Remind me not to move my head." I adjusted the towel-wrapped ice pack on my head and leaned into his arm. I sipped my drink, enjoying the feel of his soft flannel shirt on my cheek and the warmth spreading through me. Wulu jumped up to join us. He curled into a ball and flipped his tail back and forth in a lazy arc.

"This is nice," I said then yawned.

"Uh-huh. We could be doing this every night, you know." He stroked my shoulder.

"We could." I let my eyes close for a minute, feeling sleep overtake me. Suddenly I flashed them open. "Wait! I still don't know what happened to Elise!"

"*Bebé*, you know what time it is?" He gestured to the clock on my kitchen wall, which featured fork and spoon hands and hours represented by ceramic vegetables. Right now, it was red cabbage-thirty—half past ten. "Nobody's going to find her tonight. Natalia will call you if they happen to find her. Right?"

I agreed with him. The warm and cozy sensation vanished, though. Again I saw Elise's face as she lay motionless in the blue house. Barely breathing. Pale. With that crazy doll on her face. And how did it get there, anyway? For the first time, I wondered if someone else was involved. What if her supplier was pushing her to use, maybe forcing her to sell drugs herself? Maybe Elise owed a lot of money. Which could explain why her house was in such bad repair. Or if she had angered someone, she could be in danger if they were violent or vengeful.

I stared through the window into the darkness. My own attacker could be right outside. Right now.

CHAPTER FOURTEEN

Zac fixed me eggs and toast in the morning and made me promise to take it easy.

"And if you should want company on any future escapades, I'm your man. Got it? Or even if you only want a warm body at night."

My cheeks warmed.

His wakeup call a little earlier had been intensely sensual and completely enjoyable.

He planted a goodbye kiss on me that pretty much guaranteed I'd keep thinking about him all day long, then blew me an air kiss on his way out.

After locking the door behind him, I considered trying to do something to find Elise. Then scolded myself. I couldn't do anything beyond what Natalia and her crew were doing, and if I didn't get some work done, I'd be in trouble next week. I put on a Rob Thomas CD and settled into my office with a second cup of French Roast.

By eleven o'clock, I had graded all the midterms, planned the first class for next week, and pulled the draft of my conference paper up onto the monitor. Every time my mind had wandered onto Elise, I'd wrestled it back onto the task at hand.

Now, gazing at a picture sitting atop a bookshelf, I paused. It featured the two of us, Elise and me, at the summit of Mount Fuji. The thin sun shone on our ruddy cheeks. Elise grasped the top of a walking stick carved with kanji, and I had one arm slung around her neck, the other hand holding a tiny American flag aloft. We were younger. Stronger. Unburdened by concerns about serious employment or long-term relationships, not to mention life-threatening addiction. I missed our closeness of those days, when we talked about everything, sharing our feelings and adventures far from home.

"I'll look for her later," I told Wulu, who slept at my feet. "Or not." I touched the lump on my head with a tentative hand. I didn't want to go through that again. Ever. I had blustered to Zac last night, but I'd definitely ask for his company if further investigations seemed in order. For now, I was content to resume writing my findings on "The Influence of Pitch Accent on Phrase-Final Nasals in Japanese: Regional Variation."

Two hours later, I was about to rustle myself up a peanut butter and lettuce sandwich when the phone rang. Wulu awoke and barked sharply. I raised my eyebrows—Elise?—and picked up.

"I believe I mentioned to keep out of it. Don't go looking for your friend," someone whispered.

"Who are you? Where is she?" No one answered, but the call didn't click off, either. I heard breathing then a faint train whistle in the background. "Hello? Hello!"

Finally the call disconnected. I looked at the caller ID. It said only "Unknown caller. Unknown number." I stared at the phone, not seeing it. What was it about the voice that sounded familiar?

CHAPTER FIFTEEN

I left Natalia a message about the call, even though I didn't have any real information to give her. I went through the motions of fixing my lunch and munched it at the kitchen counter, not tasting it, washing it down with the last of the skim milk. I took Wulu for a walk around the block, barely noticing the buds on the trees and the daffodils blooming until I was almost home. I returned to my desk, but all attempts at concentration proved fruitless. My head ached. My life seemed to be in turmoil and mostly out of my control.

The phone rang. Caller ID read "Private Number." I wished I could block this kind of call, but I'd hate to miss it if it was Elise. On the other hand, I did not want to hear the mystery voice again. I let it ring six times. I finally picked up.

"Lauren, dear, it's Aunt Louise."

I greeted her and asked how she was.

We chatted for a moment then Louise said, "Well, I haven't seen you since Easter, and I thought we could have a little visit."

Huh? Easter was a week and a half ago. Oh heck. Why not?" Sure, Aunt Louise. I'd love to."

"Good, dear. Why don't you come for tea at four?"

Four sounded like the cocktail hour to me, but I agreed and hung up.

"What's up with that?" I asked Wulu. "I don't think I've ever spent time alone with Louise. Could be fun, could be a big bore. Guess I'll find out."

Louise's call took my mind off my worries enough to let me get back to work. By 3:30, I was satisfied with the day's progress. I was ready to shut down the computer when I remembered Jackie mentioned sending me a link to a list of her favorite wines. If somebody else wanted to do that kind of research so I didn't have to, it was fine with me.

I opened my Gmail account. I deleted the digest from the Rowley Freecycle list, the latest missive from the town Democratic Committee, and a message advertising fake Rolexes. I scanned the rest of the new messages, spying Jackie's name with a subject line "Wine List" ... then froze. The next mail was from ECgaijin. Elise's address! Elise Chase. *Gaijin*. I hurried to double-click it, and my hand slid the mouse up to Jackie's mail instead.

"Damn!" I finally opened the message from Elise.

Give it up GAIJEAN. I'm a lost cause.

I typed a quick reply, asking where she was, telling her to call me, and pressed Send. I reread the message and frowned. Why would Elise write our code word, our special name for each other, that way? It was odd and was spelled wrong. Did someone else write it from Elise's account?

Time to call Natalia. I got through this time and told her about the phone call and the email. I told her I'd forward her the message and that I'd be careful. "And I always lock my door now. It's all right if I go visit my aunt in Topsfield this afternoon, isn't it?"

"Of course," Natalia said. "Please let me know of any more calls, all right? Or emails, texts, whatever?"

I agreed and disconnected. I hoped Louise would offer me sherry or something stronger with tea. It was definitely cocktail hour.

My aunt was a woman who took spring cleaning seriously. The late afternoon sun shone through the large windows of Louise and George's sunroom. No dust or rain splatters blocked the light. I settled into a pink-and-green striped armchair while Louise busied herself in the kitchen. In the oval perennial garden outside, lines of recent raking circled points of green pushing their way lightward with promises of full bloom in a month or two. A dozen raised beds stood in formation farther back in the yard, several covered with mini hoop-houses. The scene looked like a Lilliputian's landscape nursery.

My aunt had earned her Master Gardener certification, and her gardens had been featured in *Organic Gardening Magazine*.

"Here we are, dear." Louise placed a tray on the wicker coffee table. "Sherry or tea?"

I smiled and accepted both, as well as a shortbread cookie.

After we talked for a few minutes, she said, "And how are Jackie and her new friend doing?"

"I'm not really sure. Fine, I think." Why was she asking me?

"I wanted to apologize to her again for George's bad behavior at Easter."

I nodded and waited.

"He really has a good heart, Lauren. He's just a bit opinionated. Gruff. You know." Louise studied her porcelain teacup then looked up with bright little smile. "Let me show you his latest!" She stood and beckoned to me.

Mystified, I emptied my sherry glass before joining her.

Louise led the way to a large open box in the spare bedroom. "Look!"

Four kittens slept nestled together in a soft bundle. One opened its eyes and stretched. A pink tongue started to work, licking a tiny paw, then licked its litter-mate's ear as if they were a single creature.

"How sweet they are." I pointed out a black kitten who was gazing up at us with a puzzled look. They were all awake now, stretching and grooming. "This is George's latest? Do you mean he raises kittens?"

"He fosters them for the shelter." Louise beamed. "You know, kittens whose mothers can't be found. He bottle feeds them and is as gentle as a new mother himself. It's all his project, not mine. Of course, I help out when he's at work. This litter's mother had been hit by a car."

"Are they going to be adopted?" I picked up the black kitten, wondering how Wulu would react to a little feline sibling. Yeah, right. Cute little kittens grow into big cats. That was all I needed in my small condo—two pets who might not even like each other.

"It's pretty easy to place kittens once they're neutered and have their first shots."

Driving home, I thought back to the several strange incidents involving George lately.

His behavior at Easter had been rude and bigoted. He hadn't been particularly kind to me the night I'd found Jamal's body, grilling me on my whereabouts as if he hadn't been my uncle for the last twenty years. The time after my evening class when he'd challenged me for even being in the building. Lockhart Hall, where my office had been for seven years.

Surely he wouldn't carry his bigotry to the point of killing a black student. Would he?

Louise seemed awfully eager to show me what a sweetheart her husband was. Was she covering up for him? Forestalling accusations? I shook my head to clear it.

My life had gotten very complicated.

At home, I suited up in my white reflective jacket and my running pants, put a little reflective vest and the leash with the flashing light on Wulu, and went for a dusk run. I didn't feel much calmer when I got back, but at least I burned enough calories to earn the fat glass of Shiraz I wanted.

Halfway through it, after reading the comics and skimming the first section of the *Boston Globe*, hunger hit. The refrigerator did not cooperate by yielding any more than a couple beers, two eggs, the remnants of a head of romaine, a bit of goat cheese, and a vast array of mustards and olives of all hues.

Zac was working. I couldn't hit him up for dinner. Surveying the cupboards didn't inspire me to cook a meal, since all they held were cans of soup, a box of oatmeal, a sleeve of crackers, peanut butter, and three sprouted potatoes. And dog food. Dialing Jackie's number didn't get me anywhere, either. "She's probably grocery shopping," I told Wulu. I filled the dog's bowl and headed out to my truck. Jackie always cooked.

Twenty minutes later, I rang her doorbell for the second time. My sister's car sat in the driveway and lights shone behind curtains, but nobody answered. I even thought I could hear music.

Finally, Jackie opened the door. "What are you doing here?" Her cheeks were pink, and she wore a loose white t-shirt with plaid pajama pants.

"Because I'm your sister? And I'm hungry? Because I thought it would be all right to drop in? Any of those work for you?"

Jackie looked behind her for a moment. "Can you give me a minute?"

I stared at her. "What? Why... oh, wait. Do you have somebody here?"

"It's okay, Jacksie. Invite her in." Natalia walked up behind Jackie, wearing an oversized sweatshirt, jeans, and bare feet. Her hair hung loose, and her face broadcast a relaxed ease I had never seen on her before.

"Oh, listen, I don't want to barge in on you."

Jackie frowned. "You just did." Her voice was curt, but she insisted I come in. "Chicken curry's on the stove."

In the kitchen, Natalia focused on cutting up salad vegetables. She was quick and accurate with the knife. Jackie poured a glass of Abeja Viognier for me. The fragrance of Indian spices and basmati rice infused the warmth of the room. Jackie wouldn't meet my eyes.

"Yo." I slung my arm around Jackie's shoulders and bumped her hip with mine. "What would I do without a sister like you?"

"Might lose some weight if you didn't mooch off me so often."

When she hip-bumped me back, I knew we were good. She put me to work setting the table. After I laid bright Mexican placemats with napkins, silverware, and plates, I watched my sister and Natalia move about the room like a choreographed dance, sliding by each other. A soft touch here, a consultation in low voices there.

As if they'd been cooking together for years.

A pang of longing at the cozy scene slammed my heart.

When Jackie had fetched the chutneys and lime pickles and carried steaming plates to the table, we sat to eat. Jackie and Natalia dug right in, paying no attention to my moment of silence.

"How was your visit with your aunt?" Natalia asked.

"You saw Louise?" Jackie's voice held astonishment.

"She invited me over. Have you ever been there only with her?"

Jackie shook her head. "And we haven't even had a holiday dinner there in a few years, have we? Nobody really wants to spend any more time with George than they have to," she said to Natalia, who nodded in understanding.

I told them about the visit with Louise and how she stressed George's good side. "It was weird." I then detailed my encounters with George over the last couple of weeks.

"You didn't think to tell me this before?" Natalia raised dark eyebrows.

"It didn't seem important. And, I mean, he's our uncle."

"Do you think Louise suspects George of something and that's why she went overboard on his positives?" Jackie waved her fork. "You saw him in action at Easter, Nat."

Natalia laughed. "He's quite the throwback, isn't he?"

"I don't know what to think anymore," I said. "I don't suppose you have any leads on Jamal's killer?"

"No." Natalia's tone turned serious. "And I'm afraid we have nothing on Elise's whereabouts, either. We checked lots of known hangouts and drug locations, but nobody seems to have seen her. The blue house, too." She held up her hand, forestalling the question on the tip of my tongue. "Yes, even the attic, even the shed."

Driving home, full but not feeling particularly settled, I reflected on the domestic scene at Jackie's. I'd seen a side of Natalia I hadn't before, one that Jackie must see pretty much exclusively. Jacksie. Nat. I wished my relationship with Zac was as easy.

I sat in front of my house for a moment. Natalia seemed to think George was a comical Neanderthal. I adored Louise, but love could skew a person's rational abilities. I knew that all too well. I tried not to ever think about the man I was involved with before Zac, before moving to Ashford. The intellect I so prided myself on had crumbled to dust in the face of a Hungarian's black curls, an athlete's body, and a swindler's charm. Maybe Louise, too, was blind to her husband's crimes.

I spent much of Friday working on my presentation. I kept thinking of Elise, but it sounded like Natalia was on the case, and this was the last day of vacation. I had work I had to finish before next week. So I put my friend out of my thoughts and buckled down.

In the late afternoon, I stood, stretched, and opened a window. Miracle of miracles, it was sunny and mild. The air smelled fresh, like earth and sun-warmed hyacinths. It beckoned. Then it hit me that the day might not be so nice for Elise. Where was she? Why hadn't she contacted me? I decided to use the remaining afternoon light for a long run around places Elise might be. I could at least look for her car. I pulled on a long-sleeved t-shirt and shorts with a pocket, grabbed my phone, and set out.

Route 1A wouldn't win any prizes for being a nice run. Cars whipped by at high speeds. But it had wide shoulders and was the only way to get to Elise's workplace, Northeast Biolabs. After I cleared town and a few hills with houses on the right, the road opened up. I ran past the fields and cow barn of Appleton Farm on the right and a marshy field on the left. I turned into the Biolabs drive. I jogged down to the employee parking lot as cars passed me on their way out.

I stopped in the far corner of the lot at a small red car and stared. It was Elise's. I walked around it, tried the door. Locked.

Had she disappeared into her old life? The police must have called the labs. But maybe not.

I jogged to the entrance of a mansion built a couple of centuries ago. Modern buildings surrounded it.

Elise had told me about how the labs had saved this historic building, restored it, and used it for offices and meetings.

"Excuse me," I said to the receptionist at a wide desk in an entry hall leading to a broad staircase with polished, graceful woodwork. "I'm looking for Elise Chase."

"Let me check." The young man swiveled to a computer. "No, I'm afraid she's not here today."

One more dead end. "But her car is parked in the lot out there."

"Looks like she's been out for a while. Would you like her supervisor's email?" He smiled his polite helpfulness.

I sighed. "Sure, that'd be great." I reached out for the slip of paper and tucked it in my pocket. I could at least pass it on to Natalia. Who probably already had it.

I finished up my six miles at the site of the burned-out boathouse. A huge yellow construction vehicle sat atop a pile of blackened rubble—metal, masonry, and dirt mixed with charred timber, all sorted into piles. The scene jarred with the mild weather and the daffodils blooming across the street, making the sad memories worse. I jogged on to the wharf.

Stretching at a weathered wood piling, I spied a vessel I'd never seen before tied to a heavy cleat at the end of the dock, low and almost hidden by a big fishing boat. I approached it then smiled. A houseboat was not a familiar sight on this stretch of the river.

This one had been painted yellow in the past, and looked like someone with less than perfect carpentry skills had done the finish work.

The flat roof sprouted a thick antenna tapering at its top, and several faded towels hung from a line along one side. No one appeared to be on board.

I glanced behind me at the parking area. It was empty of people.

Since childhood, I had had a fondness for houseboats. They fell into the same category as dollhouses. Abodes smaller than reality. Tidy. Inviting flights of imagination. Very different from the routine reality of my everyday world. Not that it was very routine these days.

I walked up and down the wharf, peering at it from all angles. Two white plastic chairs sat facing the rear, a rusty metal table between them. The setting sun beamed on the deck. A pot of plastic geraniums brought a spot of color. A pickle-jar lid doing duty as an ashtray was full of cigarette butts. I imagined sharing a margarita with Zac in these chairs, minus the smokes, while the boat stood anchored in some quiet cove. We might cook seafood bisque or paella together in the tiny kitchen, moving in harmony with each other like Jackie and Natalia did. And then, with any luck, move on to more amorous activities.

I stopped, peering at the back of the boat. A scrap of red was flapping in the breeze. The same shade of red as Elise's scarf. I knocked at a small gate in the boat's railing and called out, "Hello?" When no one emerged, I opened the gate and stepped onto the deck surrounding the living quarters. I had to see the cloth, see if it was Elise's. The boat rocked with a gentle motion on the water as I ran to the back. But the red cloth was only a cleaning rag. I had a strong sense something was wrong.

This was crazy. I was acting like an obsessed person. A couple of minutes ago, I was enchanted with the houseboat and my fantasy about a life with Zac. Now I had a bad feeling about this boat I couldn't shake. I put my nose to the nearest window and peered through filmy glass. A small lamp on a desk lit the corner of a living room that opened to a narrow kitchen. Cushions covered in turquoise and violet tried to brighten a beige futon couch. One door opened on a bathroom and another on a room where I could see the corner of a bed, a woven yellow covering dragging on the sisal floor. I was turning away when I saw Elise's *furoshiki*, or a piece of cloth that looked a lot like it, in a corner of the kitchen. Oh my God.

If she was in there, I had to get her out. I pounded on the door. I yelled, "Elise! *Gaijin*!" No answer. I wiped the pane with my sleeve. I couldn't see through it. I tried the handle of the back entrance. The door rattled but didn't give up its locked status. I moved back along the side of the boat toward the gate, but the curtains on those windows were drawn.

The pattern on the red cloth looked exactly like Elise's *furoshiki*. I had to find out if she was in there. I could call Natalia, but she never picked up her phone. Anybody else at the police department wouldn't believe me. A bit of red cloth in a houseboat? They'd just laugh. I rattled the flimsy door handle again, barely believing what I was about to do. But what if she was in there? What if she needed me? I anchored my feet and pushed my shoulder hard against the old door.

It gave way with a rush, and I stumbled partway in, almost falling, hearing a crash as shards of pottery and dirt spilled onto the floor. I righted myself and stepped in around a ruined geranium pot. Then I heard a sound. A motor type of sound. Maybe it was a boat approaching on the river, in which case I was totally blown. I listened and realized it was a loud car or truck. And it was getting closer.

"Elise, come with me! Now!" I stepped back onto the deck. "Damn!" From around the back end of the fishing boat, I saw a truck rolling into the parking lot and decided it was time to clear out, scarf or no scarf. Elise or no Elise. I did not plan to get caught indoors anywhere with a stranger again. I'd get the cops to help this time. Hoping the fishing boat would shield me from sight long enough, I ran down the deck and leapt onto the dock. I sprinted away from water's edge, glad for my running shoes and legs that could run.

Where East Street curved northward, I slowed, looked back for a moment. An eerie chill not due to the suddenly biting wind tiptoed its way through me. A tall man stood at the open gate and shouted in my direction. A man with bulging eyes. Dark skin. A lean, athletic body.

A body very much like the one I'd last seen with its lifeless eyes staring as if at the memory of its killer.

CHAPTER SIXTEEN

Not believing in ghosts, I ran on, rounding the bend, slowing as I thought. What was Jamal's brother doing here? Was that Thomas MacDonald's houseboat? If it was Elise's scarf I saw, how was he connected to her? I recognized him. If he recognized me, I was in even deeper trouble.

Clouds blew over the last edge of the setting sun. I heard the train from Boston clack its way northward through the other side of town. The dusk shadows misrepresented the depth of things like curbs and root-buckled pavement, so I shifted from the sidewalk to the edge of the street, continuing my musings. What if Thomas reported the broken window? If he recognized me, I could be in some legal trouble. I swore. Then swore even louder as I stepped into a hole in the roadway. Pain stabbed my left ankle. I fell hard on my knees.

I pulled myself up and sat on the curb, feeling my ankle. It hurt. So did my knees. My hands were scraped from hitting the pavement. The wind blew cold on my sweat-soaked shirt.

"Uh-oh." I heard the truck engine approaching. I tried to get up but couldn't put weight on the ankle and sat down again. Thomas pulled up across the road, put on emergency blinkers, and got out, slamming the door.

"So that was you! What were you doing on my boat? You forced my door, wrecked my plant." He crossed the street and stood looking down at me, hands on his hips. "What do you think you were doing?"

I thought I could see steam rising from his ears. I reflected on how very screwed I was as I massaged my ankle. Trespassing was certain to be a criminal offense, as was breaking private property. I didn't feel particularly safe around this furious man, either.

I looked up and said, "Listen, buddy. I've been threatened and attacked. My friend Elise Chase is missing, and I'm trying to find her, damn it. Do you know her?" I waited, sitting up as tall as I could on the stupid curb.

Thomas looked around, back at me, then at the keys in his right hand. He tapped them against his thigh.

"Why did you push in my door?" His tone was calmer now, deep and resonant. Just like Jamal's. He stared into my eyes.

"Listen, I'll pay for whatever it costs to fix it. I'm sorry. You have to tell me, though. Do you know Elise?" I couldn't quite believe how cool I sounded. I didn't feel cool, other than core body temperature. Which was dropping.

His eyes shifted away from mine. "Maybe a friend of mine knows her."

"Look. I can't find her. She's in danger, from herself if not from others. I saw her trademark scarf in your kitchen."

Thomas laughed. "Galley, girlfriend. Never spent much time on boats, have you?"

His deep laugh was exactly like Jamal's, bringing on the same rush of attraction I'd had with my student, illicit though it had been. I shook my head. "Yeah, no boats." I allowed myself a small smile "And I don't care what you call it. But I need to find my friend. And I think when I do, we might find out more about Jamal's—I mean, William's—death."

Thomas frowned. He opened his mouth to speak then swore.

Red flashing lights pulled up. I swore, too, as the cruiser headlights bore down on us.

"Are you going to report me?" I asked in my fastest, lowest voice. "For breaking your door?"

His right leg started to jitter, fast. He gave his head the slightest of shakes as a young uniformed officer walked toward us.

I looked around Zac's apartment. Lit candles decorated almost every horizontal surface. The air held promise of peppers, garlic, fish.

"So Thomas didn't bust you to the police," Zac said, his back to me as he stirred a pot on the stove." Why not, do you think?"

I adjusted the ice pack on my ankle as I watched him put the finishing touches on the meal. Sitting on one of the high kitchen stools with my wrapped and now iced foot on another, I sipped the Cabernet in my glass.

"He seemed like he might have had something to hide. He was really nervous when the flashing red lights approached, for sure."

"He could have nailed you on trespassing and trying to break in."

I nodded and sipped some more. "Boy, don't I know. I was sweating bullets. Thomas seemed worried he was being busted for something himself. I wonder what. And then all the cop wanted was to have him move his truck. From the curve on East Street."

"Yeah. People come too fast around there, and it's not very wide." Zac faced me and gestured with a wooden spoon. "So did you talk any more with him? With Thomas?"

"He said a friend of his knows Elise. What friend?" I stared at the wine in my glass, swirling it against the spherical bowl, seeing the red in the boat's kitchen. Galley.

"What happened with the scarf and all?"

"I had to abandon it when I heard the truck. I called Natalia before I came over here—she can take it from there." I was tired of talking about my stressed-out life. "So what's the occasion? My birthday's in November, you know."

"Just a nice dinner for my sweetheart. Nothing wrong with that, right?"

I assured him that any time he wanted to invite me for dinner, I would not complain.

"Okay, lady. *À table*," he announced with a bow and a flourish. "Soup's on."

He helped me move to a chair at the table. The tie-dyed West African tablecloth I'd given him covered the round table, centered with a cluster of so many red carnations they threatened to spill out of the pewter pot that held them. Zac positioned my injured foot on a pillow-topped chair. He served me a plate of aromatic seafood and vegetables in sauce on a bed of rice, kissing me on the forehead after delivering it to my place, followed by a wooden bowl filled with salad greens that glistened with olive oil topped with morsels of cherry tomatoes, pears, and pecans.

"Here's to us," he proposed, lifting his glass. "And to no more accidents."

I lifted my glass in return, nodded, and sipped. We ate in silence for a few minutes. The food was hot, delicious, and spicy. Perfect for a night like this.

"You're way too good to me, you know?" I savored a bite. "And this is good, too."

"I'm not too good to you. You deserve good. Just like my mother did." His smile faded. "Except she didn't get it."

"Oh? You've never really talked about your parents before. Only that your father died when you were young."

Zac fixed his eyes on his wine for a moment then took a long drink of it. "He did. When I was ten. But not before he beat my mother, disappeared for a couple of years, then came back to beat her some more."

"That must have been terrible for you." I reached out to cover his hand with mine. My childhood seemed idyllic in comparison. I wondered what else I didn't know about Zac. "How did he die?"

He took another bite then set his fork down.

"I came home from school one afternoon. My parents were arguing at the top of the stairs. My mother's face was bloody, and one arm hung down limp. Dad was flushed, and his breath smelled of alcohol. He had Mama pinned to the wall. There was a hole in the plaster right next to her head. He was shouting in *Kreyòl*. I ran up the stairs, pushed between them. I was terrified by Dad's rage. But I couldn't stand that he was hurting Mama." Zac looked at me. "I shoved him away from her. He fell backward down the steps. All the way."

I sat in silence. I imagined the pain of the little boy and his determination to come to her defense.

"That's how he died." Zac met my eyes. "We told the police it was an accident. They believed us. And it was. Sort of." He exhaled. "He was bad, *bebé*."

I nodded as if in slow motion. "And your mom?"

"It took her a while, but she came through it. She got her life back. Her self esteem. You'll meet her one of these days. We'll take the train to Brooklyn. Show you my neighborhood. Eat some real cooking." He nodded to himself. "Mama taught me to *fe-manje*. To cook. With my Gran's recipes."

Learning that my boyfriend, my serious love interest, killed his father chilled me. Then I thought about the boy pushed to such an extreme by abuse from his own father.

It must have been horrible for him.

My gut roiled. And now he was talking in a totally normal way about taking me to see his mother and his old haunts. I tried to get back to the present.

"Who's Gran?"

"My grandmother. Speaking of cooking, you didn't eat anything."

I stared at my plate. "It was delicious. I'm full."

"Right." Zac rose and puttered about the kitchen as if nothing had happened. He cleared plates, ground decaf beans and brewed a pot, drew out two snifters and a bottle of cognac and set them on a low table in front of the couch. He inserted a CD of Yo Yo Ma playing tango music into the Bose then lit the gas fireplace, gazing at the flames behind glass before returning to the kitchen. I watched him, amazed.

Sure, he'd had a couple of decades to process and live with what he had done, whereas I'd had ten minutes.

"If you weren't injured, I would dance with you," he said. As I leaned on him to hobble to the couch, he added in a whisper, "We can dance later. In bed."

We sat nestled together, watching the fire. The storm that had started to blow in at dusk now beat rain on the tiny deck off the living room. I began to relax, with the impact of Zac's news receding into the warm buffer of cognac and the feel of his arm around me. He was a kid, after all, protecting his mother. It surely wasn't the kind of thing he would ever do again.

As if reading my mind, he said, "So now you know something about me." He reached into his pocket with his other hand, and a nervous tension radiated outward.

"I guess. It must haunt you. Now I know why you're so overprotective."

His smile disappeared. He removed his arm from my shoulders and his hand from his pocket. He clasped his hands and stared at the fire.

The air in the room felt suddenly heavy. Leave it to me to be a mood-breaker.

CHAPTER SEVENTEEN

swore at the water of the river, black and swollen from the night's storm. The wooden bench I sat on wasn't getting any softer. I swore at my sore ankle, too, even though it was much better than last night. Where was Elise?

She had left me an urgent message that morning. Meet her at the Riverwalk at 4:00 p.m. I hadn't actually talked to her—I'd been lounging in bed with Zac—but hearing her voice had reassured me.

Clouds scudded past the sun's disk, plunging me alternately into cold shadow and brilliant sun. The days were getting longer, but air temperatures weren't increasing at the same rate. I pulled my sweater tighter.

Zac had wanted to spend the whole day together. I'd told him I needed to see Elise alone. Mostly I'd just wanted to be by myself.

Visions of him pushing his father down the stairs haunted me, even if they didn't bother him.

I wondered if I should be nervous. Maybe, but this was out in the open, right downtown, in fact. What could be problematic about talking to an old friend on a bench overlooking the river? I checked the time on my cell. 4:20. My students would be gone by now if I were this late to class. I pressed Elise's number on my phone and listened to it ring. When her voicemail kicked in, I disconnected.

I stood and hobbled up and down the brick walk bordering the water. Melting snow and the last rain made it look angry, with tree debris and beige puffs of foam surfing the eddies. The water level was almost up to the basements of new condos that had replaced a burned and demolished antique building. Oh. Two old buildings a half mile apart near the river burning down in one year. Coincidence?

My phone beeped. I opened it and stared at the new text message:

We will find each other again at the boat shop. GJ

I frowned and shook my head. Was it from Elise? GJ could be *gaijin*. Although the phrasing was kind of odd. Anyway, it had to be somebody who knew my number. If it wasn't Elise, somebody was jerking me around. Without question, that was Elise's voice earlier, asking me to meet her here. Now this. I checked the number where the text originated. It wasn't one I recognized and had the 617 prefix marking the Boston area.

Should I go to the boat shop, or what was left of it? Zac would be upset with me if I went alone and got hurt. I'd be upset with myself, for that matter. I was not inclined to ask him for help right now, though. I could call Natalia. Or Ralph. Yes. Ralph. My unconflicted friend, my unconflicted friendship.

Ralph did not answer, despite my wishing him to—a technique that never was too effective. I left him a message about my plans then set off for the boat shop ruins. I made my way across the river on the new pedestrian bridge, wove past the Ashford Museum headquarters and the police station, and took the wooded path paralleling this section of the river, which began to be tidal here, closer to the sea, and looked as menacing as at the Riverwalk. The water raced up to boulders usually only revealed at low tide before crashing over them. I slipped on a muddy patch, and my injured ankle complained. I limped on along the path.

The path ended at Green Street, and I crossed over and continued on Water Street. At the far end of the river's curve, I could see the piles of boat shop ruins hulking on the site like slag heaps from a strip mine. Heavy sheets of plywood protected the burned end of the deli. I moved toward the property as if drawn by a force. My hands twitched, and my scalp was cold with nerves. I made my way down there at a tortoise pace. I leaned on a big tree on the other side of the narrow street and waited.

Elise did not make an appearance, but neither did anybody else other than a couple walking a big black dog. They smiled and passed me with brisk pumping of their arms. I checked the time on my phone, fuming. It was 5:15.

Samuel Pulcifer's car approached from the other direction, from the wharf end, and pulled into the deli's parking area. It shut off with a rattle. No one got out. I walked toward it and slowed my pace as I neared the car. Samuel himself sat at the wheel, facing the wreckage. Again I wondered where he was staying, what he was living on. I hadn't seen Philip in a while but imagined the two probably had not reconciled.

I approached the driver's side. Samuel did not notice me. When I tapped on the window, he started then cranked it down.

"Oh, it's you."

"Were you expecting someone else?"

"Well, yes. No, not really," he went on, taking his eyes from my gaze. "What are you doing here?" His voice was rusty, like an unused tool.

Should I tell him who I was looking for? Maybe not. "Just out for a walk."

"Where's your little dog?"

"He's at home." Samuel looked thinner than the last time, and I was struck by a thought. "In fact, I need to get back to feed him. How would you like to come for some soup? A sandwich?" The heck with Elise and her cryptic messages. I was tired, and my ankle hurt.

He looked up at me. "Why, that would be nice, Missy. You're sure it's no trouble?"

I assured him it was not. "Wulu loves company, too."

A small smile came onto his face. "I had a dog when I was younger. Much younger. Long time ago." His eyes drifted back to the ruins, and he shook his head. "Well, get in, then, young lady." He gestured toward the passenger door.

"Hey, do you mind if we swing by the parking lot next to the Riverwalk? I want to see if a friend of mine showed up late for a meeting we were supposed to have."

He nodded and drove into the center of town, but there was no sign of Elise at the appointed bench. I wasn't surprised.

Ten minutes later, I ushered Samuel into my condo and seated him at the table. He scratched Wulu's head. Odd. Wulu hadn't taken kindly to him on our encounter in the cemetery. I wondered what the difference was now. I poured beef kibble into Wulu's dish and a can of beef minestrone into a bowl. I set the soup to heat in the microwave. I remembered some sliced ham I had in the freezer and took it out, glad there was at least a loaf of bread and some cheese in the house.

I tried to get Samuel to talk as I busied myself in the kitchen, but he seemed more interested in trying to get the attention of Wulu, who was busy eating. I set a glass of water on the table and watched as Samuel drank it right down. He had seemed hungry but otherwise looked like he was taking care of himself in basic ways: he didn't smell, his hair was reasonably clean, and so were his clothes. So he probably wasn't sleeping under the bridge.

"Would you like something else to drink?"

"I haven't had tonic in some time."

"Oh, I'm afraid I'm out of soda." I smiled at his use of the local word for a soft drink of any variety. "And juice."

"Wouldn't have any whiskey, would you?"

I wondered if an old man down on his luck should be drinking whiskey at all but decided it wasn't my responsibility. And maybe I'd find out some stuff. I got out the Glenfiddich and poured us each a double shot.

Samuel's eyes showed pleasure when he saw the bottle.

"Water? Ice?" I asked.

"Oh, no. Wouldn't want to ruin a good thing, would we?"

We clinked glasses. I took a sip then finished fixing the sandwich, setting it and the aromatic bowl of minestrone in front of him. The whiskey was hot and tangy going down. Smelling the soup made me realize I was hungry, too. I heated a bowl for myself as well, then sat.

Samuel chewed a bite of sandwich with his front teeth, as if he were missing the back ones. Maybe he was. His glass was already half empty.

"So, Mr. Pulcifer, where are you living now?"

He narrowed his eyes at the soup and didn't answer, slurping a mouthful.

"I'm sure Phillip would give you a bed."

"Phillip!" He pounded on the table. Wulu ran to his bed in the corner and put his paws over his head. "He's a no-good. I wouldn't ask him," he shouted. "Ever."

"I could ask him for you."

He shook his head hard, twice. "Do not do that, young lady. I shall not take charity from him. Ever again." He emptied his glass and held it up for a refill.

Again?" Did something happen in the past?" I poured him another shot.

He slumped in his chair. He put a hand to his brow and looked exhausted. "Listen, Missy, I just want to eat my dinner and be gone."

I'd pushed him too far.

But this was a chance to learn, so I kept pushing. "I was looking for someone earlier when I ran into you at the boat shop. A friend. I wondered if maybe you'd seen her around. She's tall and thin. Short black hair."

He chewed another bite of sandwich and stared at me. "What's her name?"

"Elise. Elise Chase." I peered up from my soup, wanting to see his reaction. Hoping to see he knew something about her.

"Oh, her."

I waited, not wanting to jinx this.

"Why, she's Martin's friend, isn't she?"

"Martin?"

"Pascal. The Frenchie. He and I, we were doing a little business. Before the fire."

"Oh?" I remembered seeing the two men together on Zac's editing screen.

"That Elise girl, your friend. She and Martin do business, too."

"What kind of business, Mr. Pulcifer?"

"Oh hell, Missy, my name's Samuel. Use it." He finished his soup and leaned back in his chair, looking somewhat restored. "What did you ask me?"

"I wondered what kind of business Pascal Martin is in."

A one-sided smile and raised eyebrows were all I got in reply.

He sipped the rest of his whiskey then stood. "I best be going. Thank you for the tasty grub. I don't get much in the way of home cooking now." He laughed, a sound with bitter overtones. "Haven't in some years, save my own, and that's a fact."

"Are you all right to drive?" In offering the whiskey, I had ignored the fact he would have to drive away from here.

"Don't you worry, Missy."

I couldn't give up on trying to find out where he was staying. "Do you have far to go?"

He doffed an imaginary hat, gave a little bow, and shuffled through the doorway.

I stood at the front window and sipped the rest of my own whiskey as I watched him drive away.

Elise had not shown up at the boat shop. Had it even been her who'd sent the text message?

Samuel said Elise and Pascal did business together. Was Pascal her supplier? I made a mental note to ask Natalia. She could look into it.

"I don't like it," I said, turning toward Wulu, who turned his head and opened one eye. "Why do I not have a good feeling about this?"

Wulu snuffed and closed the eye.

Zac reached out his hand and laid it on my knee. I could feel his leg jittering next to mine. This wasn't the first time I had brought him to Quaker meeting with me, but I knew he wasn't very comfortable in the silence. Many people weren't. I'd asked him to come and now regretted it.

I could have used the peace to sort through some of the conflict raging in my brain.

Elise. Samuel. Pascal. Alexa. Above all, Jamal. What a mixed-up mess. On top of my regular life, which was not exactly empty. Classes started again tomorrow, and I was completely unprepared. I had to present that paper the weekend after I turned in grades in May. And then was slated to teach an intensive summer course.

I tried to breathe in an even, regular rhythm, reaching inward for my center. Behind closed eyes, I pictured the room as a circle holding all those sitting in it with me this morning. Including a jittery boyfriend. I envisioned the circle as surrounded and infused by light. This was my silent mantra, visual rather than verbal. I extended the circle of light outward in my mind, including the troubled—Elise, Samuel, Phillip—as well as the suspicious—Alexa, Pascal, even George.

At the end of the worship hour, Friends stood and held hands before doing introductions and announcements. I realized with a start I was glad to have Zac's smooth, strong hand in mine. Glad I'd invited him, after all. During the following fellowship time, people seemed happy to have him there, pleased he had accompanied me. Cynthia inquired in detail about his video-editing experience, and Harold talked photography with him. While several regular attenders always came alone, as I usually did, it felt good to be part of a couple in this setting.

"So, some lunch?" Zac asked as we walked to my truck.

The warm cozy feeling seemed to evaporate in an instant. "No, Zac. I have to get home. I have a ton of prep to do. School starts again tomorrow, you know."

His lips set tight, and he removed his arm from around my shoulders.

"Really. My first class is at nine tomorrow morning, and I'm not ready. It's been a wild week, you know."

He nodded in silence and climbed into the Toyota.

The silence continued all the way to his apartment. I turned off the engine and reached for his hand as he started to get out. "I'm so glad you came to Meeting with me. It means a lot, you know."

"It's a weekend, Lauren. I wanted to spend a little more time with you. But you decide to work instead. I'm not happy. What can I say?" He extricated his hand and slammed the truck door behind him.

I watched him let himself into the building. He did not turn around.

"Well, damn him," I muttered, driving away. "When he has to work, I'm supposed to put up with it, but when I have to, it's a world crisis." Even though I knew it wasn't only work making me want to spend the afternoon alone. It was the antsy, claustrophobic feeling that came over me when he got too close. When anybody got too close.

I spent much of the day, as promised, alone on schoolwork. I took a break to practice some karate kicks. I studied the art in Japan, and from time to time I put myself through a practice session just so I wouldn't forget how. The turned ankle wasn't quite ready to run on, but it held up as a base for my supporting leg as I swung a roundhouse kick toward the tall mirror in my entryway. I moved through forward kicks, roundhouse-punch combinations, and even some *kata*, the stylized fighting routines I had excelled at years before. It was a good way to get my blood moving and worked better than coffee to wake up from the stupor of sitting too long.

I checked the clock at 4:00, realizing the reason my stomach growled was that I'd skipped lunch. Wulu seemed happy to accompany me on a quick walk downtown to grab a sub. Chick's Roast Beef made them just how I liked them, a toasted roll stuffed with thin slices of tender rare beef, sharp cheddar, and horseradish sauce.

As I walked back up the hill toward home, I found myself thinking about Elise. I wondered yet again if this Pascal character had anything to do with her. As I downed the sub at my kitchen table, I gazed at the framed Malian batik on the wall. It portrayed a woman pounding millet in a thigh-high wooden mortar with a pestle the size of a baseball bat. She worked with a baby tied to her back.

It gave me an idea of some work I could do. I jumped in my truck and drove to Tigedigena. Maybe Fatoumata could tell me something about Pascal. That was where I saw him first, after all. It wouldn't take that long, and I still had the evening to finish class prep.

"*Iniché*!" I announced myself as I entered.

The proprietress came forward, wiping her hands on her apron, and welcomed me like a long-lost sister. We exchanged several rounds of ritual greetings, ending up with my protesting I wasn't hungry and didn't have time to eat, a concept I knew was essentially foreign to a Malian. I finally asked for an orange Fanta and sat at the bar.

"When I was here before, mama, I saw a man," I said. "A French man. Pascal Martin."

"He is a regular, but he hasn't been around for several days. That Pascal, he likes to flirt, you know?" She gave a hearty laugh.

"I hadn't noticed, really. Do you know where he lives?"

She shrugged.

"What does Pascal do for a living, do you know?

She wiped the bar with a rag. "You're asking a lot of questions, Professor."

"Fatoumata, a student of mine is dead, and my best friend is missing. I think Pascal is involved in some way. If you can help me…"

At that, she looked up. "That's terrible." Her eyes were full, and she blinked several times. "I lost my son when he was a student, too. My Ibrahim."

"I'm so sorry. They haven't found Jamal's murderer yet, and I'm trying to help. My students are scared, because it happened on campus."

"Jamal?" Her eyes now widened. "I have heard this name. From Pascal."

"Yes. And my friend, Elise, I think she was getting drugs from Pascal, and she has a serious addiction. She already almost died." I leaned over the counter and took

Fatoumata's hand. "Listen, can't you please tell me what you know about Pascal? It's important."

She focused intent eyes on me then nodded. "I will, but I should not. These men are dangerous, they threaten."

"Who are they?"

The Malian came around the bar and sat next to me. She looked around, even though the restaurant was empty. In a low voice, she said, "You are right. He sells drugs. He smuggles them, too. I have heard he is very cruel."

"He smuggles them?" This was more than I expected. I was even more scared for Elise than before.

She shook her head. "That is what they say. You be careful, my sister. He is poisonous," she added. "He hides behind his *djembe* like a horned viper."

I walked back to my office the long way after my first class, heading down to the basement hallway. I needed some peace and quiet. It was tough to get back into the swing of teaching. Students talking about their drinking week on the beach or their experience rebuilding a home for families made destitute by the recent earthquake seemed foreign, remote to the troubles right here in River City. I meandered through subterranean corridors, holding dusty archives of dead professors' research papers. I rounded a corner and stopped. A gray metal door was ajar several inches. Voices.

"You might should listen to me!"

A woman. Talking in an Ozark dialect to someone. A double modal—might should—plus lowered vowels: "might" sounding more like "mott." I held very still. I couldn't make out the other voice, but it was of a low frequency, so it was probably a man's.

"She saw me there. I didn't do it, but I can't afford to be a suspect. You going to keep quiet or not?" The female voice was strident.

The man's voice rose. "I'll do it for you."

"You could oughta remember you owe me considerable."

I decided it was time to back away, as quiet as an eavesdropping mouse. I retraced my steps, at a fast pace this time, then sat for a while in my office, wondering who the woman was. Why her voice sounded familiar. What she didn't want to be suspected of.

CHAPTER EIGHTEEN

That afternoon, after dashing back to my condo, I dressed for Jamal's memorial service in a black linen pantsuit, for respect, with a turquoise silk shell, because I look terrible in black, and pulled my hair back with two silver hair clips. I didn't think the service in the campus chapel was going to be easy. Alexa was scheduled to deliver the eulogy, and Ralph promised to keep me company, so all I had to do was show up.

I drove on Millsbury Road for five or ten minutes before I checked the truck's rearview mirror. A gray sedan was on my tail. The next time I looked, it was still there and was riding my rear bumper. I hated that. I slowed down as I wove through town, and it kept with me, even after I took the right onto Route 114 into Millsbury. Whether I sped up or slowed down didn't seem to matter, and the car didn't avail itself of the passing lane on Route 114. What was the driver thinking?

This started to seem odd. More than odd, dangerous. I took a moment to memorize the license plate number. Just in case I needed it.

When I turned onto the back road into the Agawam campus, the car sped up until it hugged my truck's rear like a Detroit lover.

"Hey! What the hell are you doing?" I yelled into my rearview mirror. The only thing I could make out was a man-shaped head.

The car backed off then sped up again, this time starting to come up on my left. The field to my right was marshy and deserted. If this clown thought he was going to force me off the road, he was seriously mistaken. I downshifted, pressed the gas pedal, and pushed the little red truck to its max, tearing around the final corner onto the Agawam property with tires squealing.

I'd never been so glad to see those brick buildings.

The gray car didn't follow me on the last turn, so I pulled over and stopped at the entrance to the faculty lot. I shook. Several minutes of deep breathing finally calmed me down enough to drive on and park. I saw Ralph waiting for me next to his black Jeep.

"Fourakis, you would not believe what happened to me," I said, climbing down out of the cab and straightening my jacket. "Some jerk followed me and tried to run me off the road. I barely made it. Hang on a minute, I need to write down the bit of the license plate number while I remember it." I knew I wouldn't forget the color of the car, but numbers were a different story.

As we crossed the lot onto the quad, Ralph asked for details and got them. I assured him I'd call the police right after the service. If I called now and waited for them, I would miss Jamal's memorial.

We joined several somber students and our colleague Ivan walking into the stone chapel. When I visited the chapel on a bright day last fall, light from the stained glass windows colored the wooden pews like a carnival scene. Today, the fog wrapped the world in gray, and the church's meager lighting tinged the interior with a dim yellow that barely illuminated the poster-sized picture of Jamal resting on an easel in the entryway. I paused in front of his image. I remembered his vitality. I heard his deep-voiced laugh, saw the intensity of his eyes, felt the passion he had for his studies.

The quiet struck me—no music welcomed us, which might disturb others. For me, silence was the best way to enter a place of worship. A sturdy woman in a simple black clerical robe stood near the entrance to the sanctuary. I shook hands and introduced myself as Jamal's professor. I omitted the part about finding his body.

After a young man, his cornrows ending in beaded braids, handed me a program at the door to the sanctuary, I paused at the back. I held up a black-gloved hand to halt Ralph behind me.

Thomas MacDonald sat bent over in the front pew on the left. Next to him, barely visible, was a tiny woman. Jamal's mother? Behind them sat a tall black woman with two young children in tow, and behind them was Tyrone seated with Brenda Watson from the Boys and Girls Club. Toward the back on the right sat Tashandra and Li, along with several other students from my class. In between were a dozen adults and students, many of them African-American. I passed my students, acknowledging them with a little wave, then took a seat in a middle pew on the right, with Ralph sliding in beside me.

"Think Alexa will show?" he whispered, leaning in close.

"She'd better." The program listed Alexa Kensington as one of the participants. I pointed. "I hope she can find something nice to say about him." A portion of the service was reserved for comments by friends and family that I had no intention of participating in. Someone in the back clicked what must have been a CD player, and the room filled with the rich, slow tones of Etta James singing "Swing Low, Sweet Chariot."

Whoever planned the service must have selected this music. Something Jamal would have wanted? He had been too young to have preplanned this kind of thing.

Programming your own funeral was the realm of grandparents living with recognition of their own impending deaths, not an athletic man in the prime of his life.

The minister strode down the center aisle of the chapel and took her place at the lectern. She welcomed us and began to conduct the service. When she spoke of Jamal being taken before his time, I heard a sob behind me that sounded like it might be from Tashandra. The minister otherwise didn't seem to have known Jamal, and her remarks were blessedly brief. She asked those present to stand and join her in singing "Amazing Grace."

Someone near the front, perhaps Thomas, sang in a hearty baritone, and the woman behind him kept tune in an equally rich voice. I loved singing in a group as a child at Girl Scout camp. The sound of voices joined in these moving words brought me near tears. My throat thickened, and I could not continue the song. Quakers didn't sing as part of worship—one of my only regrets about choosing Friends as my faith community.

After we sat again, the minister looked around. With a puzzled look, she called for Alexa Kensington to come up. No one responded. I turned to survey the gathered mourners. Alexa was not among them. With a start, my eyes froze on the back right corner of the room. Pascal Martin stood in the shadows. He wore a black shirt buttoned to the neck, black slacks, and a silvery blazer. Why was he here?

Ralph nudged me with his elbow. I stayed turned in my seat, my eyes locked on the dark figure. Ralph poked me again.

"Yo, Rousseau. Preacher wants ya."

The minister was looking at me, saying something. Everyone was looking at me. It sunk in. The minister wanted me, as Jamal's professor, to deliver the memorial in Alexa's stead. I shook my head to clear it.

Great. Just what I had not wanted to do. Had Alexa done this on purpose?

I stood and moved to the lectern. As I tried to gather my thoughts, I couldn't take my eyes off Pascal, who now saw me, as well.

Tashandra looked puzzled, then turned to see who I was gazing at. She turned back to the front, staring at me. The student's face showed terror. She grabbed Li's arm.

"Greetings, everyone. I didn't prepare these remarks, but I am honored to be called on to talk about Jamal." Thomas MacDonald furrowed his brow at the name then sank his head into his hands, elbows resting on his knees. I realized with surprise the tiny woman next to him was Virgie MacDonald, Elise's neighbor. We'd spoken only that one time, which seemed like months ago now. Well, MacDonald—she must be Thomas' relative in some way or other, and probably Jamal's, too.

I told them how much I admired my student, his energy, his devotion to the children he worked with and whose speech he studied, his passion for learning despite being a decade older than most of his fellow students. I spoke of his love for all things Japanese and got a laugh out of the group when I told his anecdote about being asked for his autograph while visiting the countryside there.

The door at the back opened. Alexa Kensington stood in silhouette for a moment then took a seat in the left rear pew.

"I know we'll all miss him," I finished. "I hope he is in peace, wherever he is."

As I sat, the minister invited anyone present to come forward with remembrances. Brenda and Tyrone rose and moved down the center aisle. She rested her hand on the boy's shoulder. They approached the microphone set up in front of the altar, and she bent it down to the level of his small body. His low, husky voice quieted the room like the sighting of a beautiful bird in flight.

"I want to remember my Big Brother, Jamal. He taught me a lot. We had a lot of fun, too. I miss him." Tyrone was looking at a spot on the floor. Brenda, eyes full, squeezed his shoulder. The boy looked up for the first time. His eyes opened wide.

I shifted to follow his gaze. Alexa.

Tyrone looked up, fast, at Brenda then back at Alexa. Brenda's face turned grim. She took his hand. They walked down the aisle and straight outside.

A movement to the rear of Alexa took my attention. Natalia stood behind her in the back aisle. It must be protocol for police to attend funerals. *Especially for victims of unsolved murder,* I guessed. She hadn't been there earlier, though—at least not that I had noticed.

I looked at the minister, who was concluding the ceremony and inviting those present to a small reception afterward. People rose and filed out. Thomas MacDonald helped Virgie to her feet. He bent over to hear something she said. He looked over at me and beckoned.

Ralph stood. "Looks like the little lady wants to see you."

I agreed as I stood but was pulled in several directions, as if I were tied to a medieval rack. My curiosity about Thomas and Virgie was intense. My need to confront Alexa felt dangerous and necessary. What I most wanted to do was catch up with Tyrone and talk to him about his fear of Alexa. Not to mention figuring out why Pascal was there and worrying about Tashandra. How was I going to triage this?

I held up my index finger, looking at Thomas, to indicate I'd be there in a minute. "Fourakis, snag Alexa, will you? Make sure she doesn't leave?"

"How?" Ralph squinted at me.

"I don't know, get her some punch, ask her when she's going to become dean, who knows?" I spoke fast. I started toward Pascal.

He glanced at me then slid through a side door.

"Damn," I muttered then switched to "Oh, good" as Natalia followed him. Tashandra also saw his exit and looked relieved. Realizing Tyrone and Brenda had enough of a head start that it would be hard to find them, I headed for the front row.

The rack had just gotten a bit more comfortable.

Virgie looked up at me with the same sparkle in her eyes as before and said she was glad to see me again. Thomas seemed surprised at our familiarity.

"Our William is gone, though." Virgie shook her head. "Such a brilliant boy. A very attentive nephew, too. Oh my, yes."

"I'm so sorry for your loss." I knelt so my eyes met hers. "When was the last time you saw him?"

"Why, it was Palm Sunday, I do believe. Yes, he fetched me for church. Sat with me through the service."

Thomas mumbled something about wondering why a so-called Muslim would go to a Baptist service.

"Now don't you be mean, Thomas." She tapped his arm with an arthritic finger. "William was a religious boy. I don't think he ever really left the church behind, just because he wanted to be called Jamal."

Thomas' expression was stern, but he kept his peace.

We three, the last in the chapel, made our way into the adjoining hall. Most of those present at the service remained, talking in small groups, sipping punch, and munching crackers and cookies. I wondered who arranged the modest spread then decided it was probably Virgie herself. The two children were playing tag around the periphery of the adults. Ralph had indeed cornered Alexa and stood engaged in an apparently vigorous discussion with her. In a corner.

Confronting Alexa wasn't going to be easy. Putting it off, I filled a little plate with cheese and crackers and drifted over to Li and Tashandra, who stood talking in low tones. I greeted them, raising my eyebrows at Tashandra.

"Dr. Rousseau." She gave a quick look around the room. "That was him! The dude I sketched for you, for the police." Her voice was low and urgent.

"I know, Tashandra. I saw him. Did he see you, do you think?"

She nodded, eyes wide. "This is scary. I came to, like, honor Jamal, you know? I didn't think..."

I laid my hand on the side of the girl's arm. "Don't worry. Officer Flores was here."

"She was?" She sounded astonished.

I assured her the officer was there and that she followed Pascal out of the chapel. "If there are any issues, I'm sure Officer Flores can handle them. It was good of you to come. Both of you."

"Professor, how come they haven't caught the guy who killed Jamal?" Li's eyes were full, and she fidgeted with the strap on her purse-sized backpack.

I said I didn't know but that I was sure the authorities were working on it. The two said they'd see me in class, grabbed a few more cookies, and left. I hoped my students had gained more reassurance than I actually felt. Was it only three weeks since Jamal's too-early death? Things seemed murkier than ever. Well, time for a little demurking. I headed for Ralph's corner.

"Hi, Alexa."

She acknowledged me but did not seem particularly pleased to see me.

Ralph gave me a small smile. "We were just talking some politics. Right, Alexa?"

The look of exasperation on her usually unflappable face could have defined the word. "If you think your candidate would have done a better job than Mr. Brown, perhaps you might should've actually worked on her campaign."

Ralph looked amused, as always. "And how do you know I didn't?"

Meanwhile, my ears were alert. This was what I wanted, to get Alexa riled up. Might as well dive right in. "So, I thought you were supposed to deliver the memorial message, Alexa? I didn't mind doing it, but I wasn't prepared at all."

Alexa, her expression fixed with tense lines, waved her hand in the air as if brushing me away. "I was tied up with something. You did fine." Her tone was impatient.

"Yes, but you don't think you owed it to the memory of one of the best students our department has ever had?"

"Look. I was in a last-minute meeting with the dean." Her neck reddened. "Besides, I've seen better students. I've known more cooperative students. And I didn't know him from Adam's off ox! He's lucky he got any memorial at all."

Virgie, from her position near the punch bowl, looked sharply in our direction then marched over. "Listen, young lady." She pointed a finger at Alexa's face as she looked up at her. "I don't know who you are, but nobody speaks ill of the dead. Especially not of my nephew, William. And at his very service, of all places. You should be ashamed of yourself."

Sparks shot out of Alexa's eyes. With the corners of her mouth drawn down in disdain, she said, "Well." Then, as if some long-ago instilled manners overruled her apparent need to always be right, she blinked several times and said in a soft voice, "I apologize, ma'am. I was out of line. I am Alexa Kensington, chair of the department, by the way." She held out her hand.

Virgie gave Alexa a long, hard look. Then, clearly raised with the same politeness ethic, she shook hands and said, "Virgie MacDonald."

Natalia stuck her head through the doorway, bringing a wave of moist air. Her cheeks were flushed. All eyes in the room turned toward her. "Rousseau, come here, quick," she said in a short breathless spurt.

CHAPTER NINETEEN

Ralph followed me to the door. I looked back at the circle we left—Virgie, Alexa, Thomas—then back at Natalia. "What is it?" I asked her.

"Let's go. You, too." She waved Ralph out and shut the door behind us with a click. "Come on. Quick." Her voice was low and fierce.

"I was just getting Alexa to start talking," I protested.

Natalia held a finger to her lips with a dirt-smudged hand and motioned us to follow her. She wore a simple dark dress with a wool jacket, but the outfit and her footwear were utilitarian. She was clearly on duty.

We walked at a brisk clip around the back of the chapel on a cement path slick with the fog and spotted with moss. Watching my step instead of where I was going, I bumped into Natalia, who now stood with her hands on her hips.

"Oops. Sorry." Then I saw why she stopped. On the dirty mulch between two large shrubs sat Pascal Martin. One leg stretched out in front of him, and the other was bent at the knee. He glowered up at us with eyes narrowed and a look on his face like he just put something disgusting in his mouth.

"This is ridiculous. She..." he spat, pointing at Natalia, "... will not help me. She chases me, I break my ankle, and she leaves me here." He extended both arms, palms up in supplication, then winced. "I am in pain."

Natalia raised her eyebrows and turned to me and Ralph. "I need you guys to watch him, make sure he stays here. I have to get the squad car and direct my partner."

"You don't want to call campus security?" Ralph asked.

"No, Professor, I don't." At my look of surprise, Natalia continued. "Believe, me, I have my reasons, but I don't have time to explain. Just keep this one here for me. He won't hurt you." She turned to go. "I don't think." She walked off, fast, with her phone pressed to her ear.

I exchanged a look with Ralph, who cocked his head and folded his arms.

"Professor Rousseau, is it? I am Pascal Martin. I heard your excellent words at the service." The man's face transformed into a genial mask, although his eyes remained wary. "Surely you two can help me up and out of this dirt? I have done nothing wrong. I have not been charged." His smile reverted to a scowl as he looked back to where Natalia vanished around the wall of green.

"Officer Flores asked us to keep you here, we're keeping you here," Ralph said. "Questions are for later."

I wrapped my arms around myself. I didn't think to grab my coat when Natalia summoned us, and the black suit was not of a warm winter weave. I realized Pascal was staring at me.

"We have met before, no?"

I nodded, feeling grim.

"At Tigedigena, wasn't it?"

I knew he was not actually realizing this for the first time and wondered why the pretense.

Ralph stared down at him. "Did I have you in a class or something, man? You look familiar."

Pascal reached out for his injured ankle and examined it, not meeting Ralph's eyes. "No. No, I don't study here."

"But you've been around campus," I said.

"Oh, no, that is not possible." Pascal shook his head. "No, no. Why do you say that?" He shifted his eyes from his ankle to the path, gazing along its length.

"Mr. Martin, how well did you know Jamal Carter?" This was a primo opportunity, and I didn't want to waste it.

"Oh, I barely—"

"You came to his memorial service. Why?"

Pascal looked from Ralph to me and back. He moved on the ground, trying to get to his knees, but the apparent pain from his ankle and foot stopped him.

Behind the chapel was a large garden of mature rhododendrons, full budded but not yet in bloom. Student lovers in the spring particularly liked to frequent the path that wove through them.

I had walked it with Zac last summer, when our love had been fresh and uncomplicated.

"Are you the police, too?" Pascal asked. "Why are you asking me these questions?"

"We're teachers, Martin." Ralph stared at him. "But a man died only yards away from here. Jamal was a good guy." He shook his head. "It's not right. So we're trying to help. And I know I've seen you around."

Speaking of police. I hadn't called them about the gray car following me. Or told Natalia.

Ralph and I sat in the faculty pub an hour later. My second pint of beer was nearly gone. A plate formerly holding a double serving of Buffalo wings now sported only a leaf of wilted lettuce and a small bowl of pale sauce streaked with red.

"So she took him in. I didn't hear why." Ralph traced his finger over the top of the glass.

I stared at the television over the bar. Impossibly tall basketball players raced up and down the court. What I really saw were the blue lights flashing on the other side of the chapel, the closest the patrol car could get. Natalia and her partner, a gruff older man in uniform, handcuffing Pascal and ushering him away. Pascal cursing at me in French, sounding suddenly dangerous and furious. Fatoumata's horned viper. I shook my head and looked at Ralph.

"I didn't hear it, either. I'm glad Tashandra was already gone. She didn't need to see that. She felt frightened enough as it was, seeing him there."

He relaxed back in the booth across from me and stretched one leg into the aisle. As the waitress passed by, he hailed her and ordered a mushroom burger with cheese.

I patted my stomach and shook my head. "I'm all set," I said to the waitress, who stalked off, apparently deprived of an adequate order and, therefore, an adequate tip.

"No, really, why would Natalia be busting this Pascal character?" Ralph asked. "Any ideas?"

"I didn't tell you about Saturday, did I?"

When he shook his head, I related the details of meeting Samuel instead of Elise at the boat shop and giving him lunch. "He said Pascal was in business with him before the fire and that Elise did business with Pascal, too."

Ralph nodded, eyes on the TV.

"So all I can think of is, Pascal is a drug supplier. That he's Elise's supplier. What the connection with Samuel is, I don't know."

"What if he was storing stuff at the boat shop?"

"Yeah. That could have given Mr. Pulcifer some income, which he needed. And the place was huge. Lots of hiding places. Fourakis, you're brilliant."

Ralph nodded, with only the quickest of winks.

"That ties together a lot." I leaned forward. "But the fire—it must have wiped out Pascal's stash of stash, so to speak."

"Maybe he thought the local police were on to him. Even the Feds. Maybe he set the fire."

"But they said it was electrical, old wiring."

"Rousseau, did your momma never tell you not to believe the first thing you heard?"

"Yeah, no. She didn't."

Ralph's food arrived. As he dug in with his usual enthusiasm for anything edible, I rested my chin on my hand and thought. So where was Elise now? Was Samuel staying at Pascal's, wherever that was? Did Phillip know about the drugs, and was that partly the cause of the rift with his brother? And how in the world did all this involve Jamal?

I stood and told Ralph I had to get home.

He waved his napkin at me.

I dragged myself to the foggy parking lot, my legs leaden. Nervous, I kept to the lit path. It was warmer tonight, but the ominous memory of the night of Jamal's death haunted me. I did not look up at Alexa's window. I climbed into my truck. I did not check out the fir tree my headlights illuminated. I backed out and drove away.

CHAPTER TWENTY

I leaned over the counter at the Boys and Girls Club after class the next afternoon, trying to make Brenda Watson meet my eyes. "Brenda, listen to me." I looked around then lowered my voice. "I saw how scared Tyrone looked when he saw Alexa at Jamal's memorial service. I saw how fast you got him out of there."

She looked around, too, then said in a harsh whisper, "You don't know how things are around here, Professor."

"That's what I'm asking you. To tell me what goes on here," I pleaded. "And please call me Lauren. I'm only somebody who wants to help."

She sighed and checked the clock on the wall. "Meet me at Max's coffee shop down the street at five."

"In an hour, right?"

"No, wait. We need to talk in private." She wrinkled her eyebrows. "I know. The textile museum is open until six, and it's free. We can talk there. You know where it is?"

I nodded. "I'll meet you there at five, then, inside. And thank you, Brenda."

I stood in the parking lot and looked around. I realized I wasn't far from the chess club; Lawrence was right over the border from here. I never found out why Thomas seemed skittish around the police on Friday when he caught me at the houseboat. I had an hour to kill. *Carpe diem* seemed just about right.

But when I got to Knights and Kings, the chess club was closed up tight. No one answered the bell, and the lights were off inside. Odd. I thought it'd be teeming with school kids on a weekday afternoon in April. I stared at the entrance as if willing it to be busy and populated. Which wasn't really a successful approach.

In the lobby of the museum, I examined the large black-and-white photographs on the walls. Women from the 1800s sat at looms in tight quarters. Even in the grainy blowups, you could see how dimly lit the mill was and how backbreaking the work.

Brenda joined me in silence, and we moved into the museum itself, strolling past exhibits about wool and linen, shipping on the Merrimack River, and child labor protests.

In front of a picture of little boys made to work in the factories, I stopped and pointed. "Little boys at risk." I faced Brenda, folding my arms.

"Look, Lauren. I'm a single mom. I can't afford to lose my job. I have my daughter to protect."

"I'm trying to protect kids, too. Why was Tyrone so terrified to see Alexa?"

She examined the display, tapping her foot. "I don't know for sure. I tried to get him to talk about it in the car, but he wouldn't. He refused to. I've heard talk, though."

This was getting to be like pulling alligator teeth with a pair of tweezers. I waited.

"She likes to invite the kids out for an ice cream and a movie. One at a time. Only boys. They don't get treats too often, so they like to go. The first time." She met my eyes. "They're gone for a couple of hours."

"She's allowed to do that?" I was horrified.

"Well, yes. She's on the board. She's been a generous benefactor to the Club."

"Has she been CORI'd?"

"Uh, no. Board members aren't required to be."

"Great." I shook my head. "Are the kids all right when they come back? Do they seem nervous or anything? Have you had any complaints?"

"Hey, I'm only telling you what I see. Mostly they seem happy, some are quiet. I haven't gotten complaints, but I'm not there all the time."

"What about Tyrone?"

"Hmph. The second time she wanted to take Tyrone, Jamal insisted on going along, too. Dr. Kensington was mad about that, I'll tell you. She didn't want no Big Brother going with. They had a fight right there at the door. Uh-huh. And Jamal won it."

I remembered Jamal's reaction when he and the boys encountered Alexa on campus that day. "What do you think happened the first time she took Tyrone out? Has he ever talked about it?"

"I wasn't there when he got back. Jimmy, though, the guy who works the desk in the evening, he thought Tyrone looked nervous. Jimmy said Tyrone was really glad to climb in the van to go home."

"So this Jimmy also knows about Alexa's trips with the kids?"

Brenda nodded.

"What's his last name?"

"No way I'm telling you." She shook her head. "Oh, man. He needs his job more than I do. He supports a whole family, plus his mom."

"Sounds to me like Alexa shouldn't be allowed near children. At all."

She looked me in the eye for a moment then nodded. "Fine. It's Dever. Jimmy Dever. Irish."

"Thank you. We need to do something about this. Right?"

"YOU need to do something about this. Don't you see I can't?" She grasped my arm. "But who can you go to? She's on the Board of Directors."

"I'll call the police."

"I'll lose my job! Jimmy will, too. You can't do that." She looked panic-stricken.

I thought for a moment, staring at a display of union organizers who worked to end child labor. "I know who I can go to."

CHAPTER TWENTY-ONE

Tashandra and Li hung around after class the next morning until they were alone with me. I waited with my hands on my briefcase.

"Professor Rousseau," Tashandra said. "What if the guy who was at Jamal's thing Monday, you know, comes around again? What if he recognized me, and, like, threatens ME this time?" Her mouth trembled, and she clutched the strap of her book bag with whitened knuckles.

I smiled. "I don't think you have to worry, Tashandra. He was arrested after the service."

Tashandra's eyes widened, and Li pumped her fist. "Yes!"

"Why?" Tashandra asked.

"I don't know, but I do know Officer Flores chased him, caught him, and took him in. If I get any more information, I'll let you know."

Tashandra nodded several times. Her face shone.

I stopped in my office to drop off my class materials. The bonsai showed tiny buds and looked healthy despite the recent cold and neglect. I promised it more attention soon. I straightened my tweed blazer and smoothed the matching brown skirt.

Several minutes later, I sat in the fourth-floor office of the dean of the school. Situated at a corner of the Arts and Sciences building right next to Alexa's office, it featured expensive-looking cherry furniture, including a large desk. Unlike mine, it was bare of stacks of books and papers. Expansive windows overlooked the quad. Several framed Egyptian papyrus paintings as well as photographs of Athens and Rome decorated the walls, reminding me of Dean Irwin's credentials as a classics scholar. A recumbent bicycle leaning against one wall was the only quirky touch.

"Thanks for seeing me on short notice, Dean Irwin." I made the appointment before class that morning, certain I could gain an ally by convincing the dean that Alexa was a danger.

I had only met him once before, but he had seemed a man of reason and civility, if a bit cool.

"No problem, Dr. Rousseau. What can I help you with?" The dean was a tall, thin man with neatly trimmed white hair and beard, reading glasses perched on his nose. He wore a maroon v-neck sweater over his shirt and tie and looked every inch the competent academic administrator. He folded his hands on the desk and waited.

"You were so helpful to me last year. I appreciated your support in my tenure application. I need some help again." I shifted in my chair. "It's confidential."

He tilted his head to the side as he watched me.

"I'm afraid I have some concerns about Alexa Kensington."

"Oh?" His right eyebrow rose.

"I don't really know where to turn." I examined my silver and turquoise ring for a moment. Should I bring up the business with Jamal and his thesis? Or go directly to Tyrone's reaction and what I discovered from Brenda?

When he cleared his throat, I took a deep breath and rushed on. "Dr. Kensington serves on the board of directors at the Boys and Girls Club in Millsbury. I have reason to believe she was abusing children there."

Dean Irwin leaned forward in his fancy office chair, frowning and looking amused at the same time. "Surely serving on a board of directors does not require one also be a pedophile." His tone was acerbic. "I myself serve on several boards."

Uh-oh. This wasn't going well. I forged ahead anyway. "There's more." I related Tyrone's reaction to Alexa at the memorial service. Explained who Jamal was, and how I saw him react on campus with Tyrone and Ricky when they encountered Alexa. Recounted Brenda's suspicions, without naming her or Jimmy.

Irwin listened without reacting. "Jamal Carter, the student who was found dead on campus. You were the one who found him, correct?"

I nodded.

"Do you think his death was related to this alleged abuse?"

"I'm not sure. When I read his thesis—he studied the speech of the kids at the Boys and Girls Club—he was critical of Alexa's interaction with the children. He laid out the case for child abuse. And I think she suspected he was on to her, because she canceled his fellowship for no reason."

"Perhaps you are not aware she required my signature on that cancellation. I supported her decision."

"Somebody broke into my house, too. Looking for the thesis, I think. And I saw Alexa that night right before I found the body." I had to convince him of the converging constellation of facts.

"Are you accusing Dr. Kensington of murder?" His voice rose in an intonation pattern consistent with incredulity.

I never should have come.

He thought I was nuts. He was going to protect Alexa.

"I don't know. I thought, well, somebody needs to confront her." I was going to give his rational self one last chance. "She shouldn't be alone with the children!"

Irwin rose. He paced to the window, hands in pockets, then turned to face me. "I suggest you keep your ill-formed opinions to yourself, Professor. And thank your lucky stars tenure is not revocable. At least, not under normal circumstances."

I also rose. I headed for the door. "Sir," I said, looking back at the man silhouetted in front of the window, "if one more murder happens on campus, one more child is hurt, don't forget I asked you for help. And you didn't give it."

I walked away as fast as I could while hoping I looked dignified until I gained the hallway then the women's restroom. I stood at the wide opaque window, breathing hard, feeling claustrophobic in the overheated air of the old building's antiquated heating system. I raised the window. The fog swirled around the tops of fir trees like a scene from a scary black-and-white movie. I breathed in the damp scent of the evergreens—chilly but refreshing compared to the stifled feeling I had after the fruitless, possibly counterproductive meeting. I wondered if Dean Irwin would warn Alexa.

"What do I do now?" I leaned my elbows on the sill and looked out. "Why has life gotten so complicated?"

"You seem to complicate your own life, Lauren."

I whirled at the sound of Alexa's voice. "What?"

How had she gotten in here so silently? Had she already been in the restroom?

She stood a yard away, smoothing an eyebrow in the mirror. She fixed her eyes on mine in the reflection. "Making false accusations could be problematic for your future here."

"Were you spying on my meeting with the dean?"

"You might should keep out of other people's business," she snarled.

"Excuse me." I started for the door. I did not need to get into this kind of discussion in the women's bathroom.

Alexa faced me and extended her arm to the stall wall, boxing me in. She looked down into my face. "I mean it, Rousseau. I had nothing to do with Jamal Carter's death, and I would never harm a little child. Never."

Her breath was warm and close, her trademark scent cloying. I wanted nothing more than to be away from it, from her.

"No answer?" Her carefully colored upper lip rose in a look of disgust, and her eyes narrowed. She moved closer to me. "Nobody stands in my way." She glanced past me through the window then smiled. "It's a long way down."

I tried to duck under her arm, but she lowered it. In her eyes, I saw only ambition and cold ruthlessness. "Alexa, let's get out of here. We can go somewhere and talk."

Two girls laughed outside the restroom door. In a flash, Alexa turned with head high and marched out of the facility. She almost knocked the students over on their way in. The girls stopped inside the room. One gave me a puzzled look.

I turned and closed the window. "Just getting a little fresh air," I said and headed for the door.

I checked the hallway—no Alexa in sight—and made for the stairs at the end of the hall, knowing she patronized elevators as an executive right. I took each step with deliberation, trying to slow my heart rate and engage my brain at the same time. At the landing between the third and fourth floors, I stopped, stunned by what had just happened. I sat on the bottom stair. The gray cement was cold and hard but also solid and reassuring compared to my near-airborne position a few minutes ago.

"She knew what I'd told Dean Irwin," I muttered to myself. "She had to have been listening. He must have alerted her." I cursed.

How could I work with Alexa now? She had threatened me. "Who's going to believe me, though? Who can I tell? Will Natalia even listen?" I whooshed breath out through my lips then took a deep breath in.

A door clanked shut below me. Footsteps clomped up in a hurry. I rose, looking around, heart thudding in my chest. Who was it? I couldn't go back up to the dean's floor. My hands numbed as I stood between Scylla and Charybidis.

Wait. I could always call for help. I tunneled in my bag for my cell phone. There it was. I flipped it open, pressing the On button. The descending tones of death sounded: Na-na-na, na-na-na. No battery power. I had forgotten to charge it last night.

The footsteps approached. I raised my head, clamped my bag under my arm, and started down, gripping the handrail. A bulky man, head down, came into view.

"Oh!" I mustered a weak smile. "Hi, Uncle George."

He looked up, halting. "Hello, Lauren. Getting some exercise, are we?" His tone was gruff and breathless. "My doctor tells me the same thing. 'Don't use a machine when you can use your body instead,' she says. Good advice," he puffed. "You know, elevators, cars. Machines."

"Um, right. Absolutely." I nodded. "Well, see you. Love to Louise." I waved and moved down the stairs, apparently out of danger. For now.

I had office hours scheduled from two to three. When students didn't drop in to discuss papers or grades, I often accomplished a lot of class prep or research. And when they did, well, that was part of teaching. Today, though, despite knowing I should go back to my office, I couldn't bear to. I headed for home. Once there, I plugged the cell phone into the charger and looked at the land line. I needed to call Natalia, but I was sick of leaving messages all the time. I also needed to get away from everything. I suited up for a run in a long-sleeved shirt and leggings.

"Come on, Wulu. Let's get some fresh air." Stuff kept happening, but I was determined not to let being threatened stop me. Wulu barked his agreement and ran to the leash hanging on the hook in the hall.

We ran along a road lined with tidy homes, tall trees, and patches of woods behind the yards. I had to favor my ankle a little but was relieved at how much better it was. I liked to be able to hear the birds and the traffic as I ran and didn't make a habit of tucking tiny headphones into my ears like other runners did. Branches were sprouting tiny buds, but it was too cold for much of any green, other than a few valiant points of tulips poking up and a small bed of snowdrops blooming.

At least the fog had cleared.

I worked my way up a long hill that eventually flattened into an area with several low apartment complexes mixed in with industrial buildings. I smelled fresh bread, and my stomach growled. Sure enough, the next building was labeled Orowheat Bakery. I was breathing hard when I heard a telephone ring. "What a loud phone. Somebody must have left a window open," I panted to Wulu. It was awfully cold for that, though. It was spring in name only.

The telephone kept ringing. I looked around as I ran. Leaves from last fall crowded the side of the road, damp and mushy like cereal soaked in milk too long.

"They should answer that," I said as the sound grew louder. Wulu pulled me to the side of the road. I looked down at the low leaf-covered berm and stopped. I stared. I leaned down and picked up a cell phone. A ringing cell phone. This did not happen in real life.

The phone kept ringing. Was this a prank? I wondered if I was being punked. Or if one of those cameras like on the old show my mom used to watch was hidden somewhere nearby. I searched the buttons until I found one matching the Send button on my own phone. I pressed it and said, "Hello?"

A muffled voice whispered, "I'm watching you."

CHAPTER TWENTY-TWO

The call disconnected. "What? Who—"No!" I pushed buttons, trying to reconnect, to redial, to find the caller who sounded familiar in the way participants in one's dream are familiar: known and yet not known. I looked around, feeling a chill. Was that message for me? Who would be watching me? Where were they?

When I finally found the Send button and pressed it to call back, no one answered. I stared at the phone, terror mixing with anger.

I looked at my surroundings again. I was on my regular route, right over the border into Millsbury, an area zoned for mixed business and residential. No one was out walking. An old van sped by then the street was empty again. I looked at the closest street sign. I wanted to be able to remember where I found the phone. Cranton Avenue. Like the city in Rhode Island, almost. I started running again. I carried the phone in my hand and pushed my pace to the point of barely being able to breathe. Wulu trailed behind me.

"Come on, doggy, move those little legs. We have to get home."

Wulu stopped and planted himself.

I cursed and looked behind me. Pulling on the leash had no effect. I took another look around and saw we were almost to the wharf, so almost back at the condo.

"Okay, Wu. We'll walk. But fast." A dark cloud blew over the sun. I wasn't wearing a windbreaker, and the sweat from the run chilled me.

As I rounded the corner to the wharf, it was my turn to stop. The houseboat was still there. Thomas' truck was parked in front. Damn.

I'd have preferred to go straight home, but I hadn't gotten a chance to talk with Thomas at the memorial service.

"Stay here, buddy," I told Wulu, tying his leash to a light pole at the edge of the parking lot. "I'll be right back." I laid the found phone on the ground next to him and walked with tentative steps toward the boat.

"Anybody there?" I called out from the wharf's edge. All the curtains on the houseboat were drawn. I opened the little gate in the railing and stepped aboard. "Hello? Thomas?"

I heard voices inside. They grew louder, moving into the room closest to me. As I remembered, that was the boat's kitchen. Galley. Thomas' voice shouted, but I couldn't make out the words. The other voice was also male and also sounded angry. Who would Thomas be fighting with here in Ashford? He didn't even live in town. Come to think of it, what was the houseboat doing moored here?

A crash resounded then silence took over.

I didn't know what to do. Should I try to see if someone was hurt? Or clear out of there? Undecided, I lingered at the edge of the boat. A door slammed. My eyes widened when Pascal emerged around the other end of the boat, stalking toward me with a slight limp, muttering to himself as he navigated the deck, looking down. Less stylish looking than before, he wore a denim work shirt and canvas pants frayed at the hems and dark with dirt at the knees.

I froze. It was too late to leave without being seen. I was in trouble.

Pascal lifted his head. "You! What are you doing here?" He strode forward and grasped my arm. His face was red, his brow creased in a furious expression. He squeezed my muscle so tight it hurt. He had large hands for such a slender man. "*On se retrouve*, eh?"

"Hello," I said, trying to sound casual. Trying to free my arm. "I was looking for Thomas. MacDonald. It's his boat. But I guess he's not here," I said in a bright tone I didn't feel. "Hey, could you let go of my arm? You're hurting me."

He smiled. "Oh, really? *Desolé*. Terribly sorry." He did not lessen his grip, and his eyes were a cold blue above the false smile, reminding me once again of Fatoumata's warning.

Wulu barked from the parking lot, loud for such a little dog. As Pascal looked sharply over at him, I managed to twist out of his hold. "Excuse me." I turned to go back through the gate.

"You get back here." He grabbed the back of my shirt with one hand, my upper arm with the other, and twisted me around to face the back of the boat. "We're going inside to have a talk." He marched me toward the stern, where the door was. His musky scent, mixed with the smell of cigarettes and salt water, was familiar.

"No, no, I have to go. That's my dog over there." My voice rose as I realized what an awful situation I was in. No one was around the wharf this early in the boating season. Wulu was alone. And I was going to be alone and out of sight with someone who probably just did considerable harm to Thomas. How much more stupid could I get? I couldn't let him take me. He wasn't a big guy. I might have a chance.

Taking a deep breath, I kicked back and down his shin with my right foot then rammed my elbow as hard as I could into his ribs. He yelled, and his grip loosened. Enough for me to tear away, turn, and race toward the wharf. His footsteps on the wooden planking thudded irregularly after me. As I left the boat, my toe caught at the edge. I cursed when one knee hit hard and my palms scraped the pavement of the parking lot. Was I going to be dragged back on the boat? I pulled myself up to my knees, wincing at the pressure on the now-bruised one, then heard a loud rattle approaching.

Samuel's black car clanked toward us through the parking lot. I didn't know if he was going to be my savior or Pascal's co-conspirator. I looked back at the boat. Pascal stood in the gate, his face livid, his hands on the railing. He stared at me, ignoring the car behind me. "You can stop sticking your nose into business that does not concern you. Our next meeting might not be so pleasant." He smiled again, making his eyes look even colder.

Samuel stopped next to me and climbed out. He spied Pascal and waved. "Hey, there, Frenchie."

Pascal shot him a look of disgust and disappeared around the corner of the boat.

That was good timing. Odd, though. As if Samuel knew Pascal would be on the houseboat. I wondered if he also knew I'd need a little help right then.

Samuel looked down at me. "Well, Missy. You don't look so great. Need a ride home?"

I nodded with a rush of relief. I accepted his hand up and pointed to Wulu. I held onto the car as Samuel shuffled his stooped way to the light post and fetched the dog. Wulu went readily with him, straining on the leash toward me.

The cell phone. "Wait a minute." Wulu barked at me while I retrieved the phone. I joined them in the car. The prospect of driving home never looked so good.

Samuel stayed quiet on the drive of a few blocks. As he pulled up in front of my condo, I thanked him. Figuring he knew everything that went on in town, I asked, "Do you know why Pascal would be on that houseboat?"

He shrugged.

"What about Thomas MacDonald? Do you know him, Samuel?"

The old man looked into my eyes. "Some things are best not talked about, young lady."

Chapter Twenty-Three

I closed and locked the door behind me. My legs tingled with fatigue and the aftermath of fear. Wulu ran to his dish, back to me, back to the dish, and looked up with expectation on his face.

"Just a minute, kiddo. Just give me a minute." Leaning against the door, I sank to the floor, knees up in front of me, groaning when my bruised and swollen knee bent too far for comfort. Wulu ran back, gave a little bark, and licked my hand. My world was exploding. My head was, too, and I sank it into my hands.

The phone rang. I wanted to reach for it. My ebbing adrenaline fought with being too exhausted to move. I needed to call Natalia, report the incident on the house boat, have her see if Thomas was all right. Coming up with the energy to do that seemed beyond me, though. I closed my eyes for just a second. Just a minute to let the throbbing in my knee ease up.

I awoke with a start. I was lying on the entryway rug. I was chilled through. And sore. The condo was dark. Sitting up, I peered at the clock in the kitchen. It was already eight o'clock. I eased to my feet and grabbed my thick indoor sweater from its hook in the hall. After tending to Wulu's food and putting tea water on, I poured a shot of brandy, took out a box of crackers, and sat by the phone.

Natalia wasn't going to be able to do anything for Thomas now. But she should know what I went through earlier. The encounters with the dean and with Alexa. Hearing the houseboat fight and being attacked by Pascal. Samuel's curious response to my questions. I dialed.

"Don't you ever pick up?" I said aloud but left a message in Natalia's voicemail box anyway. I wondered if I should call someone else at the police department as I drained the glass of warm, strong liquor, then noticed the red message light flashing on the phone. Right.

The phone had rung after I'd arrived home, before I'd passed out.

I munched a cracker while I listened to the message. It was Jackie, inviting me to dinner. Just what I needed, a hot meal cooked by somebody else and a sisterly ear.

Two hours ago, it would have been perfect. If I hadn't crashed on the floor. Now I'd missed out.

I dialed Jackie's number. I gave her a brief rundown on the houseboat fight. A couple of minutes later, I hung up, smiling. Jackie was coming over with dinner. And Natalia.

I'd changed into sweats and started setting the table by the time Jackie rang the doorbell.

I looked past her at the door. "No Natalia?"

"She thought she should check out the houseboat first. She'll be over as soon as she can get somebody to go down there." She gestured with the casserole she held in both hands. "Any chance I can come in?"

I stuck out my tongue then gave a grand bow. "Madame La Chef, enter."

"I figured you might need some food, first week of classes and all. Plus, Natalia had a couple things she wanted to run by you." All business, Jackie set the covered red dish in the oven, turning it on to warm, and took a plastic container and a white box out of her shoulder bag. "You have wine, I assume?"

I nodded. "What's on the menu?"

"Comfort food. Orzo with sun-dried tomatoes, Kalamata olives, and spicy chicken sausage. Salad with avocado, pear, and pecans. Chocolates. What more could a woman want?"

My sister, the perfect cook. Me, the dysfunctional one. I sank into a chair, stomach growling. "Can't think of a thing at this particular moment. Well, a few. Finding Elise. Finding Jamal's murderer. Returning to a life where I don't get attacked a couple of times a day."

Jackie turned from the counter, where she was opening a bottle of Smoking Loon merlot. "A couple of times? Lauren, are you all right?"

"I will be when I've had something to eat. I don't think I've eaten since a granola bar before class this morning. And two crackers." I reached for another one. After Jackie handed me a glass of wine, I said, "Probably not up to your standards. But it's all I have in the house."

Jackie sniffed, swirled, and sipped. "It'll do. Here's to your health."

We clinked glasses.

Natalia showed up twenty minutes later, looking somber. She held up her hand to forestall questions. "Let's sit down and eat before we get into anything."

We held hands around the table for a moment that I wished would last an hour. The feeling of hands touching in quiet, the space it gave my busy brain, the blessedness of letting Light join us—I craved all of it.

Several mouthfuls later, I looked at Natalia. "How was Thomas? I know I should have called for help for him as soon as I got home, but I passed out."

Natalia finished chewing. "We didn't see him anywhere, I'm afraid."

"Really? Was Pascal on the boat?"

She shook her head. "No sign of him."

"Damn." Falling asleep on the floor hadn't helped anybody.

"I wish we could have gone in and searched. But when we knock and nobody answers, and we can't see obvious signs of a problem, well, we have to leave it at that. You heard only the two voices?"

"Yes." I went on to tell Natalia about Pascal trying to force me onto the boat, too.

"Are you an idiot? You should stay away from that man." Natalia shook her head. "Do you know how dangerous he might be?"

"I realize that now. But what's he doing out, anyway? You took him in yesterday, right?"

"We did. We wanted to question him. But we couldn't hold him. We don't have any actual evidence against him. We're trying to keep an eye on him, but resources are stretched. We didn't know he was at the houseboat." She helped herself to salad as if to hide the chagrin on her face. "Do you have any idea how he knew Thomas? What he was doing there?"

"No, not really." I added that I first ran into Pascal right down the street from Thomas' chess club, though. "And speaking of the chess club, when I went by there yesterday afternoon, it was closed up tight. Odd. It's usually bustling with after-school stuff at that time of day."

"What were you doing there?"

"Oh." I took another sip of wine. "Well, I was in the area."

Natalia looked stern. And waited.

"I was waiting for Brenda. From the Boys and Girls Club."

She raised her eyebrows.

"You know, she was the one with little Tyrone at the memorial service," I said. "She was, ah, going to tell me what she knew about Alexa. Kensington."

Natalia folded her arms. "Did we or did we not have the discussion about leaving the police work to the police?"

"Look, I'm involved in this, too. Jackie knows, you both know—it was my student who died, my friend who disappeared, and my ass that's been threatened several times now. Even this morning." I slammed down my fork, remembering the look on Alexa's face. "I'm up to here with leaving it to the police."

I told Jackie and Natalia about my encounters with the dean and with Alexa and the details of the houseboat tangle with Pascal. "So if I'm trying to figure some stuff out, you can see why, right?"

Nodding, Natalia said, "I can. But you need to tell me what happens a little closer to *when* it happens. Like beforehand. All right? This is information we can use."

"Well, here's something maybe you can use. I just thought of it. The text message I got on my phone Saturday—it said, 'We will find each other again at the boat shop.' And this afternoon, Pascal said, in French, '*On se retrouve.*' Well, translate it literally and it comes out something like, 'We find each other again.' I didn't put it together then, but I do now. So it must have been Pascal pretending to be Elise trying to lure me over there. I wonder why."

"I'll look into that. Plus I'm going to need to see Jamal's thesis. Child abuse is a serious accusation. The people at the Boys and Girls Club should have reported it."

I told her I'd make her a copy. After they left, I dialed Zac's number. He didn't pick up, so I left a message. Asking him to call me. Wondering if he would come for dinner Friday night at seven.

Telling him I'd been doing some thinking.

I ended the message with a kiss and said I loved him.

Friday late afternoon was a lousy time to hold a department meeting. Especially the first Friday after break. Everybody was tired, nobody paid attention, and, to a one, people wanted to get started on their weekends, whether that meant pizza and a PG movie with the kids or a night out drinking and dancing. I arrived early and sat at the back of the room. I wanted to be able to make a fast getaway so I could buy the groceries I needed to make dinner for Zac. A whiteboard at the front was actually clean and ready for scribing, unlike the surfaces in my classrooms. They usually bore tracks of the badly erased primary colors used to teach subjects ranging from the physics of moving objects to Marxist feminism.

When Alexa strode into the room from a side door near the front, I slouched down in my seat behind Ivan, a tall, thin man who taught Kafka in the original German, among other topics. I wasn't interested in any attention from Alexa today. Or ever again, although I supposed I should at least listen. Ralph slid in beside me, smelling like he was getting a head start on the beer portion of the weekend.

"Hey, you could have invited me to the pub, too," I whispered.

Ralph tsk-tsked. "Would I go to a pub for lunch on a work day?" he said wide-eyed, leaning toward me.

I smiled and nodded. "Yup."

"What's this meeting about, anyway?"

I pointed to the whiteboard, where Alexa was printing an agenda. "The usual uninteresting, unimportant drivel. Why do I even show up?"

Alexa began speaking about committee assignments and the need for a marketing committee.

"Marketing? For God's sake, why?" Ralph kept his voice low but sounded disgusted. "This is a college, isn't it?"

"Fourakis? Did you want to join in the effort to increase our department's enrollments?" Alexa's voice was sharp.

Ralph closed his eyes for a moment then opened them and stood. "Dr. Kensington, we are members of a college faculty. We have research and teaching to do. Why in the name of Zeus would we want to be part of a marketing campaign? Doesn't the college engage an entire high-priced firm that does marketing for us?"

I applauded without making a sound, sinking even lower in my seat. Several other tenured teachers in the room clapped out loud, however, which started a wave of applause and cheers.

Ralph stayed on his feet and folded his arms, meeting Alexa's eyes. Her neck grew as red as her power suit. She fixed her hands on the table in front of her and stared at Ralph.

"You might should value your job a little more, Dr. Fourakis." She pronounced his title with scathing emphasis, her voice steely. "As you know, our department brings in relatively few grant dollars, compared to the sciences or the School of Engineering, for example."

Something niggled the back of my brain as I noted Alexa's lapse into the non-standard double modal. And the fact that, as usual, the college just wanted to bring in the big bucks.

"Dean Irwin has asked us all to bring more students into our classes, thereby increasing revenue to the school. Which can directly influence salary increases. Depending on who helps, of course." Her amplitude quieted with triumph on the last phrase, and her eyes narrowed.

I was disgusted at her barely veiled threat to Ralph. To us all.

"We'll see what the union has to say about that kind of threat, Madame Chair." Ralph sat to another groundswell of applause. Ivan leaned an arm back and extended his palm for a high-five of support.

"Nice job, Greek," I whispered.

Ralph shook his head, casting his eyes sideways at me and his eyebrows upward. "Yeah, see if it gets me anywhere. I hate this place."

The rest of the meeting passed without incident but didn't end until after 5:30. After giving Ralph a quick hug before he was engulfed by supportive faculty members waiting to thank him, I headed for home. I took only back roads and drove slowly, trying to wind down after the week.

I stopped at the Ashford Shellfish Company for a pound of marinated swordfish tips, plus a couple of portions of their heavenly chocolate cake. I wandered through the greengrocer on Market Street, thinking about how I could explain my complicated emotional state to Zac as I grabbed a chewy baguette, a bag of salad greens, a bottle of vinaigrette, and a box of pilaf mix. I also snagged two bunches of red carnations, my favorite. You can't go wrong with gorgeous cheap flowers that last several weeks. And they looked festive on a table. Wine I picked up from the store on Central Street, a Cabernet Sauvignon. Then I selected a Chardonnay, too. We had a lot to talk about. This would have to be dinner, the complexity of which was already going to tax my abilities. It was worth it for Zac. I wanted to do something nice for him, show him I did care for him. A lot.

I unloaded the supplies and took Wulu for a walk then gave him his dinner and fresh water. The flowers I arranged in a heavy vase, and the swordfish I threaded onto two long skewers, smelling its tangy marinade of olive oil, lemon juice, and Mediterranean herbs. I knew Zac liked any meal that originated in the ocean. I opened the white wine and poured a glass. Then I set the table, whistling, with rosy sunset light giving a delicious cast to the ivory tablecloth. I noticed the blinking voicemail light.

"It's me." Zac's voice sounded strained. "I'm not coming to dinner tonight. You've been holding me at arm's length since last week. It's not really working. I'm going to take a break from us for a while. I'll call you sometime." The message clicked off.

Staring at the phone in my hand, I sat. This was disastrous. He couldn't do that, not when I resolved to show him my feelings, to demonstrate in a tangible way I loved him. Finally.

I pressed the buttons for his number but then hung up right when it began to ring. My throat thickened and my eyes stung with tears. Wulu looked up from his food bowl. He trotted over to rub against my leg. I put my forehead into one hand and reached down to pet Wulu's head with the other.

"What am I going to do now?" I put my head onto both forearms on the table.

Sitting up, I took a deep breath. I pounded the table with a fist. "Damn him, anyway. If he's not patient enough to wait for me, maybe I don't need him, after all."

My cell phone rang on the kitchen counter. I checked the number—I wasn't ready to speak with Zac right now—then hurried to open it. It was Elise.

"*Gaijin*, you have to help me! He has me trapped here."

"Elise! Where are you? Who has you trapped?"

Her voice sounded feeble. "I'm in a storage place somewhere. Maybe it's in Millsbury. He's had me here for a while. He left, and I got to my phone for the first time. Come and get me, Lauren. I'm scared."

"Of course I will. Don't hang up the phone. I'll see if you can be traced."

"No! Don't call the police. He told me he'd kill me if they showed up. Just come and find me, *gaijin*. It's a long storage place. I'm at the end of one of the rows. I think."

"You don't know anything else about the place? Street? What it's near?"

"Sounds like a Rhode Island street or something. Bread baking." Elise cursed. "I think he's coming back. Bye," she whispered.

CHAPTER TWENTY-FOUR

The phone went silent. I looked at the display. Disconnected. I stared at the phone in my hand. So that's where Elise had been all this time. Not off in an addicted haze, but a prisoner. Of whom?

I had to help her. I started to dial Natalia's number, but I paused. Elise said she'd be in danger if police came. Said the man would kill her, whoever he was. But what if I couldn't get her out? Then we'd both be in danger with no one knowing where we were.

Natalia had seemed pretty firm about needing to be in charge, too.

I paced the length of the condo and back, gripping the phone as if it were directly connected to Elise. A lifeline. Well, whatever I decided to do, I was going out. I looked through the window at the now dark world outside. I changed into jeans and a turtleneck, a warm navy fleece sweatshirt, and my running shoes. I put my phone in my pocket and zipped it up.

I had to figure out where Elise was being kept. A storage place in Millsbury. I extracted the Yellow Pages from the kitchen drawer and took it back to my office, switching on the computer when I got there.

Three storage facilities were listed for Millsbury. I opened a browser and found the addresses on Google Maps. The third one, U-Stor-All, rang a faint bell in the back of my brain. As did the name of the street, Cranton Avenue. What else was it Elise said?" Bread baking." I closed my eyes to let the memory float to the surface.

I opened them wide and snapped my fingers. That was it.

When I'd been running with Wulu on Wednesday. Cranton Avenue, near where I'd picked up the cell phone from the road. Cranton, like the Rhode Island city, Cranston. And I'd seen an Orowheat bakery sign. I'd been right next to Elise and not known it.

U-Stor-All must be in one of the other industrial buildings. I knew where to go. Now to decide who to bring along. I wished I could call Zac. That choice was gone. The knowledge saddened me. I shook my head. No time for that now.

Five minutes of calling later, I'd come up empty. Ralph, Jackie, Natalia—all out, apparently enjoying their Friday nights.

I left Natalia a message with the bare bones of what I knew, what time it was, and what my plans were. And Elise's warning. I didn't dare just call the police emergency number. They might go blazing in there and get Elise killed.

I stuffed two granola bars and a bottle of water in my bag, tore off a chunk of French bread and stuffed it in my mouth, and slid the swordfish skewers into the fridge.

I sat in the truck for a few minutes before starting the engine. I closed my eyes and pictured Elise in a nimbus of light. That was as far as praying went for me. I didn't believe in a personification of the divine to whom I could make requests. What I had was a sense of Spirit and the power of holding someone in the light of the divine.

I took one more moment and held myself in the Light. My hands were sweaty in my gloves. I had no idea what would happen, and my only weapons were my brain and my runner's legs. I realized how much of my energy over the last few weeks had been absorbed in concern for my friend. It was time that came to an end, no matter how scared I was.

It was only three miles to the Millsbury border. The landscape shifted as I drove from comfortable semi-rural residential to lower-cost housing and rental units, with abandoned and vandalized buildings showing signs of the recent spate of foreclosures.

I turned into the bakery lot and parked behind a delivery truck. I didn't know where the person on the phone I found watched me from the last time I was here. I didn't want to be seen any earlier than necessary.

Even now the night air was fragrant with a warm yeasty aroma. A smell conjuring home and hearth. Completely at odds with my mission.

How in hell was I going to find Elise? And then get her out? My stomach churned. There was nothing to do but go forward. I moved with caution around the bakery truck and tried to stay in the shadows as I walked toward U-Stor-All. The facility consisted of several low buildings in parallel, all with the trademark orange and blue coloring. An office at the end of the first building was dark. A large sign on the wall warned of surveillance cameras. A picture of a fierce guard dog filled most of one corner. Another smaller sign read "Open 8 to 8" and gave a phone number. I wondered if I should call. Bad idea. Whoever was keeping Elise might have ties to the owner or manager.

Lights on tall posts illuminated the pavement between the buildings. At the end of the last structure, the light was out. Elise said something about the end of the building. I couldn't see any cars parked at the facility. I walked with quiet steps to the darkest area, to the last section of the building. A chain-link fence barricaded the end of the drive. Was Elise being kept captive in one of these containers with no light, no plumbing, and probably no air?

Each unit had a people-type door next to a garage-type door. I was relieved to see an air vent with fixed louvers in the smaller door. I peered into the door vent of the last unit, but the louvers were slanting up, and it was dark inside, anyway. I called "Elise" in a soft voice and knocked. I thought I heard a slight sound from inside. I put my ear to the cold metal of the vent and called again, louder. I knocked again. Something bumped inside. I hoped it was my friend and not a huge rat. I stepped back. My heart sank when I saw a padlock in a sliding latch at the side.

A motor sounded nearby. It came closer, from the direction of the street. I swore, and I looked around. Between the outer fence and the end of the building was a gap of about two feet. I pulled the dark hood of my sweatshirt up over my hair and squeezed in, my eyes almost level with the top of the fence.

I heard a clank, a car door closing, and footsteps. I breathed as quietly as I could. I willed a tickle in my nose to go away. I pressed my back into the masonry wall. The footsteps grew near. I saw light swaying back and forth and realized it came from a powerful flashlight. I thought my heartbeat had to be audible, it pounded so hard.

The steps came almost to my hiding place. What if I was discovered? How could I possibly talk my way out? The footfalls slowed as the light played around the area where I stood moments before. I watched with horror. The beam swung to within inches of my right foot.

A tinny musical refrain played the theme to *Scarface*. A ring tone.

"Yeah? No, I don't see nuttin'. Calma, brother. Here nobody." The voice was raspy and spoke with an accent common among Brazilian immigrants. Many lived on the North Shore, often working in construction and service jobs. "Yeah. Sure she still in der." Footsteps. Then the car receded back in the direction of the entrance.

I waited for the coast to clear and my heart to calm. I crept back around the corner. I peered again at the lock. I dug in my pocket for my phone. Opening it, I held the light up to the padlock. It was not locked.

Number 17-F was printed above the door. A parade of identical fronts extended down to the other end of the building.

I looked around. Seeing no one, I pocketed the phone, lifted the lock out. As I slid back the bolt, I dropped the padlock. I left it on the ground. Somebody could come back any minute. I eased the door open. My hand found the light switch, but I thought the better of turning it on. My eyes would adjust.

"Elise?" I whispered. "Are you here?"

A whispered *"Gaijin"* came from the darkness to my left. I moved toward the voice then hit an obstacle at knee level. I fell forward, sprawling on a rough plastic surface. I sat up. I felt around.

I had landed on several bulky bale-shaped packages wrapped in a kind of fibrous plastic.

Elise called again. I opened my phone and cast the light around. She sat against the nearest wall. Bruises swelled her right temple and cheek. A fresh cut above her left eye dripped blood down her face, and her lips were bloody and swollen. Her hands were in her lap, locked in a prayer position with gray duct tape. Her feet, stretched out in front, were similarly bound. Her eyes sought mine.

"Oh, baby. Hang on." I scrambled over to my friend. I found a tissue in my pocket and cleaned her cut with gentle dabs. Her brow burned, and her eyes were too bright. Her pupils looked odd, too.

Elise winced and lifted her hands. "Hurts," she managed to say in a weak voice.

"I'm on it, *imoto.*" I opened the little red knife on my key ring, held up her hands, and slit the bottom of the tape between her wrists. I started to pull the end of one piece free from the skin on her right arm. She cried out, so I stopped.

Then we both froze. A car roared up to the end of the alley and stopped. Elise's eyes widened with fear. She gestured with her head to the back of the unit. "Hide," she croaked in a low, urgent tone.

I climbed over bales toward the back until I found a loose plastic tarp. I had just pulled it over me when the overhead light flashed on.

"That piece of *merde* Milton been in here," a man said.

Pascal. I held my breath.

"He took the lock." He cursed then said, "What's this? He take pity on you?"

Oh no, I thought. The tissue. I had dropped it on the floor.

"He clean up one cut. I'll give you another. You like it?"

A fist thudded, and Elise cried out.

My heart sank. My only hope was that he'd leave. But what if he didn't?

Light crept in around the edges of the tarp. I sat wedged in between two stacks of bales, with my knees to my chin. A label printed into the plastic covering of one just inches from my face was written in Spanish or Portuguese. I narrowed my eyes as I tried to read it. Seeds of some kind? What did *amapola* mean?

I heard Pascal muttering and moving about. Nothing more from Elise. Either he was leaving her alone or she was unconscious. The tarp smelled musty. The bales hiding me emitted a scent I couldn't name. Both odors started to congest my sinuses and tickle my nose. I chanted in silence: I will not sneeze. I will not sneeze. I was desperate for the incantation to work.

The noises from Pascal moved in my direction. I forced myself to barely breathe. To sit as quietly as the street performers who stood without moving for hours. The footsteps came close.

"This one's still out. Good, he'll not cause problems," Pascal said from feet away.

Who else was in here? Pascal didn't seem concerned about the man being unconscious. Was I going to have to rescue more than one person? I let air slide out through silent lips as Pascal's presence shifted back toward the door.

"Where is the damn truck?" He continued to curse in French and English. A metallic sound resonated, as if he pounded his fist on the wide door. Just as long as the fist wasn't pounding Elise.

The entry door slammed. Another door slammed, and the car roared away. I took a deep breath. I lifted the tarp from my head. The overhead light fixture cast a harsh illumination on the room. I shielded my brow with one hand and surveyed the contents. The bale-shaped objects mostly filled the space. Elise at the front slumped on a folded khaki wool blanket. Near the door was a case of bottled water—probably the reason Elise was even alive—and a few Styrofoam takeout containers sat on a cardboard box.

I rose and saw our other companion. Thomas MacDonald. He lay prone in a space near the back wall. What was he doing here?

Looking over at Elise's pleading eyes, I said, "I'll be right there, *gaijin*." I climbed over to an aisle and knelt next to Thomas. He was breathing but felt too cool when I touched his neck. I saw another blanket in the corner. I spread it over him, sneezing as a cloud of dust rose.

"I'll be right back," I whispered to Thomas. "Hang on." I owed it to Jamal not to lose his brother, too. No matter how rocky their relationship.

I hurried back to Elise, whose hands were neatly arranged on her lap.

Pascal apparently hadn't noticed any change in the tape. Thank Goddess Luck I'd stopped peeling back the tape when I had.

I promised myself to compliment Elise's quick thinking later, for putting her hands back in position to hide the sliced tape.

Now I slit the top of the tape between Elise's hands. I did the same top and bottom with her feet. "We'll leave the tape on, girlfriend. We gotta get you out of here." I put my arm around Elise and helped her up. She was never of substantial heft, but now she felt almost ethereal, she was so light. And wobbly.

"Can you walk?"

Elise nodded, shivering. I draped the blanket around her shoulders. I shepherded her over to the door and switched off the light.

"Here we go. *Gambatte, yo.* Be strong."

Elise nodded again and motioned with her chin for me to take the lead, holding onto my upper arm from behind.

I eased the door open, feeling infinite relief.

Pascal hadn't locked us in. He must have been confident Elise and Thomas wouldn't have gotten mobile on their own.

No human sounds were in evidence outside. The clouds had blown away, leaving a dark, starry night. The only noises were an empty paper coffee cup skittering along the edge of the dark building and the rustle of a cluster of leaves trapped against the fence enclosing the facility.

With our backs pressed to the wall, I stood with Elise outside. I thought for a moment. If Pascal came back while we were in this narrow dead-end alley, Elise and I were both total dead ends. Dead and ended. But if we...

A car engine approached. There went that choice. I pushed Elise into the slot at the end where I had hidden before and squeezed in beside her. The building was set at a sharp angle to the fence, which narrowed in until it met the structure at the back corner.

"Scootch!" I pressed a trembling Elise farther into the wedge of space. I trembled, too. I managed to get my cell phone out and jab at 911. The noise of the car drew closer. Headlights played on the chain links, casting a mottled pattern on the scrubby field beyond.

"Help! Millsbury U-Stor-All. Killer. Unit 17-F," I whispered. "Hurry!" I kept it open so the call wouldn't disconnect.

The vehicle screeched to a stop. I looked at Elise and held my finger to my lips. She blinked and pressed her mouth tight. *She looks so pale,* I thought. Being crammed into that slot might be the only thing holding her upright.

The area went dark, which made the light from my phone look like a blazing beacon. I quickly slid it into my pocket, keeping it open.

CHAPTER TWENTY-FIVE

A car door slammed. The garage-type door bumped and clanked as it rolled up in its tracks into the top of the storage space. In the edge of my field of vision, I saw light spill out onto the alley pavement, followed by a barrage of curses shouted in French.

"Where is she? She could not get out. How?" Pascal's voice was at once bewildered and furious.

Where are the police, I wondered. I had Elise out of danger, sort of. For the time being. Officers could come blasting in here with their sirens and guns any time now.

I heard another vehicle. The sound raised my hopes until I realized how loud and clunking it was. Not exactly the noises of a police cruiser on a rescue mission. More like a truck. The reverberation between the buildings grew closer until the fence was again lit brightly. The motor shut off, but the lights remained on. Another man conversed with Pascal.

I couldn't make out the words. The smell of cigarette smoke drifted past. Elise started to feel heavier next to me. I tucked my arm more firmly around her waist. I heard another wide door roll up. Men grunted, and voices moved in and out of the storage space; they either had to be shifting those packages into the truck or adding more to the collection in the space.

A dark shape moved in the field on the other side of the fence. The hairs on the back of my neck prickled. What was this? I thought we were safe in our cramped hiding place. The shape ran toward us. Elise moaned. I hoped the racket the men were making masked the sound. She started to slide down the wall. She was passing out.

The shape disappeared. A ghostly light appeared to my left with the fence between us. My heart thudded so hard I thought it must be audible.

"Lauren, it's me." Natalia pointed the tiniest of flashlights at her face then at us. "They're on the way. Don't worry," she whispered. "And whatever you do, don't move."

I nodded, stunned. "Thomas is in there. Unconscious."

"MacDonald?"

I whispered, "Yes."

She swore under her breath as she retreated into the dark. I thought I still heard the faintest traces of her voice. I hoped she was radioing in or whatever police did. Hoped, if the guns came blasting in, they would know about Thomas. And would be aware of Elise and me.

The effort of holding Elise up stung my shoulder. Could it hurt to let her slide down? This had to be over soon. And if she was unconscious, we weren't going to be running anywhere, even if we had to. I let her go. I leaned sideways to tuck the blanket snug around her neck. I checked her breathing. Still alive.

Pascal's voice was suddenly loud and his words clear. The other man wasn't speaking. Pascal must be on his cell phone.

"What do you mean, you didn't go inside? I saw you tried to help her. You left a tissue. Alors, Milton, you probably took her out of here, you filthy bastard." Pascal then grew silent. "What? What do you mean? Then where did that girl go? Who took her?" After a click, he cursed again.

His voice was feet away. All he had to do was look around the corner, and Elise and I would be toast. Where was Natalia?

The other man called to Pascal. "Come on, we got to finish here." The noises of hauling and dumping resumed. The headlights from the truck shone on the field beyond.

Suddenly, bright lights and sirens raced into the alley and stopped. A bullhorn blared, "Millsbury Police. Come out with your hands up. Now." Natalia ran toward us from the left side of the field. She took two climbing steps up the fence and vaulted it like it was an easy gymnastics exercise, landed, and pulled her gun. Two other officers followed her and did the same. Natalia motioned to me to stay put and moved out of my narrow range of sight, as did the other officers.

I sank down until I sat next to Elise. I closed my eyes and wrapped my arms around myself. *Finally.*

The report from two shots echoed back and forth in the alley. Someone shouted. The thin voice from a radio crackled then the air quieted. Blue and white lights strobed in silence.

"You want to come out of there now?" Natalia appeared and beckoned to me. I looked at Elise, who was still unconscious, then eased out and joined Natalia. "How's Elise?" Natalia squeezed in beside her. She knelt and held several fingertips to Elise's neck. She looked up at me. "She's got a good pulse."

"She passed out a couple minutes ago. I think she's sick or something—she didn't look too good when I found her. He had her hands and feet taped in there."

Natalia spoke on her radio then said to me, "We'll have an ambulance here in a minute." She shone her flashlight onto Elise again. "Good thing you wrapped her up."

I nodded. I was drained, the last hour finally taking its toll. My leg bones suddenly seemed gelatinous. I found myself listing toward Natalia.

"Whoa, there. I got you," she said, springing to her feet. She put an arm around me and leaned me against the wall. "Don't worry. It's just your adrenaline dropping."

I looked around. The car in front of me, until now only heard, was a gray sedan. A lot like the one that pursued me the day of Jamal's memorial service. Behind it was a large white panel truck. A dozen officers bustled about. A man I'd never seen before lay face down on the ground with his hands cuffed behind him.

Two EMTs emerged from the storage space wheeling Thomas, wrapped in blankets and strapped to a gurney. One EMT held an oxygen mask to Thomas' face. "That's Thomas," I said. "How is he?"

"He's alive."

"And Pascal?"

Natalia motioned with her head toward the other side of the alley. Pascal sat against the wall, his legs outstretched. His hands were cuffed to the garage door handle above him. A standing officer kept her foot firmly on one of his legs while an EMT cut open the other pants leg and pressed a bandage on a bleeding wound. Pascal swore and struggled.

His eyes met mine and flared. "You! You are the one." A stream of bilingual curses followed.

"Come on. Let's get you somewhere warm. Don't mind him," Natalia said.

I twisted away. "But what about Elise?"

Another ambulance approached and stopped right behind us.

"That's her ride," Natalia said. "She'll be in good hands." She walked me down the alley to a patrol car with its engine running and held open the front passenger door. The vents blew warm air as I slid into the seat. "Just don't touch anything, all right? I'll be back."

I nodded.

Natalia shut the door to the cruiser.

I watched through the windshield as two EMTs withdrew a wheeled gurney and extracted Elise from our hiding place. Soon she was the blanketed figure strapped to it. I wished I could be at her side after all this. I didn't think I could find the strength to even open the cruiser door, though. I sank down in the seat and closed my eyes.

I started when the door of the cruiser opened. Had I fallen asleep?

A deep voice said, "Thought you might want this." Zac leaned in, proffering a thick paper cup with a lid. "It's my special hot chocolate recipe."

I shut my eyes again then opened them. He was still there. "How did you know I was here?"

He shrugged. "Natalia called me. Are you going to take this, or do I have to stand here holding it?"

"You're wonderful, you know?" I took the cup and sipped the warm, rich liquid. "This is perfect."

"You're welcome." He leaned his right hand on the roof of the car and touched my cheek with his left hand. "So, you had a rough evening?"

Natalia walked up. "Hey, stay away from my witness."

"You're the one told me to come! Can I take her home now?"

"Just kidding. But, no, sorry. We have to get some information. I'll drop her off later."

"Hello? Excuse me?" I said, waving. "I'm alive here. And have my own wheels."

"Okay, okay." She smiled and held up a forestalling hand. "I have to get back down there. I shouldn't be too much longer, though. Then we'll talk, and *then* you can leave. All right?"

I watched her stride away. "Zac?" I looked up at him. "I wonder if you'd—"

"Come over tonight? I wouldn't have it any other way."

"But your last message."

"Oh, I was being a stupid man. When I heard you were in danger, *bebé*, well." He shook his head. "Let's forget that message."

"Let's not." I shook my head. "We should keep talking. About that and about everything." Zac agreed with a nod as two men with the letters "DEA" on the back of their jackets strode by. "If you are there when I get home, I will be a happy woman." I reached into my pocket for my house keys and dangled them at him. "Remind me sometime to tell you how important this cute little knife was tonight."

He leaned in and planted a long, warm kiss on my mouth. "Me and the dog await you."

I finished the hot chocolate and realized I hadn't eaten in a long, long time. I wondered if officers kept snacks in their glove compartments, but then I remembered Natalia said not to touch anything. Which probably applied to snacks, too.

The driver's side door opened, and Natalia slid in. "Time to dish. I want to hear all of it." She pulled out a notebook and a pen.

"Do you have anything to eat?"

She smiled and pulled a cheese-and-cracker pack out of the glove compartment.

I munched as I recounted the events, starting with Elise's phone call. "Is Pascal talking at all?"

"Oh, no. After showing off all the bad words he knows in all the languages he knows, he totally clammed up."

"There's so much I can't figure out. Why he had Elise here. What Thomas was doing here. What those big packages were."

Natalia looked at me. "You don't know? Those are bales of heroin. Pascal was a major drug runner. We've been tracking him for a while. But we didn't know where he did his transfers. Until tonight."

I thought for a moment. "So Elise was getting her stuff from him. But what was Pascal's relationship with Jamal?"

"We're working on that one. Listen, you get on home. I'm going to have Jeff drive you over to your truck and follow you home. No, no." She shook her head as I opened my mouth to object. "Probably should have sent you off in an ambulance, too. Short of that, I want to be sure you get all the way home and inside with the doors locked."

I frowned. "What else could happen to me?"

"I didn't mean that. Although we haven't learned who gave Pascal orders. Yet. His truck buddy might do some talking soon. He doesn't seem to have much of a backbone." She gave a short, humorless laugh. "No, you'll be fine. Go home and take care of yourself. You were foolish to come here alone, but you probably saved your friend's life, and you were responsible for our being able to finally put Pascal where he belongs. Behind bars."

A young officer appeared outside Natalia's door.

"Here's your escort," she said. "We'll be in touch."

Zac fixed breakfast the next morning: a swordfish omelet, toasted French bread, and steaming dark coffee. The man was resourceful, making dinner ingredients into breakfast. He was quiet as he bustled about the kitchen.

After a long but fitful sleep, I now sat with my coffee and watched him work. He set overflowing plates on the table, and we ate without talking, but it seemed a comfortable silence to me, not one of tension. I rose when we were finished and picked up both plates, delivering a kiss to the top of his head as I passed on my way to the sink.

"Do you think it's too early to see Elise at the hospital?" I asked over my shoulder. The clock on the stove read 9:45. "I want to get over there."

"You want company?"

I thought for a moment then faced him, drying my hands on a towel. "If you want to come along, I would be happy for your company. I don't particularly need it at this time, but I don't not need it, either. Do you get me?" I walked toward him and smiled. "I'm not pushing you away, and I'm fine alone."

"Got ya. And we're going to talk soon, yes?" He held out his hand and pulled me onto his lap.

I nestled into his neck and murmured my agreement.

"Then you go on. I hope Elise is all right."

My light mood of warm comfort vanished. "I hope so, too."

CHAPTER TWENTY-SIX

I parked my truck at Agawam College and sat at the wheel. The hospital visit had been difficult. I'd picked up an armful of yellow and pink tulips on my way, but Elise hadn't even noticed them. She was sleepy. An IV dripped fluid into her arm, and an oxygen monitor was clipped to her finger, but otherwise she didn't seem connected to any medical technology.

I held her hand in silence for a few minutes. I found a vase for the flowers under the sink, arranged them, and left. Sergeant Jeff was seated outside the door.

My stomach sank. "Why are you here? Is Elise under arrest?"

"No, ma'am."

"But why are you here?"

"I'm not at liberty to share that, ma'am."

I raised my eyebrows and prodded but couldn't get anything out of him. The nurse at the station wouldn't give me any information, either. I stomped down the stairs. Nobody would tell me anything. Again. Elise didn't seem to be getting better. And young men still called me "ma'am."

At Agawam, I opened the truck door. Spring was doing one of its showoff days. The suddenly sunny, breezy air warmed and welcomed, even though it was in the low sixties. I left my jacket in the cab and walked the long way around to the entrance on the other side of the building. Daffodils bloomed in sunny spots, and trees sported the fuzz of light green heralding the imminence of leaf. Two shirtless students played Frisbee on soggy grass.

I wandered up to my office and opened the window. The bonsai's new growth echoed the trees outdoors: a hint of new life in miniature. I sank into the stuffed chair, putting my feet on the windowsill. I grabbed a sheaf of student essays from the desk, plus a purple pen, and started to read.

When I got to Tashandra's paper, my thoughts roamed away from the task at hand and onto Alexa. While the adventure at the storage facility put the recent events at the college out of my mind for an evening, Alexa was back in it now. What was she really about? I wondered if she was as cold and ambitious as she seemed. As dangerous to children as she was rumored to be.

She had certainly threatened me on Wednesday.

The chairwoman never brought a spouse, a date, or children to any of the departmental picnics that included family and didn't talk about her personal life, at least not to me. Her office was the modern, uncluttered environment of an academic climber. I thought there might as well be a sign on the door reading Future Provost. No snapshots of dogs or children kept company with the tidy books on the shelf or the signed, original art in frames on the walls.

I shook my head and resolved to deal with Alexa later. She was my boss, after all. Since the frightening scene in the restroom, I would rather never deal with the chair again. For now, I wanted to finish my grading and get back home. Back to Zac and quite possibly my future.

Sunday afternoon found me back at Elise's bedside, after spending the last twenty-four hours with Zac.

We'd walked hand-in-hand by the river in the mild weather and eaten a quiet dinner at Ithaki. We'd made love several times and enjoyed each other's company without getting into any heavy conversations. I had put Jamal's death and everything that had happened since into a box in the corner of my mind and not opened it once.

I walked into Elise's room, glad that gatekeeper Officer Jeff was nowhere to be seen. She looked better. She had color in her face and was sitting up. I couldn't believe how thin she was, though, and noticed yellow in her eyes. I leaned over and gave her a hug then perched on the edge of the bed.

"Hey, *gaijin*. You're feeling better, it looks like."

She nodded. "Sort of." She frowned and looked away from me, picking at a spot on the thin white blanket with a shaky finger.

Was this going to be too soon to ask my friend why Pascal kept her prisoner? I decided to forge ahead. I risked my life getting her to safety. I deserved to know. "So, are you going to tell me what happened? I mean, why Pascal had you taped up like a UPS package?" I smiled, trying to keep the air light.

She stared through the window. She inhaled, blew out noisily, and faced me. "Yeah, I'll tell you. Remember the day you brought me home from rehab, *gaijin*?"

I nodded, somber. Those memories were not pleasant.

"I'm sure you thought I was heading out to get high again and stay that way."

I nodded again.

Sergeant Jeff strode in, frowning. "What's this about getting high?"

Elise rolled her eyes. "Hey, I was talking to my friend. But you said you wanted to hear my story." She gestured toward the windowsill. "Have a seat."

He looked surprised but scrambled in his pocket for a small notebook and pen then perched on the designated sill.

"I found out in rehab I'm sick. Hep C." She pulled down her lower eyelid and pointed to her sclera, which was a shade of yellow. "My liver's not doing its job these days." She shivered and pulled the blanket up to her neck. "So I wanted one more fix before I turned myself in to get help."

She'd been buying drugs from Pascal for a while. He'd been trying to convince her to sell some herself, but she'd pushed back. "When I asked him for some farewell drugs, I made the mistake of telling him I was getting clean. He accused me of planning to go clean on him, too, turn him in."

Jeff wrote furiously in his notebook.

"Jamal had already gone clean on him, Pascal said. Jamal had told me, too." Elise turned sad eyes on me. "I wasn't going to rat on Pascal. I was only thinking of myself at that point. But he didn't believe me."

I squeezed her hand and kept hold of it.

"He slapped me around and taped me up. I fought hard. I yelled as loud as I could. Then I think he must have been shooting me up or giving me something. Because I only remember parts of the days." She put her face in her hands. "Lauren, it was awful."

"You're lucky he didn't kill you."

"Believe me, I was worried about that. He said he'd let me go when he left town, but, you know, he wasn't exactly a Boy Scout. I didn't know what he'd do."

"Where was this?" Jeff asked. "In the storage place?"

"No, at his apartment. It's in Lawrence. A ratty neighborhood. Dangerous."

Jeff said, "You can describe where it is?"

"Oh, yeah. I went there more times than I'd like to admit."

"Do you know when he took you to the storage facility?"

Elise shook her head. "Maybe it was that day? Did I smell bad when you found me?" She looked at me with a worried brow.

"No. The unit smelled bad, but not you. And what about Thomas?" I asked.

"I don't know. I didn't realize he was there at first. And then Pascal went over to the corner to check on him. I didn't know who it was, only that he had another prisoner. Somebody unconscious."

A nurse bustled in and stopped, folding her arms across her chest. "What you people doing bothering my patient?" Her Russian accent was thick.

"It's all right, Marya. I need to tell them something. This is my friend, Lauren. She's the one who rescued me. I owe her my life." Elise's voice trembled, but she held her head up and cast a wan smile in my direction.

"*Zdravst vuy tye*," I said to the nurse. Marya's eyes opened wide as she smiled. She and I exchanged several further salutations. "Sorry. That's about the extent of my Russian." I put my hand up and shook my head.

"Okay. But listen, don't making her tired."

"We won't."

"*Do svidaniya*." Marya waved as she left the room.

I returned the farewell.

Jeff looked stunned. "Wow. How many languages do you speak?"

"Oh, a few." I was used to this question and didn't want to get into a description of my linguistic abilities. "Do you have any idea what Thomas MacDonald was doing there? Or how he is now?"

"I am not at liberty to tell you. Sorry. I think he's still here in the hospital, though. Fourth floor. If you want to visit."

"I might stop by there when we're done here. But I have one more question." I studied Elise. "Are you up for this, girlfriend? We don't want to exhaust you."

"I'm all right. It's good to get it all out."

"How were you able to call me?"

"Oh, yeah. He had taped my hands kind of loose when he moved me. Then he got a call and raced out of there. His cell phone must have fallen out of his coat. It was right by my feet." She scrunched herself farther down into the bed. "I had to go through some contortions to reach it. Then when he came back, that was bad. I had barely gotten myself sitting again. He looked kind of suspicious. He whacked me a few times and taped me up tight. Luckily, he didn't check the cell for recent calls."

Jeff's phone buzzed, and he excused himself to the hall.

"So what's your plan, Elise? You're really going to get help this time?"

She nodded, and her eyes welled up. "Addiction is bad, *gaijin*. It has trapped me for so long."

"But why? What are you trying to escape, do you think?"

She turned back to the window. "I had a bad experience, you know, when I had to leave Japan."

I remembered when she was framed for drugs and got deported. Lost her fellowship to grad school. Johns Hopkins, no less.

"A few years after that, well, I did something I shouldn't have. And then the first time I did heroin, it erased all of it. I kept craving it. It's no good, though."

"Will you go back to rehab?"

"Yeah, when I get out of here. For quite a while. They said I can work off some of the costs. Plus I'm getting treated for the Hep C, and those meds make me feel sort of bad, too."

"What about work?"

"My boss is great. Jamie says she'll hold my position, hire a temp for a while. Maybe I'm finally getting lucky, Lauren." She closed her eyes with a sigh.

I planted a kiss on her cheek and smoothed limp hair off her brow. "I guess I'll have to start calling you *Atariya* from now on."

"I'm an *atariya* to have you as a friend. A lucky person." She sounded sleepy.

"*Ja ne.* Bye."

I walked out, nodded to Jeff, and took the stairs up a flight. Thomas MacDonald's was the next story I wanted to hear.

The central desk was unoccupied, but a board listed a MacDonald in room 405. I looked around. The closest room number was 415. I headed toward 405, which ended up being the last room on the hall. The door was open. I knocked on the door jamb and poked my head in.

The bed closest to the door was empty. A man sat close to the bed by the window, holding the hand of a pale woman who lay still. Her eyes were closed. He spoke to her in Portuguese as he stroked her arm.

"*Desculpa. Eu queria falar com o Thomas MacDonald.*" I summoned up some Brazilian Portuguese, rusty from a decade and a half of disuse.

The man looked up, eyes wide. "*Fala Portugues?*"

I told him that yes, I spoke Portuguese. I gestured toward the other bed. "*Onde é que é o senor que estava la?*"

The man shook his head and clicked his tongue. "*Êle saiu.*"

"He left?" He'd been unconscious thirty-six hours ago.

"*Sem o consulto do médico.*"

Thomas had left without a doctor's orders. "*Quando?*"

The man told me that, an hour ago, Thomas just got up, found his clothes in the closet, and walked out.

"*Éle naõ disse aonde êle,* uh, *ia?*" I grimaced, pretty sure that wasn't quite the correct way to ask if Thomas said where he was going.

He shook his head again. Great.

"*Bem. Muito obrigada,*" I thanked him. "*Espero que ela melhora loginh*o." I nodded my head in the direction of his wife, telling him I hoped she got better real soon.

He thanked me in return, wearing one of the saddest faces ever.

On my way to the stairs, I passed the nurse's station. This time a nurse was bent over a monitor. I asked where Thomas was.

"Mr. MacDonald checked himself out this morning," the nurse said with a frown.

I looked up at him. "Hey, you were taking care of my friend Elise a couple of weeks ago, weren't you?"

"Yes, I was. And I remember you and the police officer did not help her healing process." He folded his arms over plain turquoise scrubs. "Anyway, Mr. MacDonald refused to wait for the doctor to discharge him. We couldn't hold him against his will."

"Was he well enough to go?" I took a look at his name tag. "What was wrong with him, Chris?"

Chris shook his head. "You're not family. I can't talk to you about a patient."

"You know, I was the person who found him unconscious and called the police. I basically rescued him."

"Wow." He raised his eyebrows. "I'm impressed."

The roll of the eyes made me think he wasn't, really.

"And I still can't tell you."

I stood at my truck a few minutes later.

Thomas had been unconscious Friday night. Even earlier on Friday, since he'd been out when Pascal had brought Elise to U-Stor-All.

And now, Sunday, he was out walking around by himself. How was I going to find out why Pascal even took him there? Maybe Thomas had a drug connection with Pascal, too. Pascal struck me as intelligent and crafty. The type who was likely to hire an equally crafty lawyer and who was unlikely to cooperate in revealing his story.

CHAPTER TWENTY-SEVEN

I drove home and took Wulu for a walk. Strolling along the river, with the light dancing on its gentle flow, I passed a multi-generational family with a pink-cheeked baby in a stroller, a toddler on a tricycle, and two girls working on their skateboard skills. These kids came from homes with enough food, enough money, and mostly two parents at home. Watching them playing carefree made me think of Tyrone and the other children at the Boys and Girls Club who didn't have such easy lives even though they lived only two towns away. Then I thought of Alexa, who possibly was making their lives even harder.

The conversation I'd overheard in the basement. The woman who had declared her innocence about something had to have been Alexa.

She had the same Ozark dialect when she became incensed about something, when she lost control. I noticed it at the memorial service reception, in the incident after I saw the dean, and at the departmental meeting. But who was the man in the basement? A man Alexa had some kind of power over.

I stopped, pulling Wulu close. I stared at a cloud traversing west to east, thinking, remembering the voices. I snapped my fingers. Yes. I searched my pockets for my phone, with no results.

"Come on, Wulu," I said, reversing our tracks. "I have a visit to pay."

When I called from my condo, Louise answered.

"I was just out in the garden. You're more than welcome to stop by. And we can have a nice drink."

"I'll be right over, Louise. Thanks. I hope I can see George, too."

"Yes, he's home."

I said goodbye and drove to my aunt's house. Louise greeted me out front in muddy jeans and gardening gloves.

"I'm finishing some cleanup out here. Go on in, dear. George is looking forward to seeing you."

I thanked her and let myself in. This was perfect.

After greeting George and petting the now much-larger kittens, I accepted a gin and tonic from my uncle.

"Never too early to celebrate summer, I say." In his Boston-accented voice, "summer" came out as "summah." He clinked his own drink with mine and motioned toward the chairs in the sun porch. We watched Louise move around the yard, loading up the wheelbarrow with leaves from the flower beds and brown trimmings from perennials, dump it on the compost pile by the back fence, then do it all again.

I wondered how to approach the florid man beside me. "George, I need some help." This should appeal to him. He was in security, after all. He was a law enforcement officer, even if only in the fiefdom of academia.

He nodded with confidence. "Then I'm your man."

"It's about Dr. Kensington. Alexa."

George's face paled. His left knee started going up and down. He did not meet my eyes.

Louise, suddenly right outside the window, rapped on it. She waved.

I waved back then watched her head toward a bed in the back of the yard. "I need your help. I think she was involved in Jamal's death."

George looked relieved, and his leg quieted. "Oh, no. No, she couldn't be."

"Just listen." I spoke of what I'd seen of Alexa's involvement with Jamal and with the children. I told him what I'd heard about the outings Alexa took the boys on. His eyes flashed, but he didn't interrupt.

I outlined what Jamal wrote in his thesis and voiced my suspicions about Alexa being afraid it would get out. "I don't know where to turn. I told Dean Irwin, and he totally took Alexa's side. The police seem to be getting nowhere fast. It's been a month since Jamal died!"

George sipped his drink. "If she has been abusing little children, that is wrong. The police need to know about it." His voice shook with conviction. "But Lauren, I know Dr. Kensington did not kill Jamal. I don't know who did, but she didn't. Fact."

"What makes you so sure? I saw her in her office, looking down at where I found his body. Right before I found him. At a time when nobody else was around."

"Let's just say I know." He shifted in his seat, and his leg started jittering again.

"Well, that's not good enough for me." I stood and walked to the window. I couldn't see Louise. "I thought you'd be able to help me. Jamal was a good man. He didn't deserve to die."

"Few do. Few do."

I turned back. I was going to have to do it.

"How are you two doing?" Louise asked, appearing from nowhere.

George pasted a quick smile on his face. "We're fine, dear."

"Do you need those drinks freshened up?"

"No, we're good." I lifted my half-full glass to show her.

Louise nodded and left the room. George's smile left his face. He drained his glass.

I waited until I saw her in the yard again. "Why don't you tell me what Alexa was talking about in the basement last week?"

"What? No. When?" He rose, turned to the door, turned back, and stared at me. "What basement?"

I looked back at him without moving. "I heard you down there, in the basement of Lockhart Hall. She was threatening you about something."

George sank back in his chair. He shook his head then looked outside as if to be sure Louise was still in cleanup mode. "Damn. You get around, don't you, young lady? Sit down, then. I'll tell you."

He wiped his forehead with a plaid handkerchief and held his glass up in front of him. "See this? This is my ruin, young lady. There are days that seem too rough to get through. So I pour myself a little something at work. In my office. Dr. Kensington found out." He clasped his hands between his knees and looked down at them.

"You were drunk at work?"

He nodded.

"Was she blackmailing you?"

"Sort of. I need my job. Louise, here, she's my world." He gestured at the window that stood between them and his industrious wife. "I need to take care of her, because she takes care of me. And we plan to retire in a few years, do some traveling. You know."

I sat in silence.

"If I lose my post, I might have trouble getting another one. I'm not a young man, and I made a few mistakes in my past. I was lucky to find employment with any level of responsibility."

I raised my eyebrows, but George did not elaborate.

"Anyway, Alexa, Dr. Kensington, she had me nailed to the wall that evening," he said. "She's wicked, but she didn't kill your student."

"You should tell the police, you know."

"But I can't. You don't understand, do you?"

"Listen, Uncle George. You can get help. If you came clean to your boss, I'll bet they'd understand. As long as you showed evidence of trying to quit. Like going to AA and stuff. And then Alexa wouldn't have that kind of power over you anymore. Who is your boss, by the way?"

"The campus chief. Who reports to the Provost. I think you vastly overestimate their charitable tendencies." With an ironic pull to his mouth, he added, "Another drink?"

I declined just as Louise bustled into the room, drying her hands on a towel. Her cheeks were flushed from her exertions. She laid an arm on the back of George's shoulder and smiled at me.

"You two having a nice visit?"

I nodded. George looked up at his wife, who winked at him. I suddenly felt very much an intruder into this intimate scene. I chatted with Louise for a moment then said I had to be getting home.

"Oh, won't you stay for supper?" Louise asked. "Or another drink?"

"Thanks, but I have plans to take Zac out." I didn't, actually, but wanted to get away. And wondered if Louise knew the extent of George's drinking. How could she not? And if so, why did she push alcohol on everyone?

George walked me out to the driveway.

"I meant it about the children, Lauren. You know, Louise and I married so late, we missed our chance to have a family. I know she always wanted children, though. And no little kid should be harmed. Ever." He stood taller and sucked in his considerable gut with resolve. "You tell me how I can help you. All right?"

"You mean besides stopping having whiskey for lunch at work?"

"Girly, that's already happening, believe it or not. I mean about Dr. Kensington. Anything I can do to protect children, I will."

I thanked him and climbed into my truck. Uncle George sure seemed changed. I rolled down the window. "I'll call you soon. I don't know quite how to confront Alexa, but I'll figure it out."

He pointed a finger at me and nodded. "Yes, you will." He waved then walked back into the house.

I mulled it all over as I drove home. The relatively warm weather of the weekend was prodding nascent leaves to push out from their nodes, and the green cast of the trees was striking in its new intensity. The setting sun cast long, slanting shadows.

To get anywhere with accusing Alexa, I was going to need real evidence. I resolved to visit the Boys and Girls Club again tomorrow. In the meantime, I had class prep to finish and a dog to walk. Again.

After my last class Monday, I drove to Millsbury. I sat in the truck and looked at the Boys and Girls Club building. The warm weather was temporarily behind us, leaving a cold rain splashing on the windshield. I didn't want to get out into the rain. Maybe what I actually didn't want was the work of persuading Brenda to help me again. But for the kids, it was worth it.

Brenda set her face into a mask when she saw me. She looked down at the papers on her desk.

"Brenda, I need your help."

She spoke in a low, harsh voice. "I told you too much as it is. You need to leave."

I looked around at the bustle of activity, at the fresh faces playing and studying, at one little girl whose beaded braids brushed the edges of the book she was absorbed in. "You don't have to tell me anything else. Here's what I want, though." I outlined my idea. "It's important, Brenda. You know that."

The other woman nodded with reluctance. "I know. Fine. I'll see if Mannie can get those for you."

"Is he here now?"

She inclined her head toward a door labeled Security. "In there."

Half an hour later, I left with my bag heavier than when I went in. I pressed Natalia's number on my phone after I dashed to the truck and climbed in. I brushed water off my face as the phone rang. I left her a message about the security tapes I had and that I'd be leaving them at the station for her. It was proof Alexa took kids out alone. Brenda wouldn't lose her job for telling. Natalia could combine that with testimony from Tyrone and other boys. All I wanted was for Alexa to be kept away from children.

Driving home, I thought about the events of the past few days. Alexa had an alibi for Jamal's murder, at least according to George.

So then he, too, had to have been elsewhere at the time of death.

Unless he was lying for Alexa. And why would he be? So he could be judged innocent? He seemed different, nicer, more humane the last two times I visited with him, but his bigotry about Natalia left me with a bad taste in my mouth. I wouldn't be surprised if George had some pretty deep-seated racist tendencies, too. Which he would also have in common with Alexa, at least according to Jamal.

Pascal was in police custody as far as I knew. Did he have an alibi for Jamal's death? He was a drug dealer.

But Jamal had been clean for years. Or so he had told me. Tashandra had seen Pascal threatening Jamal on campus.

And then there was Thomas. Where did he go after leaving the hospital? Was he all right? I pulled over to the side of the road. I found the Knights and Kings number in my cell and pressed the number. A man answered. Not Thomas. In fact, he sounded angry that Thomas wasn't there and told me, if I saw him, to tell Thomas to get his lazy ass in there.

"And who should I say wants him?"

"Joseph. He knows who I am. We got kids here for lessons, we got the team he was tutoring for the competition, we got parents wondering why this place is going downhill. And we got bills to pay."

"If I see him, I'll tell him to call you, Joseph. And, could you do the same for me, please?" I gave him my name and number.

"What do you want him for? You going to steal money from us, too?"

"Of course not!" I sighed. "What I want him for is complicated. But I would like to know he's all right, and I have a question for him."

The man agreed and hung up with no further niceties.

Someone had been taking money from Knights and Kings. Had Joseph meant that Thomas had been, or someone else?

CHAPTER TWENTY-EIGHT

The next afternoon, the weather was damp and chilly, although the rain ceased during my drive home from campus. I turned up the heat when I came in. I paced the condo, feeling restless.

Wulu looked up and barked.

"Good idea." I changed into running gear, including ear warmers and gloves. "Let's go, doggie."

We ran along Toil-in-Vain Road. At the top of the hill, I slowed. Phillip Pulcifer stood looking into his mailbox.

I greeted him.

"Oh, it's you." He didn't sound pleased to see me.

"How are you, sir?"

He glared. "How do you think? The family business burns down. I hear nothing from my brother, and then people report they have sighted him around town. Life is ducky, Missy."

I crouched down to stroke Wulu and to avoid Phillip's eyes.

"Hey, how's your friend doing?" he asked.

I looked up. Finally something to smile about. "Elise is doing well, thanks. I've, uh, actually seen Samuel several times."

He raised his eyebrows and waited, folding his arms over his chest.

"I don't know where he is staying. He drives by once in a while but won't talk much. A few days ago, I invited him for a sandwich after he gave us a ride home." I gestured to Wulu and myself. "That seemed to please him."

Phillip looked into the distance with a sad expression.

"Do you have any idea where he might be living?" I asked.

He surveyed the horizon for another moment then looked at me. "You know, I just might, now that you mention it. Want to go for a ride?"

He gestured to his car. We got in and drove to the house on the marsh. Phillip got out and walked to the shed. It was more an outbuilding than a shed; in a place like Mali, it might have housed three families.

Wulu barked and resisted when I pulled on his leash. He didn't seem to want to leave the car, so I rolled my window down a bit and shut the passenger door behind me. Phillip knocked on a weathered door. "Sammy, you in there?"

"Why would he be here?"

Smiling sadly, he said, "We used to hide here when we were kids. The owners weren't around much even then. We called it our clubhouse. I hadn't thought about it in a while, though." He peered through a window opaque with grime. "You call him. He might still be upset with me."

"Samuel?" I used my most friendly, rising intonation.

The door cracked open. "Oh, hello, Missy." Samuel's face appeared then he pulled the door inward. "Well, Phillip. All right, come on in. Both of you." He turned and shuffled into the dim interior.

Phillip motioned me to precede him. The shed was dusty but featured an old sofa and a small desk with a wooden chair pulled up to it. A sink held a mug, a plate, and several pieces of silverware. On the shelf next to it sat a loaf of bread, a jar of peanut butter, and a box of cookies. The window over the sink showed evidence of being cleaned or at least rubbed with a rag. I could see the marshes beyond and even a chickadee on a budding forsythia branch beyond the glass.

"Sit." Samuel waved in the direction of the couch. He turned the wooden chair, sat, and placed his hands on his knees as if it were perfectly normal to receive visitors in a decrepit shed. That belonged to someone else.

I lowered myself onto the couch and sneezed. I looked at Phillip, who remained standing. And silent.

"We were worried about you, Samuel," I began.

"As you can see, I am fine. Roof over my head. Running water. Nutritious food. All a man could want." Samuel's hand shook as he pointed in the direction of the sink. He smiled. "And not a soul to fuss over me, either. Just how I like it."

Phillip pushed his hands into his pockets and said in a tense voice, "You should come and stay with me. You can't live in a shed."

"I certainly can. You want me nearby so you can mind my business," Samuel grumbled. "It's comfortable here. I am approaching the exhaustion of my funds, however. And they have not been replenished." His elegant wording, carefully articulated, contrasted with his disheveled appearance and his surroundings. "So, all right. I'll come with you."

I was surprised at his decision to go with his brother. And I wondered about these funds and why they were exhausted. "What funds were those, Mr. Pulcifer?"

"Mr. Martin was kind enough to supply me with cash money from time to time. He appears to have left the area, however."

"Pascal Martin?"

"Indeed. We had a business arrangement. I believe I mentioned that to you previously. He stored supplies in the boat shop and recompensed me generously."

Phillip looked from Samuel to me and back. "I'm confused. What kinds of supplies?"

"Why, now, he never said. Large packages, like. Almost the size of a bale of salt hay, don't you know."

I knew exactly what was in those packages. Pascal's heroin.

This explained why Pascal had to switch to the storage place after the boat shop burned down. Explained how Samuel was able to stay on in the boat shop until the fire. And why he was around the houseboat that day when Pascal attacked me, showing up just in time.

Phillip and I helped Samuel gather up his scant belongings. When I opened the car door, I remembered this was where Natalia said Wulu was found.

No wonder Wulu hadn't wanted to get out of the car. Samuel must have moved in after that. But who had taken Wulu, and, for that matter, who had ransacked my office? It surely hadn't been Samuel.

We were driving back up the hill from the bridge when I said, "But Samuel, where's your car?"

"Oh, that fine vehicle also suffered from the cessation of funds. I ran out of gasoline and left it where it sat."

"And where might that be?" Phillip asked.

"Across the river on lower Summer Street. I walked from there, last time I was out."

I often walked Wulu on lower Summer on my way to the river. It was right around the bend from the boat shop property, too.

But I must not have been along there lately.

CHAPTER TWENTY-NINE

I was tired and distracted and kept losing track of the lecture during the next morning's class. Toward the end of the period, a siren cycled its way onto campus. Tashandra looked up in alarm. I met her eyes and shrugged then watched her sink her head onto her arms.

After class, I dropped a sheaf of papers on my office desk. I checked the elm and clipped a couple of tips, but my hands shook and my stomach agitated. Grooming the bonsai did not have its usual calming effect.

A knock at the door was followed by, "You'll have to teach me to do that sometime." Natalia leaned on the door jamb.

"It's pretty easy." I stroked the miniature branches. "What's up?"

"I have some news."

"You found Thomas MacDonald?"

She shook her head. "Pretty interesting stuff you guys called me about last night, though. Zac already sent me a report."

"So why are you here?"

"Did you happen to hear a siren during class?"

I nodded. Slowly. Staring at Natalia.

"I thought you might be interested to know Dr. Kensington has been arrested."

I kept staring. The pruners dropped open and hung from my thumb. "She has?"

"For child abuse."

I looked through the window at a gentle rain staining the tree trunk with dark marks then back at Natalia. "Really?"

"You bet." She folded her arms and looked satisfied. "Those tapes you dropped off did the trick. Our child-protection officer was able to interview a number of the children who Alexa walked out alone with. And she was not taking them to the movies."

"I am so glad you got her."

"Did somebody at the club tip you off about Alexa?" Her eyes drilled into mine. "You know it's a criminal offense not to report something like that."

I swallowed. "No, it was just a hunch I had." No way was I getting Brenda in trouble.

"Some hunch." She raised her eyebrows like she didn't quite believe me. "Now if we could only find MacDonald."

"Hey, I never told you about my conversation with Joseph, did I?"

She waited, one eyebrow raised. "Who's Joseph? You're supposed to tell me everything, remember?" She tapped her foot on the linoleum.

"I called Knights and Kings the other day. Yesterday? No, it was Monday." I related the details of the conversation with the man who seemed angry with Thomas.

Natalia said she'd check him out. "Oh, and by the way, it looks like the boat shop fire was only a wiring malfunction. No evidence of arson. With the age of those knob-and-tube wires, it's a wonder it hadn't burned down earlier."

"Did Mr. Pulcifer have insurance?"

Natalia said she didn't know. She edged toward the door. "I gotta run."

"One more question? Is Pascal talking at all?"

"Not yet. But he will. We're still working on him."

As I drove toward home after my office hours, it occurred to me Virgie might know where Thomas was. I was worried about him. It was a windy, mild afternoon, with the rain finally blowing eastward, a high pressure system promised to follow. The sun alternately shone bright then hid behind fast-moving clouds.

I parked in front of Virgie's house and got out. Looking up, I waved, certain Virgie was looking at me through the window or even through the spyglass.

Sure enough, I no sooner rang the doorbell than the tiny woman opened the downstairs door and greeted me.

I asked if I could come in. I said there was something I wanted to talk with her about.

After scrutinizing me for a moment with intense eyes, Virgie said, "Why, I suppose so. Yes, come on up."

I followed her up the worn wooden stairs. I took the same seat I had last time and refused her offer of tea. A sound came from the back of the house.

"That's some wind. Blowing things around," Virgie said. "So what can I help you with?"

"I was looking for your nephew, Thomas. Thomas MacDonald."

"Oh, Tommy. He was such a pretty boy, don't you know." Virgie looked through the window. "And so smart, too. Just like Jamal."

"Have you seen him lately? You know, he was in the hospital this weekend, and—"

Virgie waved her hand as if dismissing the news. "Yes, I heard. He got out of there, too. Hospitals are bad places. Why, my sister Jean died in one."

"So you've seen him since he left the hospital?"

"Are you certain you wouldn't like some tea? Or a nip of sherry? It is the end of the day."

I agreed to sherry.

The phone rang. Virgie excused herself and disappeared into the kitchen. I needed to go to the bathroom and wandered down the hall to find it. I peeked in the first bedroom. I liked to see how other people lived. It must have been Virgie's, featuring a lace bedspread and several bookshelves full of paperbacks. The next two doors were shut. I opened the first one.

A hand clamped over my mouth. Another hand grasped my shoulder, forcing me into a darkened room. The door shut without a noise. A lock clicked.

CHAPTER THIRTY

Thomas MacDonald pushed me to sit on a daybed. He pointed a gun at me. He held his finger to his lips. His face was slick with sweat. His right leg jerked in spasms. Patches darker than his skin lay like bruises beneath his eyes. He smelled of nerves and fear. With its drawn shades and brown paneling, the room was the lair of a predator.

"What are you doing here?" he growled. He wore the same clothes as when I last saw him on Friday, albeit now looking decidedly slept in.

My gut clenched. My hands and feet were cold. I felt light-headed, as if I hadn't eaten or slept in a couple of days. I needed to stay calm.

"I was worried about you. Did you know I was the one who found you in the storage place? You were unconscious."

"They told me. Yeah, thanks." His voice was gruff, begrudging, and shaky.

"So I stopped by to see you in the hospital on Sunday, and the nurse said you checked yourself out." I tried to swallow, but my mouth was dry with fear.

Thomas paced the room, keeping the gun pointed at me. "My momma died in a hospital. Bad places. They screwed up. They killed her." His hand trembled.

"Are you feeling all right, Thomas? You don't look too well."

He uttered a short laugh. "You try going through withdrawal. See how you like it!" His armpits were dark. He wiped his brow with his free hand.

So he was also a customer of Pascal's. I whirled my head at three raps on the door. The aim of Thomas' gun hand did not stray from me. The doorknob rattled.

"Lauren? Are you in there? Thomas Abraham, you let her out, now!"

"No. I'm talking with her."

"Thomas, you open that door." Virgie's voice was high and strong.

I willed him to obey her.

"I'm not going to, Auntie. I can't."

Her footsteps retreated down the hall.

I envisioned her going for the key to the door. I wasn't sure bedroom door locks even had keys, though. "What do you want from me?" I tried to keep my voice from shaking but didn't do too well.

Thomas moved around the room like a trapped creature. "Listen, I'm in bad shape. I need a fix."

"What about getting help? My friend, Elise—"

"Oh, her. Yeah, she's a nice lady." A wistful look came into his eyes.

"You know her?"

"Through Pascal. We both purchased supplies from him."

"Anyway, she's..." I decided to keep Elise's location to myself. "Have you tried rehab?"

"Done that before. Never sticks." He waved the gun around. "Anyway, I can't go doing anything official."

"What do you mean?" I had to keep him talking while I figured out if I could get out of here. He was a lot bigger than I was, and wrestling had never been part of my bag of tricks.

"Just can't get involved with the law. Bad stuff."

He wasn't making much sense. I decided on a wild guess. What did I have to lose?" Because of Jamal?"

Thomas stopped ranting. He planted himself in front of me, bloodshot eyes trained on my face. "What do you know of William?"

I drew in my breath. "I only know that he was murdered. And that you had problems with him."

He shook his head in slow motion. "He was stealing money from the chess club. From me." His voice flattened.

"So that explains what Joseph said."

"You talked to Joseph?" He sounded amazed.

"I was looking for you. On Monday. He was upset you weren't around. And said something about bills not being paid."

"That's it. William was taking money. For those kids of his at the Boys and Girls Club. Well, what about our kids, the ones we keep off the streets by teaching them chess? Anyway, we argued." He held out his left hand and his eyes implored me to believe him.

But I didn't. "I can't believe Jamal would steal from you, not for kids, not for anybody. Why would he?"

"Well, he did!" Thomas sounded desperate. "But I didn't mean to kill him. Really, I didn't."

"You killed your own brother?"

A siren pulsed faintly in the distance. He looked around with quick moves. His eyes shifted in panic to the door, to me, to the gun. His leg started jerking again, and his brow broke out in a new bath of sweat. I clutched the edges of the bed. I'd never make it past him to the door. What would he try to do now?

"I'm going to get out of here." His words came fast and breathy, like he couldn't get enough air. "I never should have come to my aunt's house. And you're coming with me."

"No, you go on ahead."

"Not on your life. You know too much. You'd turn me in." He gestured at me with the gun. "On your feet. Now." He grabbed my arm with his left hand and pulled me to my feet. He wrenched open a door—not the one I came in by.

Fresh air blew in, which was welcome. The fact we were leaving was not. I squinted at the sudden light as he pulled me onto a wooden landing. Steep stairs led down to the driveway, where a hard-top jeep sat facing the street. I couldn't let him take me with him.

Thomas moved his head right and left, fast, as if scanning for neighbors. "Come on!" His voice was low, gruff, and urgent. He pulled my arm, trying to make me go down the stairs in front of him, and gestured with the gun. Which was in his other hand.

I pulled back. "I'll just stay here." My mind raced, searching for a solution, for something to say to get out of going. "It'll be easier for you to travel alone."

"No. We're going." He tugged at me again. "Now."

I took a deep breath. "All right." I raised my right arm and bit down hard on his hand. He yelled and let go at the same time as I held onto the railing, took one step with my left leg, and delivered the hardest roundhouse kick I could muster with my right, connecting with the small of his back.

Thomas tumbled down the stairs. His head hit hard on the concrete pad at the bottom. He did not move.

I sank down on the top step. The sirens I heard earlier arrived. Police burst around the corner of the house, guns drawn, then stopped, training them on Thomas.

Natalia was one of them. She looked up at me.

"You okay, Lauren?"

I was shaking. I nodded in the affirmative. That was way too close of a call. I thought about Zac, how I judged him about his father, and how I now knew he did what he had to. Like I did.

Virgie appeared in the doorway. "Sorry, Professor. I got them here as soon as I could." She followed my eyes and saw Thomas at the bottom of the steps.

One officer pointed his gun at Thomas while Natalia cuffed his hands. More sirens reverberated between the houses as they approached. Thomas groaned and shifted.

At least I hadn't killed him.

"Tommy appears to be alive, then. Well, shame on him." Virgie's voice was sad. "I knew he was in some kind of trouble, even though he wouldn't say, but you can't go locking up a nice college professor. Not in my house, you can't. Maybe now he'll get the help he needs."

CHAPTER THIRTY-ONE

I heard knocking on my door just as I got into bed. When I saw it was Zac, I let him in. He told me he had to show me something.

"Now? I had a really long day. Can't it wait?"

"Believe me, you're going to want to see this, sugar." He set up his system on the table. "And nice job with Thomas this afternoon, by the way. You're my hero." He reached out his arm to draw me in close then started up the software.

I studied the laptop monitor over Zac's shoulder, brushing his dreadlocks with my cheek, not caring if my robe gaped open.

"I don't know what idiot 'lost' this tape and then found it. Probably your weird uncle George. But it might be the answer everybody's been looking for."

"Where'd you get the tape?"

"I'll tell you later. Just watch."

"Everything is so dark. I can't even see what we're looking at," I said sleepily. I had been hoping for something quick and clear.

Zac's hands flew over the keyboard. He brought up several windows within the dTective program, selected icons and items from lists, and narrowed in on an area of the video. It changed in front of our eyes. I realized we were looking at a view of the tree where I found Jamal. His body was not yet slumped against the trunk. I pointed with a shaking finger to a shape as Zac continued to work the program and two figures emerged from the darkness as if day were dawning.

"Look, there's Jamal," I whispered. "And that must be his killer."

The two men struggled on screen. I leaned in close to watch. The other man was cloaked in shadow. Suddenly, I grabbed Zac's arm. "Stop! Freeze it, can you?" He clicked a button, and the video froze. Thomas MacDonald was the other man, just as he'd said. And he held a gun. "Go again," I said.

"I'll slow it down."

As the video played with gruesome lassitude, the two men gestured as if arguing. They struggled. Then Jamal fell. Thomas knelt. He held his brother's face in his hands, kissed his forehead, looked around as if panicked. He picked up Jamal under his arms and dragged him to the tree trunk, propping him in the sitting position I had found him in. Thomas ran from the scene into the darkness.

So Thomas had told the truth about killing Jamal.

⌒∾◠

The next evening, Zac, Natalia, and I sat around Jackie's dining table as Jackie filled four round glasses with red wine. She set a steaming oval dish of lasagna on the table then came back again with a basket of bread and a wooden bowl brimming with salad greens, crescents of avocado, and crumbles of goat cheese.

"Here's to no more excitement," I said, raising my wine. The others joined me with a clink of glass. I closed my eyes for a moment then began eating.

We chatted as we consumed the lasagna and the salad, munching on chunks of bread redolent of garlicky butter. As if by a pact, no one brought up the story of Jamal's death and everything that had happened since. It wasn't until we sat with coffee and slices of apple pie that Jackie broached the subject.

"How'd you get the idea and the nerve to push Thomas down the stairs, Lauren?"

"The nerve came from really, really not wanting to be a hostage of a crazed man in withdrawal. The idea?" I looked at Zac. I wasn't going to reveal his past, but it definitely inspired me at that moment. "I realized Thomas wasn't holding onto anything, and I had a free hand to steady myself. I practiced endless roundhouse kicks when I studied karate in Minami Rinkan. In Japan. I guess you never forget how."

"You did exactly the right thing," Natalia said. "Did you learn about biting the hand that holds you in your self-defense class?"

"Yeah. But, Natalia, what I still don't know is who attacked me that night in Elise's back porch. And who ransacked my home office and took Wulu."

"Our delightful guest in lockup, Pascal Martin, has admitted he had a hand in the porch event."

"So it was him!"

Natalia nodded as Jackie got up and brought a bottle of Bahia to the table, along with four tiny stemmed glasses. "He didn't want you getting too close to Elise and interrupting the cash flow from one of his best customers. He also revealed his argument with Jamal on campus that day was about Jamal not giving him the name of his former supplier."

"Why do bad things happen to good people?" I shook my head. "Jamal was only trying to keep others from addiction. Did you find out anything about the time I found my office trashed and Wulu missing?"

"That, Lauren, your esteemed department chair has confessed to."

I stared at Natalia. I couldn't picture Alexa wearing anything less than the finest attire, not to mention knowing how to jimmy a lock and abscond with a furry bundle of loyal energy. "I didn't know she even knew Ashford. How would she have found that shed to leave Wulu in?"

"It turns out Samuel Pulcifer is her uncle. Well, Phillip, too. She's their sister's daughter. They took her to that shed, what they called their clubhouse, when she was a child."

The astonishment on my face must have been written in a script larger than marquee letters. Jackie laughed and said, "Hey, sis, remember what Daddy used to say? Close that mouth before the flies get in."

I smacked my forehead with my hand. "Samuel talked about his niece, Lexie. So did Phillip. Alexa. I get it now. And once she said she had roots in the area. That she knew Holt Beach."

"Anyway," Natalia went on, "she was so sure Jamal had written about her in his thesis, and that you had it at home, that she broke in."

"I guess it's a good thing I keep my college office so messy. She probably went in there and couldn't find it." I sipped my liqueur, enjoying the rich, slow warmth filling me. Finally, I was warm. And safe. I narrowed my eyes. "What's going to happen to Thomas? I believe him, you know, that he didn't mean to kill Jamal. They'd had their problems, but still, they were brothers."

"He claims Jamal was stealing from the chess club."

"Right, that's what he said. I don't think it's true, though." I looked at Natalia.

"More likely Thomas himself was taking the money for his habit," she said. "They'll see if he wants to cough up more information in return for a lessened sentence. Zac, do you think you'll be able to get anything more out of the video?"

"I can try."

"Oh!" I said. "What if you could slow it down enough so somebody could do some lip reading, figure out what they were saying? Like in that movie we saw, where the jealous husband hired a woman to lip read the video of his wife and her lover."

"Possible, *bebé*. Could you do that?"

"That's pretty hard. We worked on lip reading when I was studying ASL. Some near-deaf people rely on it. I'm sure I can find you an expert, though."

Zac looked at Natalia. "How'd the extra tape turn up way after all the other ones were submitted? The one that shows Jamal and Thomas?"

Natalia sighed and shook her head. "Your uncle George is a strange bird." She included both Jackie and me in her look. "He's like on some reform kick. All of a sudden he's Mr. Helpful. Searching for tapes we should have been given from the start."

I laughed. "One of them probably shows him drunk on the job and he didn't dare hand it over."

"And then he's telling me, in more detail than I want to hear, about his new sobriety and his AA attendance. I felt like telling him to button it up. Except he was being helpful. And we always need all the help we can get." She leaned back in her chair and sipped her liqueur. "I'm just glad I'm off duty."

Jackie covered Natalia's hand with her own and squeezed. "So am I, girlfriend."

I basked in their pleasure. I felt pretty good, myself. Alexa wasn't technically the wicked stepmother, but she'd acted like it. Now she was gone. In future dealings with the unpleasant Dean Irwin, I hoped I'd be able to stand my ground.

Jamal's death was explained, albeit tragically. I hoped Thomas would get treatment along with a light sentence. And Elise was on the road to healing. My friend wouldn't have an easy path, but she seemed determined to try to follow it.

Jackie was at the stereo, inserting a CD. "Dancing, anybody?"

Zac stood, took my hand, and drew me up in an embrace. Then, as the Rolling Stones' "Brown Sugar" picked up volume, he pushed me back and spun me around. Jackie and Natalia boogied nearby. As we danced, I thought about how I could now get my life back. Thank goodness I could return to working on my book. Have some time to relax, to attend that bonsai workshop I lusted after, without having to track down a murderer. Maybe I'd plant a little garden for the summer.

Whispering in my ear, Zac said, "So I just found out my niece, Marie-Fleur, is coming from Port-Au-Prince to live with me next week. I'm so glad we're together, you and me."

I stopped dancing and stepped back. "What? She is?" I stared at him. "How old is she?"

"She's eleven." He smiled, holding my hands. "You can help her out, be like her mom for a few months, until my sister Pia gets used to her new husband and all. That's cool, right?"

Me, a mother figure? Wait a minute—

-The End-

Tace Baker is a pseudonym for Edith Maxwell. Tace is an old-fashioned Quaker name, which seemed fitting for the author of a series featuring a Quaker Linguistics professor. Edith is a member of Mystery Writers of America, Romance Writers of America, Sisters in Crime and its Guppies subgroup, and is on the board of the New England chapter of Sisters in Crime. She is also a member of the Society of Friends (Quaker).

Edith has published several short mystery stories and has a new series, the cozy Local Foods Mysteries, featuring organic farmer Cam Flaherty and the local Locavore Club. The first book in that series, *A Tine to Live, a Tine to Die,* will be published in June 2013 by Kensington Publishing.

She currently resides in Amesbury, Massachusetts, but is originally a 4th-generation Californian. She has two grown sons and lives in an antique house with her beau, their three cats, and several fine specimens of garden statuary. Look for her at www.tacebaker.com, as Tace Baker on Facebook, @tacebaker on Twitter, or at www.edithmaxwell.com, as Edith M. Maxwell on Facebook, and @edithmaxwell on Twitter.

TACE BAKER

ABOUT
BARKING RAIN PRESS

Did you know that six media conglomerates publish eighty percent of the books in the United States? As the publishing industry continues to contract, opportunities for emerging and mid-career authors are drying up. Who will write the literature of the twenty-first century if just a handful of profit-focused corporations are left to decide who—and what—is worthy of publication?

Barking Rain Press is dedicated to the creation and promotion of thoughtful and imaginative contemporary literature, which we believe is essential to a vital and diverse culture. As a nonprofit organization, Barking Rain Press is an independent publisher that seeks to cultivate relationships with new and mid-career writers over time, to be thorough in the editorial process, and to make the publishing process an experience that will add to an author's development—and ultimately enhance our literary heritage.

In selecting new titles for publication, Barking Rain Press considers authors at all points in their careers. Our goal is to support the development of emerging and mid-career authors—not just single books—as we know from experience that a writer's audience is cultivated over the course of several books.

Support for these efforts comes primarily from the sale of our publications; we also hope to attract grant funding and private donations. Whether you are a reader or a writer, we invite you to take a stand for independent publishing and become more involved with Barking Rain Press. With your support, we can make sure that talented writers thrive, and that their books reach the hands of spirited, curious readers. Find out more at our website.

WWW.BARKINGRAINPRESS.ORG

Barking Rain Press

ALSO FROM BARKING RAIN PRESS

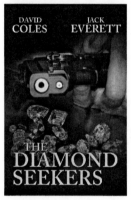

VIEW OUR COMPLETE CATALOG ONLINE:

WWW.BARKINGRAINPRESS.ORG